squirrels

in the

wall

Squirrels in the Wall

A Novel in Short Stories

by

Henry Hitz

Published by SparkPress, a BookSparks imprint,
A division of SparkPoint Studio, LLC
Phoenix, Arizona, USA, 85007
www.gosparkpress.com

Published 2019
Printed in the United States of America
ISBN: 978-1-68463-022-6 (pbk)
ISBN: 978-1-68463-023-3 (e-bk)

Library of Congress Control Number: 2019908840

Book design by Stacey Aaronson
Map of Habitat by Nicki Hitz Edson

This book is dedicated to Gloria, Slater, Ben, Zena, Jackson, and Kamille, as well as all the people and animals upon whom the characters in the narrative are loosely based.

CONTENTS

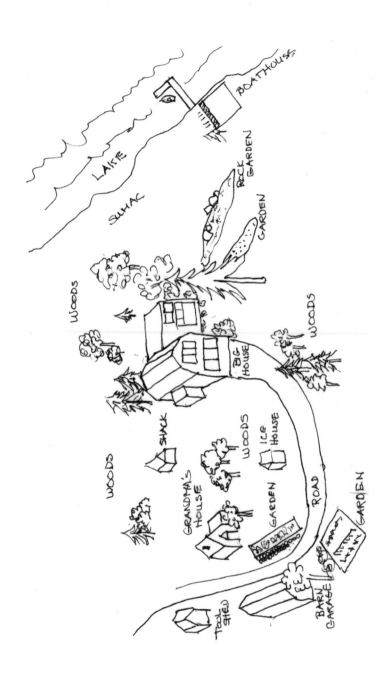

ONE

FRANK AND STEIN

— 1 —

*P*sssp, a young field mouse, paced the burrow, hopelessness filling her belly. The squeals in the nest grated on her ears. Her brothers and sisters were hungry. She was hungry. Her mama had gone out looking for nuts and such two days ago and wasn't back yet. They needed their milk. The little mice were squabbling, arguing about who should go out looking first. Psssp knew the answer. She should. She knew they were all just about old enough to fend for themselves. But she was the biggest of the litter, and the strongest, and the calmest.

Pffft, the runt, wanted to go, but he was a foolhardy mouse. He covered his small size with bluster and often got into trouble. Once he took on a neighboring mouse twice his size in a fight over a stray acorn in the burrow and lost a piece of his ear and two whiskers.

"I'll go," Psssp said at last. The others squealed their agreement. They too knew that she was the best choice.

Psssp crept to the mouth of the burrow. It was covered by a thin layer of fresh snow—an early snow that had caught the mouse family without enough food stored up. She poked her nose through the icy crystals. More snowflakes fell on her whiskers. She could hear them plunk as they hit the earth. The light blinded her. This was the first time she had seen the outside world. *Ain't nothing here,* she thought. Nothing but white as far as her eyes could see.

She looked about for her mama's tracks and sniffed for her odor trail, but of course they were both buried in the new snow. She hopped out of the hole. The snow was cold on her feet. More snow fell into her eyes, blurring her vision. *So this is the world,* she thought. *In the burrow, warm and dark; out of the burrow, cold and light. That's all there is.*

She hopped again. With each hop away from the hole, fear welled up inside her. Her heart pounded. Only a short while ago, her papa had been snatched by a hungry owl, just outside the burrow. If she didn't find her mama, would she find any food in this wasteland? If she found food, how would she find her way back to the burrow? She felt these doubts circle above her, like a patient hawk.

But she had to keep going. Safety was useless without food. Another feeling bubbled up inside of her and warmed her, a strange kind of happiness. So what if she couldn't find her way back? She would still survive.

Somehow. This much she knew. She scurried on, down the white hill.

She came to a wall. It too was white, and she couldn't see it in the whiteness of the snow. She was about to smash into it, when she felt it twitch her whiskers. It was flat, featureless, and rose straight up out of the ground. She scampered along it. It turned sharp corners. There were spaces in it from which she felt whiffs of warm air and dim scents of food. The spaces were covered with some hard, clear stuff like ice.

Then at one such space, she felt a blast of hot air and a strong smell of mouse. There was a mouse-sized hole in the clear stuff. Bravely, she jumped right into it.

Nothing was there, truly nothing. She flew through the air many tail-lengths and crashed on a hard place, stunned. More darkness.

As she shook off the shock from her fall, her nose filled with a lovely smell, milky sweet, with a hint of mold. It was right in front of her. Food! It was inside some kind of a cozy nest with only another mouse-sized hole between her and it. She leapt toward it and sank her sharp teeth into it. It was soft and even tastier than it smelled. She heard a click behind her but paid it no mind.

When she finished the gooey chunk, she tried to leap back out of the hole. The hole was gone. She slammed into a wall made of hard sticks. She bounced all around the spot she was in and found nothing but hard stick walls all around her. She tried to gnaw her way through the sticks, but only managed to chip one of her teeth. She was trapped.

— 2 —

A fter his morning ritual of gnawing on a food pellet, sipping at the water bottle, defecating four times, and running the wheel, 75413, or "3" for short, retired to a corner of his cage to meditate. He relaxed back on his haunches and lowered his pink eyelids halfway down. He slowed his breathing and made it so quiet he couldn't hear it. As thoughts came up, he noted them and let them go. He was pleased to have a cage to himself. 2 and 6 next door squabbled constantly even if they did get to mate. *Let it go,* he told himself. He knew if he could just let go of all his thoughts, he could touch the oneness of the universe and, for a moment at least, be completely at peace. And how about that Group 15 across the way? The pellet gods had put as many mice as they possibly could into one cage. *Why on Earth?* he wondered. The pellet gods act in mysterious ways. *Let it go. Count your breaths,* he told himself. He could only count to two. One, two. One, two. One, two.

The soft fuzz of the universe gradually settled upon him. A gentle radiance glowed from the point between his eyes. *Ahhh,* he sighed. *This is it. This is what it's all about. I wonder if any of the others know about this.* Really, he should tell them. It would help 2 and 6 get along. Group 15 might stop eating their babies if they knew about this radiance. He could hear 2 and 6 going at it again. "My pellet!" "No, mine!" they squeaked back and forth. *Ignore it,* he told himself. *Let it go.* But the noise

got louder and more shrill. "I'll scratch your eyes out!"
"I'll bite your tail off!" *Gods!*

"Hey, you two," 3 squealed. "You ever try meditating?"

"Fuck off," 2 yelled.

Let it go, 3 told himself again. *Slow your breathing. Glory in the oneness.* The glowing fuzz settled in again. But not for long. This time he was distracted by 2 and 6 fucking. *Gods. Is there no peace?* The sloshing about next door and with it the salty, syrupy smell filled up his brain. He felt a stirring in his own underbelly. How long had it been? Eons since he'd had any. He licked his own teensy penis. He thought about 8, the spotted mouse the gods bred him with so long ago. What a shrew she was. But could she slosh!

Suddenly the door to his cage flew open and one of the gods thrust in his enormous hand. *Oh-oh. This wouldn't be happening if I'd kept my thoughts pure,* he thought. *What do they want?* Sometimes they gave him grand Trials to see if he was worthy of living or not. They ran him through vast and terrifying labyrinths. They stuck him with needles that made him sick. They gave him shocks—all to judge whether or not he was sufficiently free from sin for them to bestow on him their Divine Beneficence. Thanks to his unswerving devotion to meditation, he had passed their tests every time. Many mice had not been as lucky.

This time however, it appeared they were transporting him to the Great Beyond. He had finally made it. He had reached the highest level. The gods placed him in another cage, covered it, and sent him in complete darkness on a vast journey, from whence he would finally reach Peace or encounter still more Trials, he knew not which. In spite of his highly developed inner tranquility, he was terrified, and kept trying to count his breaths, one, two, one, two, one, two, but he was so upset he lost count.

His cage came to a rest in an unworldly place in the Great Beyond, a place that had little light but a great deal of space outside the cage and didn't smell at all of mice. *At last they have released me from my physical being,* he thought, *from my mouseness.*

But before he had a chance to catch his breath, the gods, new gods that he'd never seen before, dropped another being into the cage. Although quite similar in size to himself, this being was not a mouse, for it was gray in color and had a ghastly odor. He suspected it of being some kind of demon, and silently thanked the gods for yet another opportunity to prove himself. This demon clearly had no consciousness to speak of, for it did nothing but cower in the corner of the cage and tremble. 3 decided there was nothing for him to do but go on with his life and his spiritual journey, so he chomped another pellet, went for his evening run on the wheel, curled up in his corner, and went to sleep.

— 3 —

*C*oony the raccoon and George the monkey were confronting Harrybear.

"You did it, Harrybear," Coony said.

"I saw you do it," George said.

"We ought to beat the stuffing out of him," put in Skunky from the edge of the bed.

"What do you think?" Coony asked Bunnywunny.

"Of course, he did it," Bunnywunny said. "Just look at his eyes."

"What do you have to say for yourself?" Coony asked Harrybear.

"Not me," said Harrybear. "It wasn't me. Maybe it was Lester."

"Who, me?" said Lester the lion. "I was deep in the jungle."

"Let's vote," said Coony.

"Guilty!" said Bunnywunny.

"Guilty!" said Skunky, Lester, George, and Coony all together. "Let's beat the stuffing out of him!"

Barney picked up the bear by the legs and started to slam its head against the side of the bed. Then he stood up on the bed in his stocking feet and began jumping up and down so that the bear's head hit against the sharp corners of the bookshelves behind the bed.

Barney's sister Pookie shouted, "Hey! That's my bear! Quit it!" She had been quietly watching Rin Tin Tin save a child from the Indians on the seven-inch-square television.

Barney kept jumping. The bed was his trampoline. One by one the stuffed animals fell off the bed and onto the floor.

"Barney! Stop it!"

Pookie lunged for the bear. With a devilish grin, Barney slammed the bear's head harder still against the shelf. A split opened in the seam that held the bear together. White cotton fluff flurried into the air like the snow falling out the window.

Finally, Pookie got hold of the bear and snatched it out of Barney's hand. "You ruined him! I'm telling Mommy. He was my favorite bear. You're sick the way you play with your animals, Barney Blatz!"

A cowbell rang from the kitchen. It was dinnertime. The playroom had formerly been a garage and was separated from the rest of the house by the back porch. It was cold on the porch. Snow filled the night sky and glistened in the light from the windows.

"Mommy," Pookie said. "Barney ruined Harrybear. He was jumping on the bed and hitting his head against the bookcase. All of his stuffing is coming out. I've had that bear since I was a little kid. I need a new one."

Mommy was setting the pork roast in front of Father, poised with his carving knife. "Barney," she said in an even voice, betraying no anger. "I've told you not to jump on that bed. That's Herzie's bed. You'll ruin the mattress."

Herziger, the dachshund, heard his name and clicked into the kitchen from his spot in front of the register that blew warm air from the furnace. He settled under Barney's chair, awaiting a snowfall of tidbits.

"You still play with dolls?" Father asked Barney roughly, cutting at the meat. "This damn knife is too dull," he yelled at Mommy. He fetched the sharpening iron and flourished the big knife back and forth along it. "You're too old to play with dolls. How old are you now, anyway?"

"Eight," Barney said softly.

"Eight years old and he still plays with dolls. Jesus, Mommy, what kind of mama's boy are you raising here? The boy's got to find an interest. A hobby. Something to engage his mind. What are you interested in, Son?"

"I don't know," Barney answered quietly.

"'I don't know,'" Father mocked as he attacked the pig's carcass with the knife. For a surgeon, his flourishes of the knife were not delicate. "When I was your age, I already had a ham radio setup. While you talk baby talk to your dolls, I was talking Morse code to England." He flung the slabs of roast onto the plates and passed the plates around. He took a swig from his bourbon. His close-cropped hair was pure white, though he was just fifty.

"All he does is play with stuffed animals," Pookie added.

"Stuffed animals, huh? I suppose that's better than baby dolls. So you like animals, do you? Maybe you'd like real animals. Maybe you'll be a vet."

"I caught a mouse today," Barney said.

"You did, did you?" Father said, pleased. "How'd you do it?"

"I made a trap with my Erector set."

"Well, maybe there's hope for you yet. Tell you what, Son. I'll bring you a cage and another mouse from the university lab tomorrow. Maybe you can raise mice, or do some experiments or something." He shifted toward Mommy. "Caring for real animals might just teach him some responsibility, too. You're no baby anymore."

The next day, Barney watched the gray mouse cower inside his trap. Later that evening Father brought him a white mouse in a huge wire cage with a wheel inside and water bottle attached to the outside, and a box of nutritionally balanced mouse pellets. Barney put the cage on a table in the playroom, dropped the gray mouse in with the white mouse, and watched them for hours, skipping *Howdy Doody, Kukla, Fran and Ollie,* and *Rin Tin Tin.*

The white one raced around the wheel, or rather, ran in place while the wheel raced around him. The gray one cowered in a corner of the cage and sulked. Barney loved them.

"What did you name them?" Pookie asked him.

"The gray one is Frank. The white one, Stein. Frank and Stein," Barney answered.

"Cute," Pookie said.

— 4 —

For the first few days of sharing the same habitat, Psssp, 3, and Barney hardly altered their behavior. 3 continued his running and meditation rituals. Psssp cowered in the corner. And Barney watched intently. Psssp didn't even eat, so 3 got fat with his extra ration of pellets.

On the third day, when Barney dropped the two pellets into the cage, Psssp finally crawled out of her corner to claim her share. 3 growled at her. He'd grown accustomed to two pellets. Psssp, weak as she was, bared her incisors.

3 was no fighter. He backed down with a squeak that said, "Oh all right, go ahead." He was surprised that Psssp responded with an understandable squeal, that meant, though the accent was bad, "I reckon I'll do that. I'm starved."

"You are a mouse, then?" 3 asked.

"What you think? I ain't one of those," Psssp responded with a nod of her nose toward Barney.

"No, you're no pellet god."

"No what?"

"Pellet god. That being feeds you pellets doesn't it?"

"So far I seen it feed *you* pellets. I don't know what it is," Psssp squeaked. "I never seen anything like it."

"That's funny. I thought all mice fed off the pellet gods. How did you eat before you got here?"

"My mama fetched sweet acorns into the burrow, and I sucked her titty milk. But food got scarce in the snow."

"You lived outside? In a burrow? How primitive. I bet you're glad to be here."

"Well, no. These pellets taste like shit. I miss my brothers and sisters. I miss the acorns. I miss racing through the burrow. I miss the stories Mama used to tell us about darting from tree to tree after nuts right under the shadow of a hawk. I reckon I miss feeling free."

"Free! Hah! Free to starve, you said so yourself. Here you have everything you need. Food, water, shelter, even companionship—if that's a need. I prefer to be by myself, frankly. And if you'll only concentrate on liberating yourself from your material being, you can have freedom too."

"I do want my freedom back. I'm going crazy here. There ain't nothing to do." Psssp's voice grew shrill.

"You haven't even tried the wheel of life. You must run on this wheel at least twice a day."

Psssp tried the wheel. She tried the meditation exercises that 3 taught her. But after three days, she was back to sulking in the corner. "I can't stand this!" she squawked. "I got to get out of here! Instead of all this meditating crap, you should be thinking up how to escape."

"Escape? Whatever for?"

"What kind of mouse are you anyway? You ought to feel what it's like to be able to visit other mice once in a while! The smells! Sniffing along the odor trails in the burrow. And the different things to eat! Acorns, bugs, walnuts, sunflower seeds, pine cones, corn, blackberries, apple seeds!"

"But you were hungry all the time."

"Only in the snow. In the warm times, we'd eat until we burped."

"Sounds lovely."

"You should try it."

"Maybe I should," said 3. "I would like to try it someday. I really would. But, meanwhile, I know something you should try that will take your mind off these things. You are a young mouse, so you may not know what's what. Let me show you."

3 sidled up to Psssp and nibbled her ear. He stroked her back near her tail. "Oh," she said as the unfamiliar feelings welled up in her. He mounted her.

She pulled away. "Stop it," she squealed. She bit him on the leg.

"Come on, you'll like it."

"I'll decide that," Psssp glared.

The next day Psssp did feel a great yearning and decided she would like it. 3 mounted her again, and she let him stay.

From that moment on, Psssp wanted it all the time. At first, 3 liked the idea, and love reigned supreme over the cage. But after a while it got to be too much. "Can't you just meditate once in a while?" 3 asked.

"C'mon! That stuff is boring."

"You're going to get pregnant and crowd this place up with mouse babies," 3 explained.

"That would at least be something to do."

Meanwhile, Barney had become an increasingly avid observer. One day he took the mice out of the cage and placed them on the bed in the playroom, in the hopes of getting an even better view of their behavior.

This terrified Psssp, who was sure they were going to be eaten. But 3 reassured her, "This god is simply conducting Trials. Do as it wishes, and you will surely be rewarded."

When the mice didn't continue their love-making on the bed, Barney picked up Psssp and stuck her on top of 3. The mice couldn't tell what he wanted. Barney turned his attention to his stuffed animals.

Psssp thought this was the time to escape. "Come! Let's get out of here!" She raced to the edge of the bed.

3 followed her. "We'll never make it," he said.

Psssp jumped off the bed and scampered toward the cold air from the porch. 3 crawled slowly after her.

Barney yelled, "Hey!" He scooped up the slow-moving 3 in his hand. He ran toward the porch.

Psssp stopped and watched 3 get caught. She hesitated before taking off again, just long enough for Barney to grab hold of her too. He dumped them back in the cage.

They had another fight. "You ain't even tried!" Psssp spat at 3.

"I did try," 3 whined.

"No you didn't."

"Did!"

"Didn't!" Psssp jumped 3 and bit his ear. He started to cry. She bit him again and again. He didn't even try to defend himself. Then they made love as never before. They vowed to really go for it the next time.

After a while, Psssp began feeling strange, sickly. "You're pregnant," 3 told her. "Gods, now this place will really be crowded."

It was a long time before Barney took them out of the

cage again. When he did, Psssp was quite fat. Barney surrounded the mice with a wall of stuffed animals: Coony, George, Bunnywunny, Skunky, Lester, a bandaged Harrybear, and a brand-new tan stuffed bear named Foobear.

Barney left the mice no room to escape. He picked up Psssp in his hand and said to her, "And what do you think, Frank? Did Foobear do it?" He pointed to the new bear. "I thought so. Frank says you did it." He dropped the mouse on the bed again and consulted the other animals.

"Coony? George? Lester?"

"Guilty," they all replied.

Coony passed sentence. "I'm afraid you're guilty, Foobear. Let's knock the stuffing out of her, gang." Barney grabbed the new bear by the leg and started to slam her head against the bookcase.

He started to jump up and down on the couch in his stocking feet. One by one the stuffed animals began to fall off.

Psssp and 3 scurried to get out of the way of the hammering feet. But it was hard to know where they would fall next. 3 got hit first. He squealed as the full weight of the boy came down on his little neck.

Psssp made it almost to the edge of the bed before the foot came down on her neck and sent her into the darkness.

— 5 —

*I*t was an accident. Barney had just forgotten about the mice. When Pookie yelled at him, "Drop that bear, Barney Blatz!" he knew something was wrong.

"Oh, no," he screamed. He jumped off the bed and scrambled to find the mice in the folds of the bedspread. "Frank!" he yelled. "Stein!" His insides ached as if he'd swallowed a rock. He picked up the little corpses with blood running from their mouths. "Please don't be dead," he pleaded. "I love you."

But the mice lay still in his hand.

Barney crumpled on the bed, sobbing.

He put the mice in a shoebox. He covered them with the rest of the mice pellets from the box. He sang over and over to himself the one dirge he knew, from Mommy's record, "Pore Jud is daid / A candle lights his haid."

He found two strips of lath and, with his woodburning set, wrote on one: "Here Lies Frank and Stein." He nailed them together into a cross. He fetched a shovel from the tool shed. He dug a hole in the snow near the back of the house where the ground wasn't frozen, and set the box uncovered in the hole. With the first clod of dirt, he thought he heard the mice squeal a final time. He watched to see if they moved. They didn't. With tears running down his cheeks, he shoveled in the rest of the dirt.

He pounded in the cross as deep as it would go. He

read from his sister's Book of Common Prayer, in dead earnest:

"Into your hands, O merciful Savior, we commend your servants, Frank and Stein. Acknowledge, we humbly beseech you, mice of your own fold, rodents of your own flock, sinners of your own redeeming. Receive them into the arms of your mercy, into the blessed rest of everlasting peace. Amen."

TWO

SQUIRRELS IN THE WALL

FOUR-YEAR-OLD BARNEY BOMBS HIS OLD CASTLE
with lead planes dropping fire from the sky like Daddy
in the war, the growl of the propeller going "Airey-airey-
airey." The castle has burned up a hundred times now.

He's all alone in the playroom of the big house his
family has just moved into. It sits on a hill overlooking
the lake. It's Grandpa's house. Grandpa's dead. Up in the
sky someplace. What's dead? The house has squirrels
that scamper through the walls. Barney can't go down
to the lake alone or even with Pookie, his big sister, because he might fall in and choke on the water and
drown and be dead.

The fall day is bright and clear. The lake is white
with the wind. The leaves of the trees in the woods are
orange, yellow, and red, the colors of fire.

Pookie comes home from school at last. She wears a
plaid dress, a jumper they call it, but she never jumps.
Her hair is cut off in bangs above her eyes. She is seven.

"Hi, Barney dear," she says in her motherly way like he was one of her dolls. He loves it. She pours him milk in a cup shaped like an elephant with its trunk for a handle. He spills his milk all over the floor.

They eat a whole package of Oreo cookies. Pookie splits them in two and licks off the cream center, but when Barney tries it, the cookies break.

"Let's explore," Pookie says. It's their favorite game.

They rummage through the closets looking for treasures and Christmas presents. In the maid's room closet—the maid long gone—the smell of mothballs tickles Barney's nose. They find a shopping bag, from Gimbels, Pookie reads. Barney wishes he could read. Inside are an orange tractor and a soft skunk, black with white stripes and a spring inside so you can make it creep up on your shoulder.

"I wonder who this is for," Pookie muses. She's talking about the skunk. She knows the tractor is for Barney. He is rolling it on the floor and going "Rrrrrrrrr."

"Me," Barney says. He likes the sound of it. "Me, me, me." He grabs the skunk from her and cuddles it on his shoulder.

"No, mine!" Pookie snatches it back in a red-faced rage. Barney doesn't argue.

They find a tea set with little metal cups and saucers, a teapot, and a little stove. The set is sealed in a box with a cellophane top, but Pookie opens it without tearing it up.

"Let's have a party," she says.

"Party," Barney says.

HENRY HITZ

"First we have to get dressed," she adds.

Barney puts on a stovepipe hat.

"Just like Abe Lincoln," Pookie says.

The hat fits him, covering his close-cut, straw-colored hair. He has a big head.

Pookie drags a black lace dress off a hanger. It had been Mommy's as a teenager. She makes Barney put it on. He doesn't mind. He likes how grown up he looks in the full-length mirror. He sticks his feet in some of Daddy's huge wingtip shoes.

Pookie puts on a black tuxedo coat and tops her head with a pillbox hat with a black veil. She sets the dishes on the imaginary table for four. She runs into her room and invites Sally, her big blond rag doll, bigger than Barney, and Harrybear, her bear. The skunk skulks on the fringes, uninvited, new kid on the block.

Pookie runs into Mommy-Daddy's room and returns with two Lucky Strike cigarettes. She gives one to Barney. He puffs on it and wets it up. She pours the tea. "Pshsht," she says. "Is everything satisfactory, Madam Barney?" she asks.

"Yummy," he says.

"Do you have a light?" she asks.

Barney pretends to light her cigarette. He scrambles downstairs to the living room, tripping over the dress, nearly falling down the stairs. He kicks off the shoes. He returns with a silver table lighter, egg shaped, with fancy bumps on it.

"Barney! No-no," Pookie scolds Mommy-like. She tries to grab the lighter from him.

He flicks it. The flame brightens the air like lightning. "Barney!" She keeps trying to grab it. He keeps flicking it, lighting and dousing the flame. "I'm telling, Barney Blatz," Pookie screams at him. She chases him. They run into the hall. Barney runs into his room way down at the other end. The top hat flies off in the rush. He slams the door and waits for her to fling it open.

But she doesn't come. She's stopped chasing him. He jumps out of the dress. He runs back to see what has happened. Something's wrong. Pookie is standing at the window in the hall. The window opens out like a door and overlooks the roof of the front of the house where Mommy-Daddy's room is. The roof is shaped like a barn, with four different surfaces.

"Look!" Pookie says. Between the wooden shingles of the roof, white smoke is oozing out. The smell is like when Mommy burns the toast. But worse. What did he do? Was it the lighter?

They go in Mommy-Daddy's room. The smoke chokes them. Barney can't breathe. He hears the squirrels scurrying in the walls.

"I wonder what it is," Pookie says. "It's too low for clouds. We better get Clifford." Clifford is the old caretaker who sings "Didee-didee-do" as he dusts the stairs every morning.

No telling where he is. Pookie takes Barney by the hand and they run through the house hollering, "Clifford! Clifford!" The upstairs, the downstairs, the basement. They don't go into the basement. It's dark and the bogeyman lives there. They don't stay long in the house.

Pookie says, "It might be on fire." To Barney, it doesn't seem to be on fire. It seems to be on smoke.

When they get outside, Barney's stomach cramps. *What did I do?* he wonders. He remembers they put Curious George, the monkey, in jail just for calling in a false alarm to the fire department. *I'm going to jail,* he thinks. *I'll never see Mommy again.* He can't share this thought even with Pookie. The darkness swoops down on him again like a giant bird. He wants to cry, but the tears ball up in his throat and choke him.

The place where they live has many hiding places. There's the main house, the boathouse, the ice house, the garage with an upstairs, the outhouse, the gray cottage, the red cottage, the tool shed, the shack, the woods.

"Clifford!" they call. They go part way down toward the lake. He's not there. They run by the red cottage in the woods, but it's still and boarded up for the winter. They take the road, then the path to Grandma's cottage, also closed for the season. Grandma has moved back to town like most of the people on the lake. Clifford's not in the garage. He's not anywhere.

At the door to the tool shed, they call again. No answer. There's smoke coming out of the chimney there, too. The smoke races across the sky in the wind.

"He must be here someplace," Pookie says, a whine creeping into her voice.

Barney has peed in his pants. They look inside the tool shed. Clifford sits on an old wooden chair in front of the incinerator. He smells of chewing tobacco and alcohol. He's been known to steal from the liquor cabinet. He's sound asleep, snoring away.

"Clifford!" Pookie yells in his face, shaking his shoulder.

"Huh?"

"I smell smoke in the house."

"I know. I been smellin' it all day."

"Come look."

"All rightee."

Pookie drags Clifford back up to the house and points to the smoke now pouring out of the roof. "Oh, shit," he says, a word Barney never heard him use before. "It's on fire."

"Call the fire department," Pookie orders.

"Hokay," he says. "Guess I better." Clifford disappears into the smoking house.

"Come on, Barney." She grabs his hand again. "Let's get out of here."

Barney pulls away. "No! Wanna see fire engines."

"Barney! You come with me this instant!" Pookie insists, Mommy-like.

"No." He runs away.

She tackles him. "C'mon, Barney. I'll tell about the lighter."

He's forgotten about the lighter. Where is it? What if they find it? What will they do to him? He thinks of stories he's heard about hell. They'll send him to hell to burn up. Maybe that's where the fire came from. They're bringing hell to him.

His will turns to jelly. He yields to his sister. She

drags him down the road to the neighbors. Just as they leave the gravel of the Blatzes' road for the blacktop of the Starks', Clifford catches up with them. "I couldn't git the phone to work. I ain't useter these dials." The family had just gotten its first dial phone.

At the Starks' garage, he hollers for Jake. Jake is the Starks' caretaker and Clifford's brother-in-law.

The Starks' lawn is even and flat. There are beautiful flowers all perfectly arranged. No woods. The poodle yaps at them. The Starks own a candy company. Barney likes them.

Jake limps out of the garage and leads them up to the Starks' house, then calls the fire department.

Mrs. Stark smiles at them and invites them in. "Well! Isn't this exciting?" she says.

Soon they hear the sirens. Barney and Pookie look over the trees toward their house. They can't see the house, but now they can see orange flames licking the sky above the trees. Barney doesn't want to go back there now, not even to see the fire engines. The sirens get real loud and then they stop. He looks at Pookie and sees the woodsman in Little Red Riding Hood. *She saved me*, he thinks.

Pookie starts to cry. "Where's Mommy?" she wails.

"It's OK, honey," Mrs. Stark says full of good cheer. "Your mommy will be home soon. Have some candy." She passes the bowl to them. The bowl is filled with the candy the Starks are famous for: Snirkles, a round, caramel-vanilla swirl wrapped in cellophane. They stick to Barney's teeth. But he eats them, one after another, until Mommy arrives. She is dressed up for the city in her gray tweed suit. She's been volunteering at the hospital. She carries a bag that reads Gimbels.

Mommy hugs and kisses Barney and Pookie. "I followed the fire engines. I never dreamed it was our house." She laughs about it, but Barney feels her holding back tears for his sake.

She goes off with Mrs. Stark, and Barney and Pookie overhear her talk about all she's lost—furniture, art, the children's toys. She doesn't quite cry, but they can tell she's sad.

When they can all see the fire is out, Mommy asks Barney and Pookie if they want to go look.

"No," Pookie says.

"No," Barney says. He is still scared they'll find the lighter. They stay behind and stuff themselves with Snirkles.

Daddy arrives awhile later, as the sky grows dark. "It was a big fire," he explains to Pookie and Barney, who are now very tired and numb. "We won't be able to live there for a while."

They eat dinner, chicken and peas, at the Starks'. They have candles on the table. When she sees the flames, Pookie starts to cry. Mrs. Stark laughs. "Of course. I'm sorry," she says and blows them out.

At the table, there's a moment when the family is close. Daddy holds Mommy's hand, which he never does. "Let's just be glad everyone's all right," Daddy says.

After dinner, Mommy gives each child a present that

she'd bought in town. "These were supposed to be for Christmas," she says. Barney gets an Erector set, but when he tries to build something, it's too hard and he hates it. Pookie gets a stuffed squirrel, and Barney wants it worse than anything. But he doesn't cry.

They spend the night at the Starks', Barney and Pookie in the same room. Neither of them sleeps. They keep smelling smoke. Pookie cries about Sally and Harrybear. Barney cries for his castle and planes, and for the terrible dark smoke in his chest.

The next day they move into a friend's house a few miles away. Pookie refuses to go near the burned house, so when Mommy goes there, she stays at the Starks' and eats Snirkles.

Barney goes and looks once. The smell is frightful and would linger for months. The roof is completely gone. He looks in the black-framed upstairs windows and sees the sky. The house is dead, he thinks. "Looks like a ghost," he says. Mommy laughs. He doesn't go back. He keeps wondering when they will find the lighter and when they will find out he started it. The next time Mommy or Daddy goes to the house, he sticks with Pookie, eating Snirkles.

One day he overhears Mommy talking to Mrs. Stark. "Did they ever find out what caused the fire?" Mrs. Stark asks.

"Electrical wiring," Mommy answers. "They think the squirrels that lived in the walls might have gnawed through the wires and shorted them out."

"Isn't that something?" Mrs. Stark says.

Barney starts breathing again. He wonders what happened to the squirrels. Are they dead? Or did they get away, too?

THREE

TOM THE SQUIRREL

By Barney Blatz, Age 9, Grade 4

Tom was the runt of the litter. His sister Sue and brother Bob picked on him. They jumped him when his mouth was filled with acorns so he had to spit them out.

Even his mother, Sally, was mean to him. When he came back to the nest, she would slap him with her big bushy tail for not bringing enough nuts. He was always hungry.

Tom's mother was different from other squirrel moms. Squirrels are supposed to live in trees, in the hollows or the branches. But Sally had found a way into the big house through a hole just below the roof. The nest was always under construction. It was warm and cozy.

Tom liked to scurry through the space under the roof. His mother warned him not to nibble on the long black vines that ran all over the house. "Why not?" he asked.

"Because I said so," she said. "Because you might die."

Tom did not want to die, so he stayed away from the long black vines.

Sally told Tom, his brother Bob, and his sister Sue to go outside and gather sticks and other stuff for their nest. At first, it made Tom feel grown up to help this way. But his sister and brother teased him all the time.

He would find a strip of white birch bark and climb the tree to get onto the roof. But his brother Bob would snatch it out of his mouth and give it to their mother himself.

One day when the sun was at the top of the sky, he was scampering on the other side of the house. He bumped into a very hard straight tree. A pole. On top of this pole was a box full of all kinds of delicious seeds and nuts. Corn, sunflower seeds, peas, rice, and other grains. He stuffed his cheeks.

While he was eating, a little bird, a chickadee, landed next to him and squeaked a greeting. She had black and white feathers. She sang him a pretty song.

He returned the next day when the sun was in the same place. There she was again. They didn't say much to each other. But Tom thought he finally had a friend. He called her Tweety.

They met at the bird feeder every day for many days. Tom started to grow bigger from eating so much.

Then one day he got to the bird feeder before his friend. While he was stuffing his face, he saw Tweety fly toward him. Then she turned suddenly and slammed into the big picture window of the house. There was a loud thump. He watched his friend Tweety drop down to the ground.

He jumped down to look at her. She was completely still.

Suddenly his brother Bob and sister Sue appeared and chased him away from his friend. They wanted to eat her!

Tom jumped his brother Bob. His sister Sue jumped Tom. They had a fight. Tom lost. Bob and Sue brought the feathers and bits of bird meat to their mother Sally. Sally was happy.

Tom became very sad. He sulked for two days.

Then on the third night, he scampered away from the nest while the others slept. He came to a place where there were two long black vines that his mother warned him about. He bit into one. He got a huge shock. Now he too was dead.

As he lay there between the wires, his body started to smoke. Then his bushy tail caught fire. Then the wood of the roof began to burn. Soon the whole house was on fire.

Sally and Bob and Sue woke up in time and scampered out of the house and down the tree.

The whole top floor of the house burned up. The squirrel family had to build a new nest.

They were very sad about Tom. They were sorry they had been mean to him.

FOUR

THE LIFE CYCLE
OF A TOAD

TOAD BIPO WAS NOT AN UNHAPPY TOAD. HE LOVED to hop and hear the leaves of the forest floor crunch beneath his feet. He loved the Great Mating on the shore of the lake that celebrated the coming of summer. And he loved to sing.

His song wasn't an unhappy song, but compared to that of his fellows, it betrayed a hint of wondering. He didn't make declarative statements like his fellows —"Tree!" "Moon!" or "Mosquito!"—but would trail off in a minor key, whistling such complex notions as, "This tree just stands here," "The moon is smaller than it was last night," or "This mosquito will soon be inside me."

Sometimes the others would sing about him. One big female toad named Pupupup had two yellow lumps on her neck just like him. When she heard his peculiar songs, she would sing back to him: "If you wonder, you wander. If you wander, you get squished."

"You must be my mother," Bipo would sing back, igniting a small scandal. A toad just doesn't ask who laid his egg.

One spring, when Bipo was just awakening from his six-month nap, he wondered if he was the first to wake up. He did not remember where he was. It was dark in his burrow. He remembered strange dreams, but nothing about them. He knew one thing for sure. He was hungry.

As he dug his way out of his burrow with his spiny fingers, he came to an earthworm. With a sleep-slowed roll of his tongue, he scooped it into his mouth and delightedly chewed the soft salty worm-flesh.

The light—"the sublime light of spring"—dazzled his somnolent eyes. He blinked. It was still afternoon in the woods. Bipo had to be careful. It wouldn't do to be snatched by a hawk on the first day of spring.

He couldn't see the lake, but he remembered where it was. He hopped toward it, his legs painfully stiff. He jumped in the icy water. He stayed in just long enough to get the dirt out of his pores and suck a long cool drink through his skin.

He retreated into the woods and hid under some leaves. Peeking his head out, he could see the black boughs of the wet trees, still skeletal against the clouds. He could see the jagged loam of the forest floor. But there wasn't a single toad.

He wanted to sing for the sheer joy of being alive and to find out if any more toads had awakened yet. But he didn't dare take the risk while it was still light. Who knew what hungry skunks or seagulls might be lurking about? So he waited, terribly alone, quietly foraging for ants and potato bugs, watching the darkness ooze across the still wintry sky.

Was he the only toad in the world? Perhaps the toad-eaters had gone on a rampage over the winter and eaten every toad but himself. Perhaps the others had failed to dig deep enough burrows and had frozen with the lake. What good was it to be alive if no one else was?

As evening fell, the sky cleared some, and Bipo could see his old friend the moon rising. He started to sing, a high-pitched trill, a whistle—"bu-rr-r-r-r-ip"— that grew louder as the night wore on.

"Bu-rr-r-r-r-ip," he finally heard. The welcome voice of another toad! Bipo hopped happily toward the sound.

It was a familiar chirp, too. Could it be? He saw the other toad hopping out of the lake and back into the woods. He could see the two big yellow bumps on the back of his neck.

Blipy.

His oldest friend.

They'd been tadpoles together. They'd survived the famous pike attack, when most of their fellow tads had been swallowed in one gulp by a walleye. They'd watched each other in amazement as they'd sprouted legs and taken their first tentative gulps of air.

Bipo and Blipy hopped over each other, the traditional toad greeting. They sang of the full moon now rising in the east. They sang of good times when they would flick the plentiful insects from the air with their long tongues. They sang of the Great Mating, when they would spend days in the water cavorting with the females as they laid their eggs, oblivious to any danger.

The two toads continued their leapfrog through the woods, admiring the scilla, the tiny white flowers sprouting in scattered clumps. At one such clump, they felt the leaves move beneath them. Another toad was waking up from the Big Sleep. A larger toad, a female, peered toward them groggily, unseeing, blinking. From the triangle of bumps on her back, Bipo knew she was different from himself and Blipy, that she had not been a tadpole with them and was therefore fair game. He remembered her name, Popo. They sang a welcome song to her, "Burr-rip-rip-rip," and she smiled sleepily at them and lumbered off to splash in the lake.

In the next few days, the rest of the toads in the colony awakened from their sleep, and the nights came alive with singing.

One night, Bipo was hopping happily, following a swarm of slow-moving baby mosquitoes, scarfing numbers of them deliciously with his tongue. Suddenly, he sniffed that he was in a strange place. The toad colony inhabited a section of the woods marked by the distinctive smelling secretions from the toads' poison glands. Now Bipo detected no such toad-scent. His good sense told him to turn back. But in the distance, he saw a space glowing with light, like the sky above the lake, but somehow different. Curious, he hopped toward this new edge of the world.

When he got to where the trees ended, he stopped

short. He blinked incredulously at this broad expanse of treeless earth, like the lake, but sloping, green, and apparently solid. The space was covered by thin, green leaves, arranged in an unreal symmetry. He froze in place, too fascinated to return to the woods, too terrified to venture farther.

Finally, he hopped back the way he had come, calling his friends, "Blipy! Popo!" When he found them, he sang them into following him, to show them the "green earthen lake" he had discovered. Blipy stopped at the edge of the toad-scent and refused to continue. He repeated Pupupup's warning, "If you wonder, you wander. If you wander, you get squished."

"You frog!" Bipo called Blipy, a terrible insult. "Come on, Popo." He got Popo to go to the edge of the world with him. Terrified, she begged him to return. But Bipo hopped right into the green earthen lake. He didn't sink. But he was terribly exposed. A sharp-eyed owl could snatch him in a tongue-flick. He jumped back into the woods himself and quick-hopped fearfully with Popo back to the colony—another risk, since the quick-hops of panicky retreat are far more visible from the sky than the deliberate, intermittent hops of normal toad-travel.

In the days that followed, Bipo kept to himself, as most toads do, and didn't think about his discovery. Blipy and Popo had told him to just forget about it. "You're a daredevil," Popo told him.

One evening, the story about the "green earthen lake" slipped out in his song, causing a furor among the older toads. "How dare you stray from the toad-scent," they chastised him. Some really old toads re-sang, in their gruff voices, the old legends of evil lands where huge four-legged insects rolled over toads and flattened them. The other toads distanced themselves from Bipo, as though he were the messenger from the evil lands.

Bipo decided to stick to love songs like the other toads, in preparation for the Great Mating. But his love songs did not attract the female toads the way those of the other males did. Was there a hint of melancholy in these songs, too?

One big night the females all plunged into the lake and dared the males to follow them. Bipo and Blipy eagerly did so. The males swam about the females and tried to climb on top of them. Sometimes the females playfully pushed them aside. Sometimes they let them joyously plant their seeds in their egg sacs. Then, while they still embraced, the female would ooze her long string of jelly-wrapped fertilized eggs from under her tail like a slithery worm.

Bipo and Blipy both climbed on the back of Popo. But Popo dove deep in the water until one of them, Bipo, had to let go. She resurfaced, swam around, and said to him, even while Blipy clung to her back, "I'm sorry, Bipo, you're just too much of a daredevil."

Bipo was devastated, though he understood her reasoning. Popo figured if he was a wanderer, then their offspring might wander and have a poorer chance of survival. Besides, toads don't form attachments. No female toad usually cares much which male toad fertilizes her eggs, as long as he does it long and hard. No male toad cares which female's eggs he fertilizes. But Popo's spurning of him made him want her all the more, and he just couldn't get excited about any of the other females.

Later that night, he traveled to the edge of the world again, just to think things out. Something about that forbidden green earthen lake gave him perspective on his whole life. This time there was another light, like a moon, moving across the green lake. Something large and shadowy moved behind the light. The something was as big around as a tree, as tall as a bush. He dared not move even to retreat. The earth-bound moon revealed strange sights in its light. He saw another world dappled with clumps of gorgeous flowers, all different: reds, blues, yellows, whites, pinks, oranges, rounded, fluted, puffed up, frilly, some simple and delicate, some intricate and convoluted, some as small as himself, some as tall as the thing behind the light.

Then he saw thousands of insects swarming in the light: moths, mosquitoes, gnats, dragonflies, pincer bugs, katydids. Bipo's stomach rumbled and took over his judgment.

He took one hop onto the green earthen lake toward the light. He waited to see what would happen. Nothing. He took another hop. He was drawn, inexorably drawn. The closer he got, the more insects he could pick off with his tongue. Flit. Flit. What do the other toads know? Far from being an evil world, this is paradise. Closer still to the light, the insects were so thick he could pick off three of them with a single tongue-flick.

Then the light shone right on him, blinding him like the first daylight of spring. He tried to hop out of the light, but it followed him. He quick-hopped in panic. The light stayed right on him.

Then it was dark. A terrible clammy claw squeezed his body. He tried to hop. He squinched his eyes closed and spurted gushes of milky poison. The claw lifted him into the air. He could scarcely breathe. He went numb.

The grip suddenly let go. Bipo fell. Not far. Just a short way. He landed with a plop on a hard surface, like the lake when it's frozen.

Yet he was still moving. He was still, but he was moving. It made no sense. He hopped as far as he could to get away. Smack. Ouch. He hit something, and landed in the same spot. The sense of motion stopped. He looked around, taking long, slow breaths to calm himself.

There was light all around him, as if coming from four moons at once. The sky above him was round and black, interspersed with star-like bits of light. Visible around him were all sorts of angular shapes, but not a single tree, rock, or leaf.

He peed. His pee, warm and smelly, collected around his legs in a round lake. So he was in a round place with hard, invisible boundaries, and a round black star-studded sky.

Then he saw, one leap away from him, the most hideous monster imaginable. Its white eyes that moved together were as big as Bipo's whole head. Its mouth, a tongue-flick away, was big enough to swallow him in one gulp—better than grinding him up between its big, white, square teeth.

Bipo felt suddenly guilty for all the insects he had so joyfully snapped from the air, for this creature was about to do the same thing to him. He resigned himself. He closed his eyes and braced himself for a snap of the tongue that was sure to come. If you wonder, you wander, if you wander, you get scarfed. Justice be done.

But the tongue didn't come. Instead, thunder. An awful scraping sound, followed by light filling in where the dark sky had been. A gentle rain came, a sprinkling of water, a downpour of dry grass, and two flies. With more scraping thunder, the sky returned. He was grateful for the flies. He was no longer alone. He refused to eat them.

Time passed, interminably. The light in the monster's hive was so strange he couldn't tell day from night, but he ceased to care. The monster either molted and grew new skin of a different color all the time or changed colors like some lizards. Interesting, but not that interesting.

He slept a lot. He liked his dreams, sad as they were. He dreamed his whole life, from egg to tadpole, to adult, to the Great Mating. He regretted that he hadn't fertilized more eggs, but he was glad that there had been some. He hoped that his offspring weren't so devilishly filled with wonder.

He finally ate the flies. He got sick drinking his own pee, though sometimes the monster would turn his world upside down and pour it out, bumping him against the hard sky.

He stopped eating. He let the flies collect inside his world. He looked forward to a time when they would eat his remains, as he'd seen them do to the dead fish on the shore of the lake.

One evening, when Bipo was perhaps only days away from death, the big-eyed monster scraped off the sky to his tiny world, carried the world out to the green earthen lake, and turned it upside down. Half-dead, Bipo fell to the ground.

He tried to hop. Ouch. His legs were stiff. The air was cold now. He could smell fall. Brown leaves were beginning to cover even the green lake. He hopped laboriously back into the woods.

When at last he reached the magnificent toad-scent, he tried to sing. "Brp." His voice was hoarse. But soon he was singing with the delight of a newly land-bound toadlet.

The night was quiet. Crickets, he heard, but no toads. Mating season was over. Toads stop singing when the time comes to fatten themselves up for the winter. Could the Big Sleep have already begun? He didn't think so. He hadn't shed his skin yet.

He called Blipy, Popo, Pupupup. No answer. He scoured the toad-scent area. He plunged delightedly in the lake. He hopped toward the center of the woods again. "Bur-r-rip!" He heard it. Blipy! He was sure.

"Bipo!" Blipy called. They jumped over each other again and again. Then Popo appeared too.

"Bipo, Bipo, Bipo," they both sang. "We thought you were dead."

"Me? Not a chance," he boasted. "But let me tell you what happened."

Blipy and Popo listened politely while Bipo sang a long disjointed song about the monster with eyes the size of toad heads, skin that molted once a day, drinking his own pee, worlds of angular shapes, and four moons. Other toads came to hear the strange song, dangerously raucous for this time of year. When he came to the part about the monster dumping him unceremoniously on the green earthen lake, they shook their heads.

Bipo looked at the other toads. Their eyes blinked at him, weirdly reminiscent of the giant eyes of the monster. They didn't believe him. "You look weak," Pupupup sang. "You best spend your time fattening yourself up for winter."

The toads hopped away. Only Blipy and Popo lingered. "Popo!" Bipo pleaded. "You believe me, don't you?"

"Bipo," she sang, not unkindly. "I think you are a very sick toad. I wish you well. But I don't know what you are singing about. Perhaps you ate a scorpion. Your song, Bipo, it isn't possible."

"Blipy?" Blipy just looked at him with blank eyes and shook his head. Then the two of them hopped off.

In the nights remaining before the big sleep, Bipo did his best to fatten himself. The other toads avoided him. When he wasn't digging his burrow, he sang to the new toadlets snatches of his story, treating it as one of the legends, a warning to them to stay inside the toad-scent. When the other toads caught him, they glared at him fiercely until he hopped away.

Once, when secretly singing his story to a group of toadlets, one asked where this green earthen lake was. He found himself leading them toward the edge of the world to show them.

But when he saw the vast light beyond the trees, he realized he was endangering them just to prove himself. This won't do, he thought. "Let's go back now," he sang. "It was just a story. The others are right. Don't listen to me."

After that, he stuck to digging his burrow, and even that he did half-heartedly. As he licked off his old skin, he knew the time was coming. When the cold finally drove him underground, he knew he might not be deep enough. This time when he settled in for the big sleep, he wasn't sure if he would wake up again in the spring. He didn't even know if he wanted to or not. He would decide in his dream.

FIVE

THE CLEARING

BARNEY, WHO WAS ONLY SEVEN, WAS ALL EXCITED about going camping with Daddy, but I was older, almost ten, and didn't like all the work it took putting up the tent, lighting the fire, getting dirty as heck. Daddy woke us up at eight in the morning. Mom made pancakes, and we used the real maple syrup in Mason jars that Daddy gets from a grateful patient. Then she packed our rucksacks with liverwurst sandwiches and Coca-Colas.

We had to go on a huge hike before we got to the campsite. Daddy said it was a quarter mile! Can you imagine? Not only did we have to lug our rucksacks, Barney and I each carried a heavy wooden army cot. Barney could barely drag his. He got as far as the barn before he dropped it. Daddy looked back at him with that disappointed look he gets. I managed to drag both his and my cot all the way to the end of the driveway. Then I dropped them and started to cry.

That disappointed look again. But Daddy said, "That's OK. I'll come back and get them. Let's just get to the site."

We hiked past the gate to Tannery Row where a lot of rich people live. Herziger, the puppy, followed us. The next driveway led to the farm—Daddy's and Otto's farm. We trudged up the gravel road to the top of the first hill and then left the road for a narrow path into the woods.

The path was barely visible. I wondered if I would be able to find it on my own if I needed to. Even at midday, the woods were dark.

Daddy liked to give lessons. "Those trees with the white bark? Those are birches. Indians used to make canoes out of the bark. The big trees are oaks. Then all those pine trees. I think I overplanted."

There was a hush in the woods. We came to the clearing. It was round, cleared of trees, and half the size of a tennis court. Daddy said in a lowered voice, trying to scare us on purpose, "No one knows who made this clearing. It couldn't have been Indians because these woods are only fifty years old. Used to be fields. Kind of mysterious. Someone was camped here, built a campfire circle, and everything."

Barney played with Herziger in the dirt while I had to help Daddy put up that smelly green tent. It had specks of white stuff all over it that made Daddy sneeze. "Just a little mildew," he said. "Achoo!"

The tent had wooden poles and walls. I had to hold all the poles while Daddy fit them together. Then we had to drive the stakes in the ground. The day was sunny and hot. Finally, we did get it up, and I felt pretty good about being able to help him, but I was sweating. Not that he thanked me or anything.

That Herzie follows Barney everywhere. All day long Barney throws the ball and Herzie just watches the ball with no idea of what he's supposed to do.

Daddy went back down the hill to get the cots, and I got Harrybear out of my rucksack.

By the time Daddy came back with the cots, it was time to eat our lunch. I love liverwurst, but Barney hates it. Sometimes I think he just hates things that I like. He gave me his sandwich, and I gave him my apple. So he had two apples for lunch.

Daddy put the cots together. "There's only two cots," I said to him.

"They're for you two. I'm not staying the night. You guys need to learn how to be on your own."

I glanced at Barney. We both felt a jolt of fear. "Ha ha," I said. "You're kidding, right Daddy?"

"No, I'm not. You'll be fine. I'll stay until it's time for you to sleep, then I'll come get you in the morning."

This was not OK, but you don't argue with Daddy.

We spent the afternoon gathering sticks for a fire. We made a pile of them in the circle of stones. Daddy tried to show us how to light a fire by rubbing sticks together, but it didn't work. Finally, he used his Zippo lighter.

We put our hotdogs on a stick and roasted them. Then we put marshmallows on a stick and roasted them. Barney's marshmallows kept lighting on fire and burning to a crisp. "I like them that way," he insisted.

We sat on logs while Daddy told us a story. "That guy who made this clearing? His name was Smokey Joe, and he was what you call a hobo. He was wandering these woods about fifteen years ago, before the war, during the Depression. He was as poor as a church mouse, but there were a lot of poor people in those days. Not on Pike Lake so much, but on the farms around here. They'd help plant the corn and whatnot, but when they were done, they had no place to go. Smokey Joe found this place. He'd catch rabbits and squirrels and roast them right here."

"You're making this up, right, Daddy?" I asked.

He winked at me. "One day toward winter, the farmer who owned the land before we bought it saw the glow of the fire in the woods. He rode down here on his horse with his shotgun. He confronted the hobo.

"'Get off my land!' he said. 'You're trespassing.'

"'I got no place to go,' the hobo said.

"'Not my problem,' said the farmer.

"The hobo grabbed the farmer's leg in his saddle and pleaded, 'Please, sir, help a poor man.'

"But the horse panicked and reared up, and the shotgun went off and shot the hobo. No one ever knew who he was or where he came from. The farmer buried him right over there behind where the tent is now. Sometimes if you listen real careful, you can still hear him crying."

We got quiet, and, scared out of our wits, we heard the wind in the trees. It did sound like crying.

"OK, you two, time for bed," Daddy said, even though it was hardly dark yet.

"I have to pee," I said.

"Of course. Just go behind the tent."

"Where the hobo's buried?" I asked.

"That was just a story, Pookie."

"But there's no toilet."

"Toilet? You don't need a toilet. Just pull your pants down and pee on the ground."

"That's disgusting."

"It's what people did for centuries. When I was a boy, we didn't have toilets out here. We had an outhouse. Just a hole in the ground."

Terrified, sure I would see the hobo rising like steam from his grave, I went behind the tent, but I couldn't pee for the life of me. I just pretended to go.

I watched Barney pee against a tree, and I was jealous of boys who could do it so easy.

"I have to go poo," Barney whispered to me, probably afraid to tell Daddy.

"Just go on the ground like I did."

He pulled down his pants, but he couldn't do it either.

We crawled into our sleeping bags. Daddy kissed us, which he rarely does. "You'll be fine. See you first thing in the morning."

Barney called Herzie, but he followed Daddy out of the woods, hungry. Barney and I both held our breath as Daddy left us. Barney started to whimper.

"It's OK, Barney," I said, though I wasn't at all sure that it was. It was really dark in the tent.

Barney's whimper became a cry, then a sob, then a wail. I crawled into his cot with him and cuddled with him until he fell asleep. Then I went back to my cot and fell asleep. I dreamed about that hobo, but he was a nice man and protected us during the long night, keeping away the wild foxes and bobcats rumored to roam the woods.

When Daddy came to check on us, it was still dark. "I was worried about you," he said. He smelled like whisky.

"What time is it?" I asked.

"About midnight. Boy, it stinks in here." He shined his flashlight on me and saw that I had peed in the sleeping bag and it was soaking wet. Then he shined the light on Barney's cot. His sleeping bag was open and right on top was a pile of poo. But Barney was gone!

"Where's Barney?" Daddy asked. "You were supposed to watch him."

"How could I watch him? I was asleep."

"You should have heard him leave."

I started to cry.

"We'll find him. He couldn't have gotten far. You stay here. I'll look around."

"I want to come with you."

"OK." He held my hand as we trudged through the woods looking and calling. "Barney! Barney!"

We went all through the woods, and farther up the hill to where Otto lived. His house was quiet.

"What am I going to tell your mother?" Daddy asked. "She thought I should have stayed with you."

I was beginning to think we had lost Barney forever. He could be a brat sometimes, but I would miss him. And it was partly my fault. I should have heard him leave.

We got down to the big house and woke up Mommy. She panicked. "How could you lose him, Robert? I told you to stay with the kids." Mommy hardly ever gets mad at Daddy.

"They need to learn independence, Trudy."

"At age seven? Call Chief Lutz. Have them search." Chief Lutz was the police chief of the Pike Lake Village.

"Did you check his room?" I asked quietly.

Sheepishly, Daddy and I went into Barney's room where he was sound asleep in his bed like a baby. Daddy gave me a hug.

Though I hated him sometimes, I kissed Barney on the forehead.

THE NEXT MORNING, Daddy dragged us back up to the campsite. He made Barney carefully carry his sleeping bag with the poo on it back behind the tent and dump the poo where the hobo was buried.

"You need to bury it, Barney," Daddy said.

The shovel was way too big for him, but he managed to dig a little hole and scrape his poo into it.

Then Daddy took the shovel and dug. And dug. And dug. He stopped to rest. "We're going to build an outhouse here," he said. He made me dig a little, but I didn't get much farther than Barney.

Daddy kept digging. The sweat poured off his brow. But he dug and dug until the hole was way over his head.

We were starving. Mommy brought us liverwurst sandwiches and Cokes at lunchtime. Barney ate his this time.

Mom helped us fold the cots and take the tent down. She had brought the car, so we just had to haul them back to the road.

Daddy kept digging until he could hardly get out of the hole.

We drove back to the big house in silence. As we got home, I asked him, "Did you find Smokey Joe's bones?"

He smiled at me, clearly tired of the whole adventure. "No, Pookie. That was just a story. Next week we'll build an outhouse up there."

"OK," I said, though I was sure I could find something else to do. He forgot about it anyway. The outhouse never got built. The hole is still there though.

SIX

WOOF

THEY CALL ME HERZIGER, BUT MY REAL NAME is Woof. They call me a dachshund, but in reality, I am just a dog. I live with my mother among a pack of wild humans in a big house on a lake.

Mama (they call her Tootsie) is always complaining about the humans. "They chase us around in their deadly cars, beat us with newspapers when we do what comes naturally to us, and feed us raw horsemeat and stale, dry, tasteless kibble," she tells me.

"Mama," I tell her. "You're the one who chases cars."

"That's just my way of getting even."

It's true we've had to train them to feed us. It's fairly simple. We howl our heads off. They hate that. They hate our noise. We can get them to do lots of things just by making our noise.

Are we free? This is a question that has puzzled canine philosophers since the dawn of legend. I don't know if we're free. Humans keep us behind closed doors that only they can open. But you'd be surprised how effective a good howl can be. If we bark loud and long, we almost always get what we want. That's certainly one definition of freedom.

I think Mama exaggerates how bad things are for us. She just likes to complain. We've got it pretty good. I'm inclined to think we are free. "We could always run away," I argue with Mama.

We know of dogs in the woods who have run away and now run "wild," who spend all of their time hunting rabbit to feed themselves. They're slaves to their hunger. It's a trade-off. The humans provide us with food and shelter, and in exchange, we don't eat them.

The wild thing is: they love us. Humans! What a breed! They are so starved for love that all we have to do is curb our natural hostility toward them just a bit, and they slobber all over us with their love. I have this one human, they call him Barney. I call him, "Hmmm," a high-pitched squeal. He's young for a human, maybe seventy in dog years. (We don't know how long they live, but there's one in my pack that is at least three hundred and fifty). The boy just can't keep his hands off me. He is always hugging me. He's up on me so much, sometimes I hump his leg just for a joke. He doesn't get it.

Mama and I are very close. I'm the only one left of her only litter. She has just started telling me things now that I'm fourteen. She tells me how for years, when her Time came, the humans would just lock her up— even though all her male friends came around and she would have given her canine teeth to mate with any one of them, or all of them. Then one spring they took her all the way to this awful prison to breed her, with a complete stranger, a dachshund, who cared only about getting off and nothing for her. My father. Whom I will never meet.

She tells me she had five pups, but that all of them but one—me—were sold off.

"Did they give you the money at least?" I ask her.

She laughs. "No, son. They let me keep you. That's all."

"Why me?" I ask.

She nips my neck gently. "Because you're cute. Because that boy, Hmmm, liked you."

I dimly remember my brothers and sisters. I do remember frolicking with them and cuddling with them at Mama's teats, wallowing in the sticky smell of warm milk.

Mama tells me one of the many oppressions we dogs suffer at the hands of men is that we cannot breed freely with whomever we like. When I hear this, I grow defiant. "We'll see about that," I snarl. I'm just beginning to notice some powerful fragrances in the air.

I tell my friend Wow what mother has told me. He's what humans call a Great Dane, but we just call him a giant dog. He scoffs at her weakness. "I suppose small dogs do have problems," he says. When I'm with Wow, I imagine we can do anything. No mere human can stand in his way. He's bigger and stronger than any of them. He smells as fresh and powerful as the woods. We roam around the lake, looking for adventure, sniffing for bitches.

One day we find a big house giving off the sweetest scent imaginable. We know her, of course. Wa-Wa, the poodle, and is she hot! We know all the dogs in the area. The smell brings tears to our eyes. It's sweet and pungent and hangs in the air. It tingles like the smell of lilac blossoms, but with the mouthwatering sweetness of a dog who has just rolled in dead fish.

Wa-Wa lives in a big white house with a perfect lawn rolling down to the lake. An old man, the one they call a caretaker, is riding a little tractor around on the lawn, cutting the grass, but the dogs get so thick cavorting in front of him that he has to stop. Thank goodness. Machines like that give off a high-pitched whine that drives us dogs crazy. The house is surrounded by dogs. Collies, spaniels, setters, Labradors, schnauzers, beagles. To us (since we don't make these foolish distinctions), we are big dogs, little dogs, black dogs, brown dogs, gray dogs, spotted dogs—you name it, all the males in the neighborhood have come courting here. The noise is terrific.

At first, the dogs content themselves with pissing around chunks of rival territory. It's like a game to see who can piss the most the fastest, but it's in the spirit of fun, and the lawn in front of the house eventually divides fairly evenly among the dogs.

Then the old man yells. "Get out of here, damn dogs! Go home!"

Wow and the bigger dogs discuss attacking the man

but decide that would only bring retaliation. Instead, they satisfy themselves by crashing through the perfectly arranged flower beds and knocking over the largest blossoms. The man retreats into the house.

"Git! Git, dogs! Git!" he yells behind him.

Frustration runs high. Near the door to the house where the smell is especially strong, a couple of dogs are play-fighting. The rest of us surround them, egging them on with our barks. The dogs get rougher and rougher. After a while, we all forget it's just play. The fight turns real, and the salty, intoxicating scent of blood fills the air.

But good old Wow, our natural leader by virtue of his size, steps in. With a bark that terrifies both combatants, he breaks up the fight. We all laugh at ourselves for getting so carried away and thank Wow for keeping a cool head.

As the dogs begin to realize that no matter what they do, the bitch is not coming out, they turn their ardor on each other. Wow and I make quite a scene when I stick my butt in the air so he can hump me. He gets his big pecker all the way in there, too. It hurts, but the smell of his hot breath on my neck is delicious. The dogs surround us and laugh their hard-ons off.

Just then the old man comes out of the house again, carrying a shotgun. "Fuck with my garden, will you!" he growls. *Blam!* He fires into the air. *Blam! Blam!*

There are enough hunting dogs among us to know what guns can do, and they recommend we disperse. We scatter like a flock of chickens, taking care to run through and destroy as much of the flower beds as we can.

One day when Wow isn't around, Mama asks me if I want to go down the road with her to see our friend Ruff. There's nothing else to do, so I go along. It's a hot muggy day, and our tongues hang out even when we stand still. A car speeds past, ignoring us. Mama has to chase it of course.

"Yip-yip-yip-yip!"

I hang back and wait for her senses to return. "One day you'll be sorry," I tell her.

We cut through the woods to avoid the hot alfalfa fields.

Ruff, a rare dog whose human name and dog name are the same, lives in a tiny farmhouse that smells of potatoes and manure. The old man who works for Wa-Wa's humans lives here, too, but he acts completely different around Ruff. You can't figure humans.

Ruff is what humans call a mutt, but dogs would call her a medium-sized, shaggy, gray dog. Mama tells me Ruff smells like her Time is coming soon. She gives me a wink.

"Mama," I whine. I'm not interested. Somehow, anyone Mama recommends doesn't really turn me on. Besides, I've known Ruff since we were pups. She's like family.

Ruff is in the house, but she starts to howl when she smells us coming. Her human lets her go just as we scramble out of the woods into her piss perimeter. She yips and yaps in greeting and bites necks all around. We sniff rears. I can't tell about her Time, but I'm sure Mama knows about these things. We chase around the farmyard. We chase the cat until it creeps under the house to a place we can't squeeze. We scare the chickens. We sleep for a time in the shade of the barn.

I have a dream about Wow licking me off, and I wake up with my slick pecker sticking out of its sleeve. *What the hell?* I think. Mama's asleep. Ruff is stirring in her nest of hay. I sidle over and mount her.

Ruff goes berserk. She jumps out from under me, spins around, and snaps at me, catching a piece of my ear in her pearly teeth. I smell my own blood. Ruff glares at me, growling softly but fiercely. "How dare you just jump me like that!" she growls.

Mama rouses herself and, with her infallible instincts, figures out exactly what's going on. She tramps right in between us and prances about with her laughing bark. Then she swings by the house and comes back with a juicy bone in her mouth. When Ruff sees her, she squeals, "Hey, that's mine!" and takes off after her.

We play "Get the Bone" for the rest of the afternoon. We've all forgotten the tension between Ruff and me, though when we part to go home for supper, I look at her differently. On the way home, Mama grumbles about me being so insensitive. "First, Son, you have to wait until the scent is really ripe. Even then you let her make the first move." I don't say anything. I'm annoyed because now I can't seem to help thinking about that stupid Ruff.

On the way home, Mama is quiet and keeps her distance. She seems inordinately mad. I know her moods. I know she gets depressed sometimes. I usually leave her alone. But for some reason this time, I catch up with her and give her a questioning look.

She slows down and cries a bit. "I never told you what happened to me after you were born, Woof. The next time my Time came, they took me to the vet, you know, the one who gave you those shots. He gave me a shot. I fell asleep. When I woke up, my belly ached and there was a cut in my gut. He had done something that changed me. That delicious yearning just went away. My scent went dry as kibble. My Time stopped coming. It just went away and never came back. It's a terrible feeling, Woof, like a hole where love used to be." She whines some more. When we get back to our own piss perimeter, she stops. "I can't face them right now, Woof. You go back home. I'm going for a run in the woods for a while."

I know she's lying. What she's really going to do is go out on the highway and chase cars. I know that's how she lets off steam.

By the time I get home, it's dark, and the humans make a fuss over me. They feed me my horsemeat and kibble and call for Tootsie. They call and call and call.

The mother, a human female, is funny. I call her Humom. Some days she bustles about and takes care of everyone. Some days she forgets to feed us. After dinner she takes off on foot into the night to look for Mama. She doesn't find her, of course. Mama comes back herself before Humom does. When Humom does get back, she pats us both and closes us in the playroom where Mama and I sleep on a human size bed.

A few days later, I meet Wow at the top of the wooded hill behind the house. It's another hot, wet day. We can smell the coming rain. We chomp a bit of grass, but the sun is still blazing in the sky. We decide to stick to the shade of the woods.

We tromp slowly through the underbrush, our tongues hanging out. We chase everything that moves—squirrel, chipmunk, rabbit, field mouse, butterfly—but without much conviction. We rest in the shade of a rusted water tank, in which we can smell a soggy dead rat without difficulty.

As soon as I open my mouth, I regret it. "Ruff's Time is coming," I say.

"Mmmm," Wow says. "Now that's a choice morsel."

The way he says that rubs me wrong. Somehow, Ruff isn't just another bitch in heat. So I drop it.

Wow doesn't though. "So," he says. "Shall we go for her?"

I stammer. "Um, I said it was coming, it's not here yet," I say.

"Oh," he says with a funny, hurt look. I've seen the look before, when I've hesitated to share a bone with him. It's generally followed by an angry growl that persuades me not only to share the bone but to eagerly offer him the whole thing.

Not this time, buddy, I think.

The next puff of wind from the other side of the hill brings with it the strong pissy smell of a deer. "Mmmm,"

Wow says. He gives me a look. Few animals challenge Wow the way deer do. Rarely does he encounter an animal anywhere as big and fast as he is. And one that only eats vegetables is irresistible since it offers no threat.

Deer are boring to me. They're way over my head, with my pitiful stubby legs. I'm a good sport though, and I lumber along after Wow as he takes off at full speed after the deer scent.

It isn't long before I lose him completely and find myself all alone in the woods. It's too hot to run anyway. I wander a bit, not really sniffing for anything, just enjoying the woods. I even find myself ambling away from the diminishing scent of Wow and the deer—and toward something else, but I don't know what.

At the bottom of a ravine, I'm hit with a smell I've smelled before but never known what it was. It's a dog smell, but it's not a dog smell. The piss is sweeter, fresher, as though it eats live game. The smell just sits there, hanging in the air. I follow it, curious, but careful. It's coming from a tree. I sniff around the bottom of the tree. There's a hollow under the tree and among the roots, such as a bunch of rabbits might make, but larger. I should know better, but I'm bored, so I bark, poised to hightail it out of there in case it's a skunk or a weasel.

I hear some rustling from inside the tree and draw back behind another tree to watch. After a while, an animal emerges from under the tree. It's very quiet. Its eyes are sharp like a cat's and blink against the light. It's about the size of Ruff and has the shape of a dog but with a long bushy tail tipped with white. Dogs are color blind, but this creature is the same tone of a setter I know whose human name is "Red." It moves like a cat, too.

I've heard both human and dog legends about such a beast, though I've never seen one before. Dogs call it "Er-er-er," which means something like, "wild night grandfather." Humans call it a fox. It slinks right up to me, without saying a word. I bark to scare it, but that er-er-er is not afraid of anything. It stares at me with an utterly unnerving confidence. It yawns. Politely but firmly, that yawn says, "Please go away. I'm sleeping."

I don't argue. This thing is too much for me with its silent stare. I move on. The fox returns to its den.

But it has upset me for some reason. Its stare speaks of a purity of life that I can barely imagine, mired as my life is in the compromise with humanity. I know what it is: freedom. Freedom from having to be somewhere to get fed. Freedom from the cloying "love" of humans, which is more about them than it is about us. A sense of being a part of nature, not imprisoned in some artificial habitat.

I strut about as wild as the fox. I close my mind to the sophisticated thoughts of dogdom and listen only to my instincts. I stalk through the woods as if looking for prey, for rabbit, for squirrel. I perk up my ears and sniff my nose to be flooded by the sounds and smells of the woods.

The next thing I know I'm hit with a blast of the dead fish smell of ripe bitch, and not just any bitch either. Ruff. I'm right up on her piss-perimeter.

Before I see her, I can hear her in the yard licking herself. What a smell! Holy dogshit. She smiles at me coyly. My tongue hangs out and slobbers, and not just from the heat. I feel the air against my unsheathed pecker. She squeals a greeting. I try to squeal back, but I'm speechless. I sniff her awkwardly. She laughs and moves away. Did I do something wrong? My heart's beating so fast I can't hear myself think. I do hear Mama's voice in my brain saying, "Wait," but I'm up against the power of nature itself.

I approach Ruff again, questioningly, tentatively. She giggles, moves away, and sits again. I can see that her hind parts are swollen and juicy. It's all I can do to keep myself from jumping her. I think she even wants me to, but I can't quite believe it either. Me? I'm too little for her. My little thing will never satisfy all that yearning I smell. And why does she keep moving away? I manage her name. "Ruff." She lets me get closer next time, but she moves away again, though not as far. My balls are throbbing. I can't stand it. Finally I get one leg up on her. She bites my neck, but it doesn't hurt. She pulls away again, but only about half my length. I swing the other leg over.

Just then there's a raging bark swooping down from the hill from the way I'd come. Ruff jumps out from under me. Both of us turn toward the sharp noise. My body stiffens as my pecker goes limp.

It's Wow. Any other time, the sound of his deep, sharp bark would delight me, but not today. I poise myself toward the sound of him crashing through the underbrush as if he were my worst enemy. When he hears I am not greeting him, he slows his approach.

I won't glance at Ruff for fear she'll somehow show me she'd rather have him. Who wouldn't? Besides, dog law says he's the biggest so he goes first, friendship or no friendship. But I say, law or no law, he doesn't.

He strides up to us and laughs at my fierce stance. "Hey, Woof, it's only me," he says.

I growl at him and stare with all the confidence of that fox.

Wow ignores me. He goes right up to Ruff and struts around her, licking his chops disgustingly as he sniffs her fragrant rear. His big thing hangs down the length of my tail, the girth of my leg.

"No," I yap at him with all the ferocity I can muster. He does glance at me and pause his obscene dance, but only for a tail-wag.

I refuse to look at Ruff, but it sounds like she's reacting to Wow with the same kind of infatuating tease that she used on me, damn her soul. I lose my head.

I leap at Wow's neck and manage to break the skin of his shoulder. He stares at me, first in amazement, then in fury. He knocks me silly with his huge paw and shows me that he can fit my whole head in his mouth. But I'm inconsolable. I go for his underside and sink my teeth into his balls. This enrages him still more and soon we are all over each other, no holds barred.

Ruff howls her head off at us, but I hardly hear. The blood smell has me crazed. I'll kill this dog—if I don't die first.

From the corner of my eye, I see the old man come out of the house with his gun. "Stop it, dogs! Go away! Git!" he yells. He fires the gun in the air, *blam!* Wow starts to leave like any sane dog, but I jump at his rear haunch and take out a kibble-sized chunk of flesh.

We keep at it, ignoring the old man. He fires a couple more times, then retreats into the house. Mostly Wow draws back his pointy-nosed self and tries to get me to listen to reason. "Only if you leave," I spit at him.

"C'mon, Woof, the law's the law."

"Eat your law."

"If you don't stop, I'm going to have to hurt you," he threatens. Since I can't see out of one eye for the blood, it seems to me like he's already done this.

I'm only vaguely aware, but I can smell other dogs arriving on the scene, amazed that the fight has continued despite the gunshots. They approach gingerly, but relentlessly, no more able to resist a good dogfight than a bitch in heat. Luckily for them, the other dogs don't come on to Ruff, no doubt waiting for Wow to have first dibs after doing me in. But they may be surprised.

Then I hear my human, Hmmm, running down the road, calling. "Herziger! Herziger!" There is terrible fear in his voice. Out of the corner of my eye I see him plow into the pack of dogs surrounding Wow and me. But they're not about to let some toy-sized human mess up the fight of the century, the fight between the giant and the runt, the colossus and the dwarf. The other dogs jump Hmmm, and soon it's his blood I smell.

In other circumstances, I might have let sentimental

duty snap me to my senses and jumped into the other fray to protect my human. But I have other things on my mind. I am going to win first dibs on Ruff or die trying.

I'm holding my own with Wow. His size is not such an advantage when I can jump from underneath him and nip at his chest and balls. I am tiring though. My eyes and mouth are filled with blood. I've only got three working legs. There are open wounds oozing all over my little body. I'm beginning to forget what the fight was about. I know it's too late for me to do much with, what's-her-name, Ruff.

Then I smell a great cloud of dust and hear Humom's car, followed by Mama's yip-yip-yip. Mama jumps right in between us, glaring back and forth at Wow and me with a look that makes us ashamed. I'm secretly grateful and pull back to lick my many wounds.

I look around and discover that Ruff isn't even in the yard anymore. I smell that she's gone inside the house. My body suddenly floods with pain. I see blood gushing out. I glance at Wow and see that he isn't hurt at all.

Humom is making a big fuss over Hmmm. He has a small bite in his leg. She's got a blanket on him and is carrying him to her car. When she has him lying down in the back seat, she turns her attention to me. "Look at you, bad dog. I suppose I have to take you to the vet. It looks like your leg's broken." She dumps me on the floor in the back, next to Hmmm, who is crying.

"Here goes the ambulance," Mom says as she takes off down the road. I hear Mama chasing after us, yip-yip-yip. She wants to come, too. I whimper. "That damn

Tootsie," Mom says. "Get out of the way, stupid dog!" The car swerves.

Then there's an awful thunk and an ear-splitting squeal. "Oh, no," Mom moans. "Not now."

Mom stops the car, and in no time has Mama in the back with us. She's been hit by the car, and she's hurt worse than me. Her eyes don't focus. She can't hold her head up. Her body alternately spasms and goes limp. She whimpers all the way to town. My eyes flood with tears. *It's my fault*, I think. Then I pass out.

When I wake up, I'm in a cage suffused with the sickly sweet smell of death. There's no smell of Mama anywhere near, though I can smell all kinds of other dogs, cats, and sick birds.

When they finally take me home with bandages on my leg and ears, I still can't smell any more than a mere trace of Mama. Hmmm, himself with a bandage on his leg, finally tells me, tearfully, "We had to have her put to sleep, Herziger. I'm sorry."

Put her to sleep! You mean you killed her, I think. *Some kind of love.*

That night the sky breaks open and the air fills with thunder, lightning, and rain. I curl up under Hmmm's bed.

After that, I don't see Wow or Ruff for a long time. I mope around pretty close to home. Sometimes I do go into the woods and visit the fox though. I love to look into his clear eyes and wonder what it would be like to have such dignity, such freedom, and to be so free from doubt.

SEVEN

THE BIRDS
AND THE BEES

— 1 —

Z -z-z was used to the big blur violating the Hive from time to time and knew better than to waste her life in panic. If she stung it, she would die. It was only stealing honey. The Hive had resigned itself to giving up some of its honey as rent for the safe dwelling the blur provided.

The other, smaller blur bugged her. It only showed up some of the time. It just stood there. It didn't take honey. It just watched. She could smell its fear. It wasn't her job to guard the Hive, but she kept her eyes on this blur anyway. It seemed to have no function, and that was suspicious.

With a warning dance, she told Z-z-z-z, a guard bee, to keep her eyes on the smaller blur.

"Why?" Z-z-z-z danced back.

"It doesn't do anything."

Z-z-z-z flicked her antennae in agreement. They both knew the legends ZAH-ZAH told in the evening that each blur had a special duty. One steals the honey, one tends the flowers, another builds their incredibly huge but clumsy hives with their stupid rectangular cells. It was generally understood among bees that blurs, while social beings, had not yet discovered the hexagon.

Z-z-z's function was to find the richest flowers and to dance their location to the other workers, who would go there and gather nectar and pollen. She liked her job. She knew the Hive was all-important. Only rarely did she even think of herself as independent of the Hive. Usually when she thought "I," she thought of the whole Hive. The Hive was the being, she was merely one of its parts. Her nurses had simply assigned her the job while she was busy transforming herself as a pupa. She would have liked to be Mother, but only seven or so of the forty thousand female bees in the Hive got picked for this job, and the first born of these killed all her rivals. She was certainly glad she wasn't a stupid drone who hovered around the Hive all day hoping for his big chance to get ZAH-ZAH. But the drones had their role, too. Useless as they were, a few of them, and only a few, would mate with the Mother, and father the next generation.

As bad as she would talk about the drones, there was one she was fond of. She had done a stint nursing him when he was just a white-hulled nymph, and she'd presided at his hatching. Bz, he was named by the consensus of midwives. There was something about him. Of the five hundred brothers competing for the honor, this one would father the next generation, she was sure. He had strong wings. He was demanding and arrogant, insisting that she wait on him antenna and leg, but such traits are forgivable in one who would be the next Father.

As the days grew longer, she noticed that each time she saw the small non-functional blur, it was a little closer to the hive. It really gave her the creeps.

She buzzed of the creature among her friends. "Why doesn't it take our honey? What does it want, anyway?" She found herself politicking in her circle for a cautious appraisal of the do-nothing blur.

"You worry too much," Z-z-Z-z, another guard, told her. "It's just a blur."

Z-z-z wasn't consoled. She took on an unofficial watch of the do-nothing, hovering around its monstrous eye—a vulnerable spot, bees know. She examined the strange eye closely. A single peep-hole. How could it see anything? It could only see in one direction at once. And round. No wonder they don't know hexagons.

Then once it took a swipe at her. It brought its long limb within a feeler's breadth of her stinger. She spasmed as the panic flooded her body. She unsheathed her stinger. But she absorbed an extra gulp of air and calmed herself.

The blur disappeared. The next time it returned, it was covered with webs and had no place vulnerable to her sting. She kept her distance, eyes wary.

— 2 —

𝘉 arney first learned about the birds and the bees from Jake. Clifford, the caretaker, took him to Jake's once a week or so after school in his '41 Ford pickup. Jake's farm was a quarter mile down the road from the Blatz place by Clifford's ancient odometer. Jake's daughter was married to Clifford's son. Jake's daughter had taught Barney nursery school, years ago. He was in fourth grade now. Jake worked for the next-door neighbors, the Starks.

Jake smiled a lot and smoked a pipe. He had a bushy scrub-brush of a mustache that was at once comical and dignified. Occasionally, he even looked at Barney. Most adults didn't even see him.

Jake was a beekeeper. One day, Jake asked Barney, "You like bees, Son?"

Barney shuddered and shook his head. "I got stung once." His voice was shrill with disuse. He was not a talkative boy. He kept remembering when he stepped on a yellow jacket and screamed. He'd never known such pain.

"Oh, honeybees don't sting. They sting once and they're dead. That's the same as a hero dying in a war. There ain't that many heroes. Honeybees just the same as people. They don't want to die. It's all birds and bees, Son."

Barney smiled shyly, hopeful the old man would continue.

"See, birds and bees spread the pollen that mates the plants so they can grow. Take it from an old farmer."

Barney knew the family myth that Jake and Clifford had once owned a big farm together but lost it from laziness. That's why they're caretakers now, the tale went. Now what they called "the farm" was two acres of alfalfa, a small field of clover, a vegetable garden, a flower garden, a red barn used as a garage, a handful of chickens, a dog, a cat, and three hives full of honeybees in wooden frames.

"You like honey?" Jake asked.

Barney nodded yes.

"You ever taste it fresh?"

Barney shook his head no.

"Well, c'mon then." The two of them went out back to the "apiary" as Jake called it. Barney stopped fifty paces from the hives. "I told you, they don't sting. Not if you're careful." But, paralyzed, Barney wouldn't budge even with Jake tugging his arm. "Watch, then," Jake said.

Jake, without a net or glove, walked right up to one of the boxes and reached into the top section. He broke off a piece of the honeycomb and crushed it in his hand. He made Barney lick the honey off his hand, an unpleasant sensation until the taste came through. The sweetness coated his throat and buzzed all the way through him. He licked Jake's hand clean until he tasted pipe smoke.

This gathering of honey became a weekly ritual, with Jake chipping away at Barney's fear. Barney's father had told him, "Just stand still," when he was around bees. He would do just that, as each week Jake would edge him closer to the hives and fill him with a new piece of bee lore. "Of all the females, only the queen gets laid."

The next week, "The male bees are all drones and only a few get to screw the queen. Those that win die right away. The others are killed by the workers when they return to the hive."

Then, "So only about five out of forty thousand bees have sex. All the rest die virgins. That's rare in nature. Even a flower gets its pistils jiggled."

When Barney finally got close enough to see inside the hive, Jake stuck a pith helmet on him, way too big, wrapped his head in nets, and slid huge gloves on his hands. Barney pretended to be a robot so he wouldn't have to feel the fear gurgling in his stomach.

"Look at that architecture!" Jake exclaimed as he pointed out the honeycomb. "Perfect hexagons. All exactly the same size. No one knows how they do it."

Barney read all the books in the library about bees. He would even ask Jake show-offy questions. "Have the queens mated this year yet?"

"Not yet. Wait until around the first of July."

"They dance to give directions, don't they?"

"So they say. But if you listen closely enough, you can hear them talk."

Barney listened as hard as he could. He stilled himself and squinched up his face. He heard a soft oscillating hum. He listened and listened. The hum changed ever so slightly from time to time.

School finally let out, and he started coming to Jake's to listen to the bees without Clifford, on his Raleigh three-speed bike. He came every day around noon. He learned to recognize the drones as they made their daily practice flight.

He came at sunset one night after supper. He heard the hum change as the sun went down and learned the bee word for sunset.

One night Barney heard the bees talking English— not English, exactly; something it sounded like he could understand.

After hours of listening, he figured out what they were saying. They were calling his name.

He didn't believe it at first. He heard his father's voice inside him say, "That's just your imagination."

But the bees insisted. "Barney, Barney, Barney," they called. He moved closer to the hive. He thought of Winnie-the-Pooh being summoned in his tummy by his honeypots.

One day, Jake showed Barney a microscope and said, "Lookie here, Son, I'm not much on the science, but my bee supplier says I ought to art-i-fish-ally in-sem-in-ate my queens, so I can get a stronger strain. I need your help."

"Yeah?" Barney brightened.

"Yeah. You have to watch every day around noon and catch the queen right when she's ready to do her mating flight. You can't miss her. She's twice the size of the others." Jake gave Barney a cigar box to put her in.

— 3 —

As the summer days grew hot and heady, and the stored honey plentiful, Z-z-z found it increasingly hard to concentrate on finding new swatches of clover, crabapple blossom, and phlox. All she could think about was Bz. The other workers too became caught up in the drama of who the next Fathers would be. Each drone had its fan club of workers, feeding him, grooming him, flattering him, catering to his every desire. Every day the drones would venture forth into the world hopeful that this day would be the day the virgin Mother chose for her deflowering. Z-z-z would pretend to go out herself in search of new foraging grounds, but she would instead watch the entrance of the hive for any sign of the Mother.

She would also watch that troublesome, do-nothing blur. Every day it would come closer to the hive by about three dance-circles. The way it followed the flight of the drones with its head, she was worried that it might interfere with the mating. Blurs have been known to do this. There were legends of Mothers being captured by blurs and being replaced by terrible smelling new Mothers, already full of ripe eggs.

Then one day, with the blur just a few dance-circles from the Hive, ZAH-ZAH herself appeared on the threshold. She took a couple of awkward practice flights, having rarely used her wings before. Z-z-z flew up to warn Bz the moment had arrived.

When she returned to the Hive, she saw the blur was chasing ZAH-ZAH. Z-z-z unsheathed her stinger to attack the blur. She buzzed the blur's eye, covered with webbing. ZAH-ZAH twisted about in the air and finally flew free of the blur, at the cost of some of her stamina. ZAH-ZAH now headed straight into the air. Z-z-z followed her. Against the dazzling violet of the sky, Z-z-z could dimly make out the great pursuit of the large Mother by the dark cloud of eager drones.

When the drones caught up with ZAH-ZAH, Z-z-z could see that Bz was right out in front. He would be one of the new Fathers! Higher and higher, beyond the tops of the trees they flew until Z-z-z could barely see them any longer. At the last second, she saw ZAH-ZAH falter, and then she felt the tumultuous vibration as the first winning drone coupled with her.

She hovered awhile, waiting to see the new Father, his abdomen ravaged, dead but proud, plummet to earth. It wasn't Bz. Z-z-z herself sank back to earth with disappointment. Two more drones followed the first into triumphant death. Neither of them was Bz either. All that coddling. He had been strongest, but because that blur tired out ZAH-ZAH before her flight, she didn't fly as high or as fast, and the weaker drones had won out in the end. Z-z-z was sick.

The Mother returned to the Hive, glowing with satisfaction, her dead drones' sex organs dangling from her rear. Right away she began to lay her eggs in the specially prepared hexagonal cells.

Z-z-z was despondent over Bz's failure. He too returned to the hive, expecting her and her cohort to continue taking care of him. No way. Z-z-z was fed up with the whole business. She ignored him.

Bz and the other drones became desperate. They didn't know how to feed themselves. They became increasingly demanding, while their worker-helpmates shunned them with increasing hostility.

Finally, an hour or so after Bz's return, Z-z-z had had enough. She attacked him, snapping at him with her powerful mandibles. Though he was bigger than her, he was weakened from hunger and, anyway, had no stinger. She wouldn't use hers unless she had to, but if she had to, she would.

The other workers followed her example and began attacking "their" drones.

The Hive was in complete uproar. Z-z-z snapped and snapped at Bz until his wings were tattered and big chunks of flesh fell away from his thorax. Soon he gave in. "All right, all right, Z-z-z, have it your way," he buzzed. "I'm leaving." She followed him all the way to the landing platform. She watched him take off on his dilapidated wings. He would be dead in two days, she thought. Her abdomen quivered with a small spasm of grief.

— 4 —

*B*arney failed to catch the queen. He hoped Jake wouldn't be mad. He didn't see the actual mating. But he continued to watch the bees for a long while. He saw the workers throwing the drones out of the hive. He found himself watching them now with a surprisingly complete absence of fear. He threw off the pith helmet with the netting. He heard the bees calling him again. "Barney, Barney, Barney." He decided right then that, to make up for his failure to catch the queen, this would be the day he would get himself some honey.

With no special gear but gloves, he lifted the lid on the top super.

— 5 —

Suddenly, Z-z-z felt the whole Hive shake and saw that do-nothing blur. It was going to capture the Mother. She flew at its huge eye. The Hive will prevail, she thought nobly. And I'll be rid of this blur for good.

— 6 —

Barney broke off a big chunk of the honeycomb and reset the lid. A bee landed just under his eye. He brushed at it with his hand. He danced around to shake it loose.

— 7 —

*F*uriously, Z-z-z backed herself into the huge eye. She felt the blur quiver as her venom entered its system.

She retracted her stinger. But of course it was caught. She jerked it loose, and pulled away a large chunk of her own abdomen. The pain was excruciating. She knew it was over. *Well,* she thought, *I've done my job the best I could.* She plummeted to earth for the last time.

— 8 —

*B*arney screamed. He dropped the honeycomb. He ran all the way home, screaming, forgetting his bike.

His mother put him to bed and applied a baking soda plaster, but the pain kept throbbing and the swelling didn't go down for days. Except to pick up his bike, he never went back to Jake's apiary. He forgot all about the bees.

EIGHT

DEATH MASKS

THOUGH HE'D BEEN DEAD FOR TEN YEARS, Dr. Barnard Rudolph Blatz, the First—physician, sculptor, inventor—still puttered in his studio, sculpting dust. *Ashes to ashes,* he thought. "Thought" isn't quite right. Radiated. He knew he was dead, but he could hardly remember being alive and, not at all, the act of death. It was as if his powers of awareness had simply grown gradually dimmer and dimmer over a time that was itself slowing down.

The shack of a studio stood at the top of the hill near the rusting rainwater cistern. The shack was a remnant of the old house by the lake that had belonged to Dr. Blatz's father. The grandfather had had it moved when he built the new house in the 1920s. The shack was painted a dull olive green to blend with the woods. It was constructed of vertical planks with moldings covering the cracks between the planks, as was the style with houses built in the previous century. The roof sagged, and moss grew between the shingles. There was a bay window overlooking the steel tank of the rainwater cistern.

From his dabbling in the affairs of the spirit late in life—his consultation of mediums, séances with his dead father—he knew that by now he should be altogether free of the cycle of suffering we experience as time. But something was keeping him mired in the material world, residing in this shack, nesting like an ethereal squirrel among his own sculptures—a collection of plaster death masks of the leading physicians of Milwaukee, including himself.

The masks, stored unceremoniously in rotting cardboard boxes on a loft in a corner of the shack, were prototypes of his unfinished magnum opus, a series of busts of the venerable founders of the Milwaukee Medical Society. His own death mask was his little joke, his last work. Days before his death, he had buried his face in plaster-coated muslin. Now, a spot between the eyes of this mask seemed to be the center of his being, such as it was. He might not have even known how stuck he was if it weren't for his grandson disturbing his repose.

As the brilliant foliage of the fall trees gave way to skeletal branches etched against the white sky, Barnard Rudolph Blatz, the Second, had taken to visiting the shack nearly every day. He was a tow-headed boy, frail, with pale skin and thick glasses, always sloppily dressed. He painted a skull and crossbones in radium paint on the door. He seemed to be settling here, establishing his own laboratory. It was here that the boy, seated at his grandfather's broken-down roll-top desk and using his grandfather's own medical instruments, stuffed butterflies in killing jars, pulled the legs off daddy long-legs, watched the spasms of their legless bodies in the microscope, and designed rockets to the moon.

At first the old spirit had welcomed the boy's visits, a breath of warm air breaking the monotony of death. His son's wife, Trudy, had been pregnant with the boy when the grandfather had died, and he had felt him becoming "quick" in the womb with his own hands. Having this opportunity to observe his namesake growing up gave his existence, such as it was, purpose. He was pleased the boy shared his scientific bent.

But something about the boy troubled him. He was far too solitary for his own good. Sometimes the boy sat in the overstuffed chair and read through a musty copy of *Gray's Anatomy*, breathing heavily on the diagrams of the reproductive system.

The boy kept a cat here, too, a scruffy orange tabby, no doubt a secret from his family. The grandfather remembered how dreadfully allergic to cats his son Robert, the boy's father, had been. As soon as he saw a cat, he would go into a sneezing fit that would last for hours, sometimes days.

The cat came and went during the day and night, but was always around when Barney came every afternoon with his can of tuna.

The boy liked to talk to the cat, Pussy. "So what if I'm no good at baseball, Pussy? I'll be a great scientist. I'll discover how to create life, or how to build a rocket fast enough to get to the moon. I'll show them. Do you want to go to the moon, Pussy?" He seemed inordinately angry. He'd punctuate his soliloquies with violent gestures, slamming musty pillows about until their feathers covered the floor, or smashing glass bottles against the cistern.

The rainwater cistern had been the grandfather's invention, too. The new house was to have three water systems. There was a well for drinking water, but this water was too hard for cleaning purposes, so there was another tank for lake water. But, as his microscope showed, the water from the lake was full of bacteria. So, for the sole purpose of his wife Louise washing her golden hair, he had built this rainwater cistern with its pipes commingled with those of the other systems.

He could still see Louise sitting on a stool at the gleaming new porcelain basin in her satin nightgown, smiling indulgently at him, as she let down her magnificent hair to try out the system for the first time. When she turned the tap, her smile wilted. The rainwater had a most disagreeable odor. When he checked the cistern, he discovered a large dead rat floating in it. Though he had the caretaker Clifford fish out the rat, drain and clean the tank, Louise had never again tried to use the rainwater to wash her hair. She began visiting a professional hairdresser in the city, and the cistern began to rust.

A small ball of concrete hung on a rope along the side of the tank measuring the water level, and sometimes Dr. Blatz could hear it ringing against the steel tank in the wind. The tone, which varied in pitch depending on the amount of rainfall, from a resonant bong in the fall to a tinny ping in the late spring, always reminded him of the lilac smell of his wife's hair. Many times, he wished he could visit her—she was still among the living—but, for a spirit, he was surprisingly immobile.

One day, as the pitch of the tank lowered toward winter, Barney the Second appeared in the shack so seething with anger that, to the grandfather, it looked as if his aura was on fire. It was difficult to piece together the story. There had apparently been some confrontation with his parents. "How dare they" he shouted at the cat. "I hate them! I hate them! They know I want to go to Chicago with them. They know I have to see that V-2 rocket they have at the museum. I told them! But no! They say I have to stay here with Pookie and Mrs. Chipmunk! How can they do this?" He grabbed the cat and looked as if he was about to slam it against the wall. Alarmed, the cat jumped out of the boy's hands.

Then with his bare hands the boy smashed all the windows he could reach in the place. Blood spattered all over the old furniture and boxes of mildewed medical books. When he stopped his raging long enough to notice the blood, he screamed and ran back down to the big house. *Now he'll get some attention*, his grandfather thought.

What distressed the grandfather most was the evidence that the child was badly neglected. No one seemed to be paying the slightest attention to what he might be up to in this secret hideaway. It reminded him of all the time he had spent puttering in his various studios. He too had neglected his own son, Robert. He remembered when Robert was just a boy of five building a snowman in the backyard in Milwaukee. It was Sunday, the maid's day off, and Louise had gone to church. Barnard agreed to keep an eye on the lad, and then, preoccupied in his attic studio, had forgotten all about him. By the time he remembered, the boy was screaming to come inside and had come down with double pneumonia.

With so many windows broken, the rain and wind blew freely through the shack. A few days later, the boy returned with his father, Robert. The grandfather gasped to see how old his son had become. His hair was all white, his ruddy face wrinkled. His lower lip poked out in a familiar pout. "Shit," Robert said as he surveyed the damage. "This was pretty stupid, Barnard. Breaking all these windows. I thought you had more sense."

Right away, the father had a sneezing fit. "It must be all the dust and mold," he sputtered.

Father and son awkwardly unrolled a sheet of translucent fabric to cover the first of the broken windows. Their movements were stiff; they didn't speak to one another as the boy held the fabric and the father pounded nails. It was clear to the grandfather that both of them were klutzes.

Watching them work reminded the grandfather that Robert had not wanted to join him in the medical profession at all at first. He had wanted to be an engineer but had flunked calculus in college. So, at the grandfather's urging, with trembling, uncoordinated hands, Robert had become an eye surgeon and joined the grandfather's eye-ear-nose-and-throat practice in Milwaukee. The grandfather remembered how pleased he had been to have his son following in his footsteps. He wondered how much pressure he had applied. It was then that the pout implanted itself permanently on Robert's face. Working together became a terrible strain for both of them after a while. Robert's entire being was channeled into keeping his hands steady for the four hours a week he had to maneuver his scalpel millimeters from the optic nerve. He did well, but there wasn't much left of him after that. He would sometimes relax, but it took three or four drinks.

It pained the grandfather to see the fear and tension between father and son, so much like that between himself and Robert. Helplessly he blew back and forth between them as if to warm the air, but of course he only chilled it.

Finally Robert broke the leaden silence. "You know, most of this stuff belonged to your grandfather. You could show some respect."

Barney said nothing.

"If I had done something like this when I was your age, your grandfather would not have spoken to me for weeks. He was always a severe and distant man, but if I had stepped out of line like you did, he would have cut me off completely."

Is that true? the grandfather wondered. *I was not severe. Distant, maybe, but not severe.* How he wished he could speak to his son, as he hadn't done when he was alive. If only he could just say he was sorry. He started to blow about the shack in a flurry of frustration. He blew in circles around father and son.

"Brr," Robert said. "Winter is here." Barney and Robert inched closer together to share their body heat.

That was the most he could do, thought the grandfather.

One afternoon, Barney the Second barged into the shack with a friend, a hefty, dark-haired boy named Jeffery. The grandfather smiled upon this development, perhaps signaling the end of the child's awful isolation. "Hey, this place is spooky," Jeffery said. "Do you think it's haunted?"

"Naw," Barney said. "It's my lab. I come here all the time."

"Barney, the mad scientist. It would make a neat clubhouse."

Jeffery sat in the overstuffed chair. Barney showed him the *Gray's Anatomy*. Jeffery turned red in the face and giggled over the cutaway drawings of the vulva. The cat jumped in his lap. Jeffery absently stroked it. "What's the cat's name?"

"Pussy," Barney smiled slyly.

"Pussy! That's a good one. Pussy, meet pussy." Jeffery giggled, showing the cat the diagram in the book. "Do you think cats really have nine lives?"

"Sure. Sort of," Barney answered. "They always land on their feet. Watch." Barney scooped up the cat and dropped it upside down from the level of his chest.

"That's not much of a drop. Could he do that from higher up?"

"Sure." Barney stood on the desk chair and dropped the cat. "He could even do it from the top of the roof."

"Really?"

The grandfather stirred himself. He didn't like where this was heading. He shifted himself across the room, and a cold breeze swept through the shack. The boys didn't notice, but the cat raised its hackles, arched its back, hissed, and darted out the door. The grandfather noted his power.

The boys seemed to forget about the cat. After a while, Jeffery asked, "What kind of club shall we make it?"

"How about, 'The Moon or Bust Club'?"

"Don't you know anything but science, science, science? How about a baseball club? Or a model car club?"

"I think I know how to build a rocket," Barney said. "Listen to this." Barney read from a book called *The Real Book about Space Travel*. "A jet engine. A jet is the simplest of engines. Fuel stored in one tank is mixed with air in the combustion chamber and ignited. The resulting explosion pushes hot gasses out the rear of the plane and creates thrust."

"That doesn't sound too tough," said Jeffery said.

For the next several days, the grandfather watched the grandson work feverishly over plans and drawings. He watched him collect supplies. Two small orange juice cans. A length of copper tubing. A spool of solder. *How could he solder anything without electricity?* the grandfather thought. The old spirit become alarmed at the answer, when the boy showed up with the grandfather's own brass blowtorch and a can of white gas.

The boy spoke to the cat. "We're going to get out of here, Pussy. You and me, we're going to the moon."

Barney turned the valve on the blowtorch and lit a match.

The grandfather stepped up his attempts at intervention. It took all the strength he had, but somehow, he managed to swoop down from his perch in the loft in the corner above the half-empty paint cans and oily rags, and breeze icily past Barney's face. The match went out. Barney shivered. He looked around. The sky was growing dark. He gave up his fruitless attempts to light the blowtorch and retreated to the big house. The grandfather heaved a sigh of relief.

Several days passed before Barney returned. His friend Jeffery was with him. They were both full of excitement. Barney showed off his plans. He held the pieces together awkwardly. "We'll solder the copper tubing to a hole in the bottom of one can with the blowtorch and then onto the side of the other can. The gas will drip from the first can and mix with the air in the second can. All we have to do is ignite it."

"How are we going to do that?" Jeffery asked.

"With the blowtorch. If we can get it lit."

Barney topped off the fuel in the blowtorch again, though it was already full. He pumped the pump until he couldn't pump it anymore. He opened the valve.

Again the old grandfather felt the need to intervene.

Again he swooped down from the corner loft and chilled the air close to their faces.

His hands shaking, Barney lit a match. The cold wind of the grandfather blew it out. He struck another. Another. Another.

Finally, despite the grandfather's efforts, the jet of gas from the blowtorch caught and spurted fire across the shack like a flamethrower.

Jeffery screamed and ran out of the door.

Barney quickly shut off the valve from the blowtorch, but not before an oily rag in the corner caught fire. And then another. And another. Barney stood there open-mouthed, staring at the spreading flames.

Dr. Blatz realized his mistake. In blowing out the matches, he'd exacerbated the situation by allowing more gas to accumulate. He thought quickly. The cistern. Barney! The cistern! he would have shouted if he had had a voice. He mustered every last iota of his strength, and found himself breezing past Barney, out the door of the shack to the cistern. A wind came up on the hill. Suddenly the concrete ball hanging on the rope swung against the tank with the mighty ring of an Oriental gong.

Barney grabbed an empty paint can, ran to the cistern, and turned on the tap in the side of the tank. He filled the can and doused the flame. Again and again he emptied the can of water in the corner, now smoldering.

Exhausted, the grandfather retreated into the box of death masks, into the spot between the eyes of his own mask, eyes now circled with eerie black swirls from the smoke. He heard the other masks click together as he settled in.

The fire was out now. Only the rags had burned. Little of the shack or its sundry contents were damaged, except that the boxes in the loft were smudged with smoke. Perhaps Barney had heard the faint click from within one of the boxes. The grandfather felt him take the box down from the loft and look inside.

He peered at the faces of the death masks. He looked at his grandfather's face, which he seemed to recognize, with the black streaks radiating from the hollow eyes. "Grampa!" he sputtered. Barney stiffened. His hair bristled. He dropped the box and screamed. He ran out of the shack.

That night Barney the Second returned with his father. The moon lit up the skeletal trees. The father held a large flashlight. The grandfather started when he saw the huge shadows cast against the wall. The skull and crossbones glowed in the dark on the door. The father cursed as he stumbled into the shack and was seized by another sneezing fit.

"You were lighting a blowtorch?" Robert said, a quaver in his voice. Hearing his son's voice, gruff, yet full of emotion, stirred the grandfather's spirit once more. He could tell that Robert was a couple of sheets to the wind. He could see his son's white hair glisten in the moonlight. A warm breeze wafted through the shack.

"I guess that wasn't too bright," Barney admitted fearfully.

"But how did you ever put the fire out?"

"I don't know. I just thought of the tank out there. I figured it had water in it."

The father crouched down to the son's level and put his arm around him. "You're right. It was real dumb to play with that blowtorch. But it was real smart the way you put the fire out. I guess one dumb and one smart just about cancel each other out." He ruffled the boy's hair.

The grandfather's awareness grew suddenly keen. *So this is what I've been stuck here for,* he thought. To scare the boy into straightening himself out. To reconcile father and son. And, that's not all. He remembered. The father had made him a deathbed promise. With his last remaining strength, the grandfather jiggled his death mask, and a click emanated from the box on the floor.

"What are these things?" Barney asked, pointing to the box.

Robert looked inside of the box himself. "Jesus!" he said. "I see why they scared you! They're death masks. I'd forgotten all about them. Your grandfather made them by smearing plaster of Paris on the faces of his dead colleagues in the medical profession. He had a plan to make a series of busts of the giants of Milwaukee medicine. He got sick before he had a chance to finish it. He made me promise on his deathbed to commission another sculptor to finish the project for him. I forgot all about it after he died."

"Is it too late now?" Barney asked.

At these words the grandfather felt himself smile.

"Too late?" The father laughed uproariously. He

stumbled again as he tried to pick up the box, which broke apart in his hands. "Too late? For a series of amateurish busts of a bunch of old farts that everyone in town has mercifully forgotten? No, Son." The father sneezed. "It's not too late." He sneezed again. "Grab the other end of the box." Another sneeze.

The grandfather and his venerable colleagues were hauled out of the shack. Then the box dropped into a pile of leaves. With horror the grandfather watched while father and son took each mask out of the box and hurled it against the steel tank of the rainwater cistern. The masks smashed against the tank and scattered on the forest floor like snow.

When the father took hold of the grandfather's mask, he hesitated. "Should we save this one?" he asked Barney.

He answered himself.

"Naw, it's ruined anyway. These things have haunted me long enough. Goodbye, old man," Robert said as he raised the mask behind his head.

The last sound the grandfather heard was the giddy laughter of father and son as his own mask smashed into a thousand pieces, finally releasing him to soar up toward the moon, free from time at last.

NINE

THOUGHT IT WAS
A GONER

ONE DAY I RUN UP ON MY STUBBY DACHSHUND legs and wag my tail to greet my human, Hmmm, coming from that mystery place they call school on his bike, I smell right away, and soon see, he's got a perfectly horrible scraggly striped cat stuffed into the front of his jacket. At first I think maybe he just wants to torture it or something like that; that might be fun. Hmmm is always doing things like that, pulling the legs off spiders and such. But when I see how he is with this cat, I'm foaming with rage. What does he need with a cat? He's got me.

He takes the cat up to the old shack on the top of the hill in the woods behind the house, his hideout. He talks to it in a way he never talks to me. "This is your new home, Pussy. That's a good name for you, you sweet thing. Sorry I can't let you stay in the big house, but Father's allergic to cats." He sits down with her in a

moldy-smelling overstuffed chair with the stuffing coming out and strokes her for what seems like hours. The
cat purrs while I lie down at his feet and whimper. He
pays me no mind at all, like he's forgotten I exist. The
smell of the cat, sharp and pissy, is making me sick. I'm
getting madder and madder.

My whimpers turn to growls. I rub up against
Hmmm's leg to get his attention. The cat sees me and
raises its hackles. "Easy, you two," Hmmm says.
"Herziger, I think you're jealous." I don't care what he
thinks I am, I snap at the cat. The cat springs off
Hmmm's lap and lands right in front of me on the floor.
It puffs itself up and glares at me straight in the face
with its pale beady eyes.

I jump at the cat's neck. The cat scratches my snout.
I smell my own blood. Hmmm shouts, "Stop it!" and
sweeps the cat up in the air. He stuffs the cat under his
arm and with his other hand comes down hard—crack—
across my back. He's never hit me before. I squeal and
draw back.

I don't know what I'm going to do. Since they put
Mama to sleep, Hmmm has been my only companion. I
was growing rather fond of him, but this is a low blow. I
begin to dream of that cat in various states of death: in
my mouth with its neck broken; flung from the roof by
Hmmm himself; drowned in the lake.

Hmmm has to keep the cat a secret from his family,
because Gruff—Hmmm calls him Father—goes into un-
controllable sneezing fits at just the thought of a cat.
But the secret doesn't work very well. Gruff doesn't

even know about this cat and he starts sneezing whenever Hmmm is around.

After the third night of sneezing when Hmmm comes home, Gruff ask Mom, "Can I be allergic to my own son?" He's laughing about it.

"Maybe it's that sweater he's wearing. Barney take that sweater off," Mom tells him. That stops the sneezing for that day.

But the next day, the sneezing fit resumes, and Hmmm isn't wearing a sweater. Gruff, who has the white hair of someone about 350 in dog years, turns dark in the face and starts sneezing, one sneeze after another. Mom fetches his breathing medicine, but nothing seems to stop the sneezes. "It's something about that boy," he says, not laughing any more. "Just what is it that you've been up to, Son?"

"Nothing." Hmmm rarely says more than a word or two in Gruff's presence.

"Go take a bath, Barney, and change your clothes," Mom tells him. "Maybe that will work." It does work, and for a while, Hmmm has to take a bath and change his clothes every evening before Gruff comes home.

If I could speak human, I'd tell the old man about that cat, and then Hmmm would have to get rid of it. For a while, I just stop greeting Hmmm when he comes home. I fool around off by myself, chasing squirrels. I try to ignore the wretched little human and that stupid, foul-smelling cat altogether. But I get so lonely and bored.

I try to hang out with Hmmm's sister Ra-ra, called Pookie by the humans. I sit at her feet under the piano and dream as she plunks the keys. But my dreams get interrupted every time she plays a sour note, which is every third note, and otherwise she's not interested in me. When she's not playing the piano, she plays with her stuffed animals—her bear, her raccoon, her lion. A dog like me is too alive for her. She can't so easily put words in my mouth.

Hmmm doesn't tell her about the cat either because cats cause her to sneeze, too. But only when she actually knows about them.

So, in desperation, I start greeting Hmmm again. He seems extra friendly. "Have you stopped being mad at me, old Herziger?"

I resume my place at Hmmm's feet, with the cat purring in his lap in the overstuffed chair. Hmmm pats his free leg to invite me up and join the cat. I don't know what gets into me, but I do it. I jump up there, carefully avoiding any contact with the hateful creature on his other leg. I expect some violent reaction from the cat to my invasion of its newly claimed territory, but it just keeps on purring. Luckily, cats are stupid.

"There's no reason why you two can't be friends," Hmmm says.

I can think of lots of reasons, but I let them go. After a couple days of this truce, I don't even worry if the cat accidentally rubs me sometimes, though the smell makes me want to throw up.

After a while, Gruff's wild sneezing fits don't stop after Hmmm's bath. I know it's because the cat hairs are all over me, but I keep quiet. A bath is the last thing

I want. I stay out of Gruff's way as much as possible.

It isn't until one day when Gruff is home all day that he discovers that I make him sneeze, too. It is early in the morning, before Hmmm is awake. The sky is clear, the air is crisp, the leaves on the trees have turned their brilliant shades as they do when it starts to get cold. I follow him down to the lake. The water is so still that the woods around the lake are doubled in their reflection. In the boathouse he has a boat that I have watched him build with his own hands over the past year or so. We often spend these early morning times together. He talks to me.

"She's almost done, Herziger. One more coat of varnish."

The varnish smell hurts my nose, but I stick around anyway.

I know nothing of boats, and, in my opinion, humans would be better off if they walked on all fours, instead of constantly busying their forelimbs. But I'm impressed with this boat. He calls it a "lapstrake," meaning he has had to steam each of a bunch of planks to curve them just right and overlap them for the hull.

I find a patch of sunlight at the door to the boathouse and curl up in it. Gruff sneezes. Mostly he talks to me of our mutual problem, Hmmm. "I'm worried about our boy Barnard," he says. "He doesn't seem interested in anything. He's sullen. He keeps to himself. He won't talk to me. You spend more time with him than anyone, Herzie. What's wrong with him?"

If I could talk human, I'd tell him that Hmmm is

very interested in this boat, that he comes down here all the time to admire it.

"You know what the worst of it is?" Gruff continues. "He's exactly like me. I'm raising another crabby, antisocial dilettante just like myself."

He sneezes again.

Then again.

He looks at me.

"Herziger," he says sharply. "Could it be you? Are you the one making me sneeze? We just may have to get rid of you."

I decide to make myself scarce. Even though it's freezing cold, I take a quick dip in the lake and hope for the best. When I see Gruff again, he doesn't sneeze and seems to have forgotten his threat. Luckily, humans are not the brightest creatures, either.

Even a dog with as sensitive a smeller as mine will eventually get acclimated to even the worst smell. At first that cat—Mu I've come to call her—smelled deadly sharp and eye-watery like the vet. Now she smells more like the cod liver oil Mom sometimes feeds me for worms. Hmmm keeps her locked up in the shack now, and boy does it stink with Mu shitting in a box full of sand in the corner by the oily rags. Of course, Hmmm never cleans it out. This also means I don't get to hang out with Mu much when Hmmm isn't around. I'll go up and sit under the shack sometimes, and we'll kind of whimper at each other through the floorboards. We complain about humans, how they never seem to love you enough. But it's hard to communicate through the floor. We don't know each other's language. We both know human of course, but only to understand it, not speak it.

When Hmmm gets home from school we go up to the shack, and then Mu and I are together. When we sleep together on Hmmm's lap to the rhythm of Mu's gentle purring, it's like our dreams merge together. It's really strange. Winter is coming on, but we dream of sleeping in the hot summer sun. This, it turns out, is both of our favorite activities. I can't tell you how I know Mu is dreaming the same dream. I just know.

Another odd thing happens: both Hmmm and I learn to purr. It kind of seeps into us with the shared dreams. It starts as a faint vibration in the back of our throats. We don't even notice at first, but gradually we realize how much calmer both of us are after cuddling with old Mu for a while. This purring business gives me a sympathetic connection with the cat that I'd just as soon not have, but there it is.

One day, Hmmm is doing some harebrained experiment, trying to build a rocket or something, in his shack of a hideout, and the place catches fire. It's just a small fire, and Hmmm puts it right out with water from the old rusted water tank nearby, but Gruff has to come up there to check.

The old man isn't too mad about the fire, but he's furious about the cat. "I can't believe you've been keeping this thing up here all this time," I hear Gruff shout in the dark woods on their way down from the hideout. "Concealing it from me when you knew it was making me sick. You have to get rid of it. I don't care how, but by tomorrow, that cat better not be anywhere near this place, understand?"

"Yes, Father."

It's about time, I think.

The next morning, Hmmm sets off for school on his bike, even though the air is so cold you can see your breath. That cat, Mu, is stuffed inside his jacket the same way it was that first day. Does Mu know what's up? She might have heard them talking. Anyway, she is squalling inside the jacket, clawing at Hmmm's chest.

"Don't scratch me, Pussy," Hmmm tells her. "You'll be all right." He's got tears in his throat.

I want to make sure he's really getting rid of her. I follow them at a fair stalking distance. It's been a long time since I've ventured so far from my piss perimeter. I'm dazzled, frightened by the strange smells. I walk way off to the side of the road. A car killed Mama. I won't let that happen to me. We go way out onto the highway that curves between the lakes.

Finally, Hmmm stops and lets the cat go. They can't see me, but I piss a little on the nearest tree, and return home, pissing here and there along the way—I don't mean anything by it, I just seem to need to piss a lot.

That noon that smelly cat comes proudly prancing down the road and rubs all up on me. "Thank you," she purrs. She's convinced it was me that led her back, of all the ridiculous ideas. That night the old man sneezes his head off. "You didn't get rid of that damn cat, did you?" Gruff growls at Hmmm.

"I tried. She came back."

"It's your responsibility, Barnard. I better not find it here tomorrow night, or I'll be forced to take drastic action, understand?"

"Yes, Father."

The next afternoon, Hmmm cajoles Mom into driving him far away to dump the cat. I jump into the car to convince them to take me, too. Mom smells of soap and flour.

She drives and drives through the rolling hills. She talks to Hmmm. "I know this is hard for you, Barney. I know you like the cat. But sometimes we have to make hard choices."

"I know, Mom." I can tell he doesn't want to talk. He's on the verge of tears.

"Your father loves you very much. It's just hard for him to show it."

"I know, Mom."

After a while she stops. "Ten miles to the middle of nowhere, that ought to do it," Mom says. The place she's chosen is out in farm country and smells of manure.

Hmmm puts Mu down on the shoulder. Mu squawks and clings to his shirt. "Bye, Pussy," Hmmm says. Tears streak his face.

On the way back, he cuddles me the whole way. By the time we get back to the house, I'm not unhappy that cat is gone, but there's a hollow place inside me. I try to purr with Hmmm like Mu showed us, but nothing happens.

Two nights later the whole house wakes up to shrill caterwauling in the dark. The cat is back.

The next morning at breakfast, Hmmm's sister Pookie sings:

"The cat came back the very next day

"The cat came back, they thought it was a goner

"But the cat came back, it just couldn't stay

"Awa-ay."

EVEN GRUFF LAUGHS, but then he says to Hmmm, "You and me are going out this morning and getting rid of this cat once and for all."

Hmmm and I go outside to try to persuade that stupid cat to get out of town. She greets us right at the door, smiling and prancing happily. I have to admit I'm really glad to see her, but I know it's dangerous for her, so I growl at her. Hmmm just tells her straight out, "Pussy, get away from here! If Father catches you here, something terrible is going to happen."

The cat looks bewildered by our reactions, but she doesn't budge. It isn't long before Gruff comes out of the house holding his hand over his nose and handing Hmmm a burlap gunnysack. "Put the cat in the bag, Barney," he orders, though his gruff voice is now oddly tender. He sneezes.

Hmmm grabs the cat and stuffs her in the gunnysack. The cat squalls in a way that makes the hair on my neck stand up. Now she knows she's in trouble.

"We'll launch our new boat, too." He brandishes a dark bottle of champagne in the air. "Bring the cat," Gruff says.

I follow them down to the lake. At the shore, Gruff tells Hmmm, "Pick up a few of those rocks and put them in the gunnysack with the cat."

Hmmm hesitates. "Come on, Barney," Gruff says in his tender voice. "I know this is hard. But the cat makes me sick. You have to choose. Me or the cat?"

Slowly, Hmmm picks up two rocks and puts them into the gunnysack. He looks as if he's swallowing the rocks himself. The day is cold and gray. The clouds rage in the sky. The water puffs every which way. I chomp some grass. It looks like rain.

Gruff hands Hmmm a piece of rope from his pocket. "Tie up the bag," he says. "Do you know how to tie a square knot?"

The cat is clawing the bag, but her claws get caught in the burlap. Hmmm ties the rope around the top of the gunnysack. Mu is still jumping around, trying to get out. "That's a granny knot," Gruff says gently. "The end that's closest to you stays closest to you." He takes Hmmm's hands in his and gently directs them. "Now, that's a square knot."

The rowboat is still upside down on a rack in the boathouse. "You grab the bow," Gruff tells Hmmm. They flip the boat over and slide it into the water. "Hope it doesn't sink," Gruff laughs. It doesn't, though some water does collect in the bottom. "It will leak some until the wood swells," he says. "All right!" He is pleased. He takes the bottle and tries to smash it against the bow. It doesn't break. He hits it a few more times. "Shit," he says.

Finally he hits the bottle against the rocks in the bag with the cat. It breaks. He flings the champagne toward the boat. "I christen this boat *Barnard's Boat*. It's yours, Son. I built it for you."

Hmmm is moved, smiles. "Really?"

"Really."

"Gee. Thanks, Pa." This is the first time I've ever heard him call Gruff anything but Father.

"Let's go," Gruff says, grabbing the oars and climbing aboard the boat.

Hmmm climbs in after him. "Don't forget the cat," Gruff says with a chuckle. Hmmm snatches the bag almost casually, as if the cat were already dead. "Grab the dog too. You come too, Herziger. You've got your own peculiar relationship with this cat. It's unnatural. If you were a normal dog, this cat would have been dead a long time ago."

Hmmm throws me into the boat, too, now filling with more and more water, up to my knees already. Gruff rows the boat out onto the lake. I climb up on the seat in the bow. The cat in its bag is soaking in the water as it fills the boat. I remember how she hates water. Actually, I don't remember. I never knew it before. She is telling me. A faint ultrasonic squeal that the humans apparently can't hear comes from the bag. Stop them! she is saying.

I catch Hmmm looking wistfully at the lump of a cat and then bittersweetly—confusedly—at Gruff. Gruff seems to catch the look, too.

"You row, Barney," he says, changing seats and

handing him the oars. "Keep going up wind, toward the waves, so it'll be easier to get back." Hmmm rows. The humans are silent.

Not Mu though. Mu is still emitting this subliminal song that tugs at my heart. She is reminiscing about sleeping in the hot summer sun. I can see the butterflies dance in the air. I can hear the locusts. I can smell the tangy intermingling of dog and cat sweat. I can't keep from whimpering back at Mu: I'm sorry. What can I do?

Surprisingly, she answers: Stop them.

I start to bark.

The barking backfires. It seems to remind Gruff of the cat. "OK, Son. It's time," he says, his voice quavering.

Hmmm stops rowing and glares at Gruff. The boat drifts. "You do it," Hmmm says.

"No, Son, I'm afraid it's your job. Believe it or not, I know how you feel. I had to shoot a horse once, Blackie, we called her."

He leans back to tell the story.

"I loved that horse. I suppose you know there weren't many cars when I was a boy. There were some, my father had one, but horses were still the main way we got around. And Blackie was my horse, a jet-black stallion, fast as the wind. I rode it everywhere. One day I rode it too hard." Gruff's voice cracks. "I tried to get him to jump a fence on the way home. He missed and broke his ankle. I fell off and hit my head."

The old man rubs his head as if he has just hit it. "When I came to, my father was standing over me, holding a deer rifle. 'You've got to shoot him, Son,' he said to me. I begged him to set the leg, at least try, it didn't look like a bad break to me, and he was a doctor. He shook his head. 'Once a horse breaks his leg, he's no good any more,' he said."

Gruff takes a deep breath. "So I did it. I aimed the gun at the horse's head, closed my eyes, and blew poor Blackie's brains out.

"And now it's your turn. I'll count. On the count of three, you fling that cat into the drink. Here goes. One . . . two . . . three . . ."

A shriek comes from the bag as Hmmm heaves it over the side, and a wail comes from me as if that cat were a part of my soul. It feels like it's me terror-struck inside that tomb of a bag, my hair standing straight up. Bubbles gurgle up from the water as the bag sinks. Hmmm breaks into tears.

Gruff does something—two things—I've never seen him do before. He hugs Hmmm and cries himself, as the boat drifts home.

I crawl in between them myself and cuddle. You can't figure humans.

By the time we reach shore, the boat is full of water up to the bottom of the seats. "I'm afraid your boat leaks pretty bad, Barney," Gruff says.

TEN

🐿

GUNS ON THE WALL I

WHEN HE DIDN'T SEE HIS MOTHER'S STATION WAGON in the driveway by the barnlike front of the house, Barney knew no one was home. His friend Jeffery spun his bike around in an artful skid, just missing the tall pine tree that defined the parking circle. Barney wished he could do that, but his bike was fancy, a Raleigh three-speed, with chrome hand brakes that stopped the bike cleanly. Jeffery's was just a plain bike, a Schwinn, but he could beat Barney, and he had customized it by taking off the fenders and chain guard and painting the frame with orange flames. On this spring day, they were riding from their school in Rockland, two miles away.

Jeffery lived in one of the many small bungalows that were crowded around Elk Lake, in between Rockland and Pike Lake, where Barney lived.

On the way into the house, Jeffery, big and soft, got down on all fours while Barney rode around on his back all over the lawn, Barney's favorite game. "You're my brontosaurus," Barney told Jeffery. Every now and then, Jeffery would buck Barney off, and Barney would giggle uncontrollably. The knees of Jeffery's jeans stained green.

Inside the quiet house, they skipped up the broad wooden staircase and all the way down the hall to Barney's room.

Barney's room had picture windows looking out on the woods and the lake. The walls and ceiling were covered with knotty pine. The knots terrified him at night, mimicking fearful monsters, but in the daytime, he liked the manly, rustic flavor of the wood. It was like a hunting lodge.

On one wall, next to his framed collection of butterflies, was a real Japanese flag, stained with real blood, that his father had brought back from the war.

On another wall were three guns hanging horizontally on hooks. They were old guns, antiques that had belonged to Barney's grandfather. They hung in descending order by size and age, a geometric timeline, the longest and oldest on top, a rusted muzzle loader complete with ramrod. It was dated 1809, and Barney imagined that it had been used in the War of 1812.

The middle gun was in the best condition of all, except that the spring was broken and it only "fired" when rigged with rubber bands. This one was also a muzzle loader and dated 1850. It had a big "U.S." engraved on the side, so Barney was sure it was an army gun utilized in the Indian campaigns.

The third, shortest, and newest, was a breech loader,

a shotgun dated 1862 and certainly used in the Civil War, because what good is a gun without a war?

"Let's play cowboys and Indians," Jeffery said, eying the guns.

Barney rolled his desk chair under the guns and fetched them down from the wall. "Let's play Civil War. I'm the North." He took the two biggest guns and climbed onto the bed. "This is my fort."

"Civil War, Civil War. We always play Civil War," Jeffery complained. "Just because your granddaddy was a general or something."

"My great-grandfather. That's right, a general." Then he added, persuasively, "They're my guns." Barney stuck the two guns out of the ramparts of his bedstead. "You attack," he ordered Jeffery.

Jeffery took the smallest of the guns, the breech-loading shotgun, the only one left, and trudged out the door. A few minutes later, he returned, blasting away. "*Boom! Bang! PPKKK-CCCHHH! PPKKK-CCCHHH! PPKKK-CCCHHH!*"

Barney fired back. They kept this up for a long time, until finally Jeffery, crawling on his elbows on the floor, reached the bed. He leapt up suddenly and then crashed down right on top of Barney with his full weight. The shooting stopped. "*Aaaaaaaaa!*" Barney screamed.

"The South wins again," Jeffery declared.

"That's not fair," Barney whined.

"Sure it is. Everything's fair in a war. Hey, do you think this gun would actually fire if we had some shells?" Jeffery asked.

"I don't know." Then he blurted, "My dad has some shells downstairs."

"Well, let's try it!" Jeffery said, his eyes lighting up.

"I don't know if we should," Barney said.

"Aw, c'mon, chicken. I've fired plenty of guns before."

"I don't know if the shells are even the right size."

"How are we going to know if we don't try?"

"My mom will be home soon." Jeffery looked so sad, Barney couldn't help adding, "But I suppose we can look."

Barney led Jeffery downstairs to a closet under the stairs. He rummaged through one of his mother's purses and came out with a ring of keys. He took the keys through the kitchen to the pantry where the guns and the liquor were kept. There were two padlocks on the cabinet, one on each side, to keep Clifford, the caretaker, from stealing the liquor. At first there had been just one lock, but Clifford had removed the hinges. Barney opened the locks and then the door.

Inside the cabinet were more guns. There was a 16-gauge shotgun, a .410-gauge shotgun, a .45 automatic, and a weird, long, single-shot .22 pistol with a removable rifle stock attached to the handle.

"Wow!" Jeffery gasped. He fondled each of the guns. He picked up the .45, a genuine army pistol that Barney's grandfather had carried in World War I, and aimed it a Barney's head.

"*PPKKK-CCCHHH!*"

"Hey, don't point that thing at me!" Barney demanded.

"Aw, it's not loaded. See, no clip." After lovingly aiming all the guns, away from Barney, Jeffery said with a crazed look in his eye, "Barney, let's go hunting."

Barney turned red and glanced scornfully at Jeffery.

"C'mon! Why not? There's nobody home."

"Jeffery! You know better. We can't, that's all."

But Jeffery was too excited to be dissuaded. "C'mon, Barney! We know what we're doing. We've both been hunting with our dads. We don't have to take all the guns. Just the one's you've fired."

"The only one my dad let me shoot was the .22."

"OK. You take the .22, and I'll try your Civil War gun. We'll leave the rest here."

Barney knew they shouldn't. He liked the non-working guns all right, but the others scared him, especially the noise, and he hated hunting with his father. "No, Jeffery," he said decisively. "I'm the one who will get in trouble."

"OK, I'm going home then."

Barney was quiet again.

"You want me to go home?"

"No."

"OK, let's go then." He took one of the shotgun shells from the boxes on the floor and jammed it into the breech of the old shotgun. It fit badly. He stuck a few more of the shells in his pocket. He handed the .22 to Barney, and then a handful of the short bullets for that gun.

Barney shut and locked the cabinet. With the guns

on their shoulders, they marched out of back of the house and into the woods. Barney's hands were sweating, his stomach gurgled, his heart raced.

"There's a squirrel!" Jeffery squealed. He raised the ancient shotgun to his shoulder. The squirrel peered at them from the base of a tree, nibbling acorns. Jeffery fired.

Click.

Nothing.

"Aw," he said. "You try."

Barney knew this squirrel. It had a broken tail. He had named it Squeaky. It had a nest in the tree next to one of the windows of his room. He couldn't remember how to get the bullet into the .22. He jammed it in somehow, closed his eyes, and pulled the trigger.

Click.

Nothing.

The squirrel darted up the tree.

"We need to go back and get some real guns," Jeffery said.

"Wait," Barney said. "Follow me." He ran out of the woods down the front lawn to the lake, golden in the afternoon sun. He led Jeffery into the boathouse, a weathered gray building with water in the middle of it. It was musty inside. There was an old pump. A canoe. A rowboat. An iceboat. Everything was covered with swallow droppings.

"Look!" Barney said. He pointed to a small silver cannon about the size of a breadbox. It had two wheels. "My father uses it to start sailboat races."

Jeffery's eyes grew big as bicycle wheels. "Let's fire it!"

Barney grabbed one of the blanks that were in a box next to the cannon, wheeled the cannon out the door, and aimed it toward the lake. He opened the breech and shoved the blank inside. He gave Jeffery the string to pull. "Go ahead. Fire!"

Ka-bloom!

Jeffery smiled as if he had just fallen in love.

There was a shout from the top of the hill. "Barney!"

Barney looked at Jeffery. "My mom!"

They looked up and saw her coming toward them. They went up to meet her, guns at their sides.

"Barney! What was that noise?"

"Just the blanks from the cannon, Mother."

She had a round, red face, and brown hair in a fresh permanent wave. She was dressed in dark green suit, high heels, and a little gray hat with a veil. She managed to look stylish and frumpy at the same time. She was tiny standing next to Jeffery.

"You took those guns out?" There was fear in her voice.

Barney said nothing.

"You know better than to fool with your father's guns, Barney. Jeffery, I think you better go home now."

"OK, Miz Blatz. See ya, Barney." He handed Barney the old shotgun. Barney glared at Jeffery. He knew he'd be the one to get in trouble.

"I'm disappointed in you, Barney," his mother said with a scowl.

A FEW YEARS LATER, Barney and Jeffery parted ways for a long time. It was a gray, muggy day at the end of summer. Barney would be starting ninth grade in a new school soon, a fancy boarding school back east. Jeffery would be going to the local high school. They sized each other up in the driveway.

Barney was wearing Madras plaid Bermuda shorts and a light blue polo shirt with an alligator on the left breast.

Jeffery wore a dingy white tee shirt with the sleeves rolled up, black engineers' boots with their twin buckles, and faded, soiled jeans, held up by a thin purple suede belt with the buckle at the side so the crack of his ass showed.

"Jeffery, you look so boppish," Barney said.

Puttering tensely down by the boathouse—the silver cannon no longer there—Jeffery cocked his head from side to side and acidly mimicked the remark right back to Barney: "'Jeffery, you look so boppish.'" Then Jeffery asked, "Hey, do you still have those old guns?"

"Yeah. Why?"

"I'm taking metal shop next year. I bet I could get them to work."

"Metal shop?" Barney sneered. "I think I'd just as soon they didn't work. Guns are so crude, don't you think?"

To be continued . . .

ELEVEN

LET NOTHING
YOU DISMAY

Pike Lake, Wisconsin, December 28, 1958
Holy Innocents' Day, Ha!

Dear Mike,

I swear my father would freeze time at 1913
if he could. I don't know how Mother puts
up with him. I'm afraid he's also making
Pookie and Barney into screaming neurotics.
They're even more nervous than I was at
their ages (sixteen, thirteen), though
Pookie seems to be coming out of it.

    A couple days before Christmas, Father
gets it in his head that we are going to
have a "traditional" Christmas. That
doesn't just mean turkey and plum pudding,
no sir. It means we have to go cut down our
own tree from the farm. And that's not all.
It also means we have to kill our own
Christmas dinner. Can you believe it? And
you know, once the old man makes up his

mind, there's no talking him out of it.
Usually he hates things like holidays.
Really, I think he hates "family," although
to be fair I guess he sometimes thinks the
individuals in it are sort of OK. Mostly
he's very withdrawn from the family, in a
world of his own. But then he'll get this
fixation, like a "traditional" Christmas,
and look out, here comes Mr. Family!

Winter at the lake is always so strange
anyway. No one, and I mean no one, lives
year-round here except my parents. They've
got Pookie in some awful Episcopal boarding
school and Barney in the local public
school, which was two rooms until not too
long ago. If he weren't so obsessed with
his laboratory and stuff, I'd suspect
Barney's brain of atrophying there.

It's cold, as cold as New England, but
not as soft somehow. The trees are harsh
against the sky, which itself is bleak. New
England winters have a purity to them
comparable to the splendor of their autumn
colors, but not Wisconsin. The snow is not
as plentiful and not as clean either, I
guess sullied by the smoke from those
Milwaukee factories. The snow-covered
frozen lake looks like a desert.

The day of Christmas Eve is one of these
harsh days, the temperature hovers around
ten degrees. Father wakes Barney and me at
seven o'clock sharp so we can go out and
cut the tree down and pick out a goddamn
chicken. I want to just tell him no.
"C'mon, Dad, how about we go into town and
buy a tree and a turkey like everyone else?

That's tradition." But you don't argue with
Father like that anymore than you call him
"Dad." You just don't.

So off we go into the freezing morning,
on foot of course—there weren't many cars
around here in 1913. "I'll make men out of
you boys yet," our father threatens us.
Barney and I exchange glances. I've been
trying to subvert Barney a little from his
so obviously becoming his father's son,
with his science and his silence. I'm
giving him Lady Sings the Blues and Catcher
in the Rye for Xmas, which ought to shake
him up some.

It's about a half mile to the lower
field where the trees are—trees our father
planted eight years ago, of course. He's
got me carrying the ax, and Barney carrying
the bucksaw. First, he can't make up his
mind which tree to cut. He has to look at
every one, while Barney and I freeze our
butts off. He can't remember how high the
ceiling is in the living room. It amazes me
how someone can be so outwardly successful
(an eye surgeon no less) and yet so
generally incompetent. Finally he picks one
which I'm sure is way too big, and has
Barney crawl under it in the snow to cut it
down with the saw. Which Barney is unable
to do, of course; this is a setup.

After Barney tries about six times to
get the saw caught, Father finally grumps
at the boy, "All right, come on out of
there. I'll do it myself." I look at
Barney, and I know he feels like warmed
over shit inside. Father slices right

through the stupid tree. We drag the tree
to the road to pick up on the way back.

Now for the fun part.

At the top of the hill is the farm that
Father owns a piece of, where his partner
raises chickens. We go into the chicken
coop, and there are some fifty hens puck-
puck-pucking around. Again, he can't make
up his mind which one. He does ask our
opinion. "Which one do you boys think is
the biggest?" It's really hard to tell, and
anyway I wonder if the biggest one is going
to be all that tasty, but I pick one with a
ruffled wing.

"Barney, you catch him," he orders.
Barney gives me a helpless look and then
chases the bird all over the coop. He
finally corners it and reaches around its
wings to grab its legs. The chicken turns
around and scratches Barney's face with its
beak, but I have to hand it to him, the kid
doesn't let go.

Guess what! Now it's my turn. Father
helps Barney hold the poor thing over the
wood block and then says to me, "OK,
Charlie, chop his damn head off."

I want to remind the old man that I'm a
city boy, that he didn't get on this
country thing until I was away at school,
and furthermore, chopping this poor
chicken's head off is the very last thing
in the world I want to do. Here I am,
twenty-five years old—you'd think I could
stand up to the bastard by now. But it's
like I don't need one more of his huffs
like he gave Barney for failing to fell the

tree, and so I just go along and swing that
old dull ax and miss the chicken's neck
about three times before I finally do hit
it. Blood spurts out all over both Father
and Barney, and they let go. The chicken
runs around all right, but not like a
chicken with its head cut off, because it's
head is still on, even though it's bleeding
profusely from a rather nasty gash in its
neck. I go off into a corner to throw up.

Surprisingly, Father doesn't huff in
disgust at my failure, but instead says,
"That's just what happened to me after my
first operation. You'll get over it.
Barney, catch that bird again." Barney, not
about to fail a second time, catches the
chicken again, more easily this time since
it is slowing down, and Father brings the
ax down again onto the chicken's neck, and
this time the head actually comes off, and
the chicken lets out this utterly
otherworldly scream.

I'm still queasy as hell and it doesn't
look like old Barney boy is doing so well
himself, but we manage to trudge through
the snow after Father, who holds our
chicken upside down by the feet, dripping a
Christmasy red trail of chicken blood in
the snow all the way back to the house.
Barney and I pick up the tree on the way.

When we try to set up the tree, it is
way too tall as I suspected, so we cut off
the top and are left with the most
ridiculous looking Christmas tree ever,
shaped like that parabolic conic section
they used to have in our analytic geometry

books. Mother and Pookie do most of the
decorating, using a lot of the ornaments
that Mother has made over the years:
baker's dough bells, twisted-straw angels,
pipe-cleaner Santas. Mother would be a real
artist if she put all the creativity she
puts into Christmas crafts into something a
little more original. Actually, she did
block-print the curtains in the living
room, cane the dining room chairs, weave a
runner for the sideboard. And, decorate the
place herself, interestingly if a bit
incongruously. There's a Klee print over
the fireplace, facing the heavy-framed
portraits of Father's illustrious ancestors
on the opposite wall, over the antique sofa
with the Danish modern coffee table in
front—you get the picture.

Pookie has become quite the young lady
at her Episcopal school. She's filled out
and has bleach blond streaks in her hair—
looks a bit like Grace Kelly. It's hard for
me not to see her as just a snot-nosed pain
in the butt, but I have a good feeling
about her, like she's developing a good
heart somehow, in spite of this family.
She's even been reading Oscar Wilde and
Gertrude Stein. She's delightfully filled
with enthusiasm, even for Father's newly
discovered obsession with tradition.

When we get to the lights for the tree,
Father, up from his nap, suddenly insists
that we have candles. In this day and age?
Can you imagine? Mother even argues with
him, "Robert, don't you think candles would
be a fire hazard?"

"Nonsense," he says. "We used candles
for years and never had a problem."
Unfortunately, there are some candles along
with some antique candle holders made for
putting candles on trees in the ornament
boxes, so candles it is.

Meanwhile, I feel so different being
here. This is the first time I've been
"home" since you and I, well, you know. My
shame is cast against the wall like the
shadows from the candlelight in the dusky
afternoon. Suddenly I'm feeling so sad that
you and I just can't seem to give into it
completely.

I'm suffocating in the house, so I take
a walk by myself out onto the frozen lake.
The lake makes these rolling thunder noises
as it freezes. Most of it is covered with
snow except out near the island, where it
has just frozen over. The water underneath
the thin fresh ice is black. I'm fearful it
will crack, but I walk on it anyway. Close
to the island is a community of ice
fishermen with little huts and holes in the
ice. When I was a kid, I used to hang out
with these fellows sometimes. They were
always friendly. I want to approach them
today, but I'm suddenly afraid they will
see that I'm different, that I'm queer. I
shudder with the cold and run back to the
house.

I'm dying to tell someone about you and
me, but I don't think Pookie could handle
it at sixteen. Then there's our Uncle Fred.

Uncle Fred arrives, late, about five.
Let me tell you about our mother's brother.

He's a gourmet cook for one thing and has
of course been left the task of cooking the
chicken. He is very fat—like he couldn't
have seen his thing for twenty years, that
fat. He sells insurance for a living (ho-
hum). He's so German he drives a black
Mercedes 300 coupe, which really looks like
Himmler's staff car. He's a total drunk,
even to the point of straight vodka in the
morning. He loves to make anti-Semitic
jokes that make my mother cringe, like
"Hitler was half right, he should have
killed the other half, ha ha ha."

And, get this, an open secret in our
family: he's queer.

I wonder which would be worse for my
family, knowing that you are my lover or
that you are Jewish. Obviously, there's a
lot I don't like about the guy, but I also
have some sympathy for him, maybe because
Father can't abide him. As soon as he
waddles into the back door, laden with
packages, already tipsy, I know I'm going
to tell him about us before the evening is
out.

I've whipped up a huge batch of eggnog
—"traditional" for Father's sake, real
eggs, whipping cream, and Myers's rum
(though he won't touch it, preferring his
straight bourbon)—and I'm deciding that I,
for one, am going to enjoy this Christmas
Eve. Pookie and especially Barney help
themselves to the eggnog, too, so with
Mother and her bourbon and water, we are
off to a festive start.

Mother has spent the afternoon cleaning

the chicken. She worked in silence, while I tried to help her, but what do I know about plucking chickens? For that matter, what does she know? Turns out, nothing. It's just like Father to have launched this huge chicken plan, assuming that Mother would do all the dirty work. She did what she could, reading instructions from the Settlement Cookbook, but even I could see that the plucked bird still had the stalks of feathers sticking out all over it, to say nothing of remnants of entrails in its body cavity. Fred, seeing this decrepit excuse for a chicken, hits the roof. "Ach, Gott, I'm supposed to cook this?" His German is put on, since he was born in Milwaukee. "This looks like it was run over by a truck."

"It was Robert's idea for the boys to kill our dinner for tonight," Mother says, emboldened by Fred's presence to leak just a drop of her annoyance at Robert. Though if you asked her if she was mad, she would deny it to kingdom come. In fact, denial is the way Mother gets through life.

"And a terrible idea at that," Fred adds, loudly so Father, watching the traditional It's a Wonderful Life on the traditional TV in the next room, is sure to hear. "Since when has Robert taken an interest in the culinary arts?" Fred is not much fonder of Father than Father is of Fred. "First, we've got to dunk the bird in a pot of boiling water, just for a second. Does the good Doktor have any surgical tweezers around at least?"

He does of course, and after Fred has
blanched the thing, he has me pick over the
chicken with the tweezers to remove the
last bits of feathers. The chicken finally
makes it to the oven about six thirty.
Normally, the whole family, Mother in
particular, would be frantic about eating
so late, since Father has a bad habit of
getting outrageously drunk and ugly if
dinner isn't served at six on the dot. But
it's Christmas. And besides, the rest of us
are not exactly stone cold sober ourselves.

Mother does serve the traditional beef
tartar—raw ground hamburger—to keep the
hunger wolves at bay. She leaves Fred and
me in the kitchen alone for a few minutes,
and the words just kind of slip out. "I'm
in love with a man, Fred."

His mouth drops open. It's like he has
no idea how to react. I suppose he has such
incredibly mixed feelings about his own
sexuality that he can't just welcome me to
the brotherhood the way I want him, too.
"Oh, Charlie," he says as if I told him I
have cancer. "Does he know?"

"Of course not. You're the only one I'd
have nerve enough to tell. I knew you'd
understand."

He stares at me with this cold look in
his eye, and suddenly I can't remember how
I know he is queer. He's never told me. I
met his houseboy once, and it was just
painfully obvious they had something going
on. Certainly Mother has never openly
acknowledged the situation. I once raised
the question to her as discreetly as I

could: "Do you think Fred might be homosexual?"

She answered me something like, "Well, I don't know. Fred caught TB in the Army and when he came back, he was just never quite the same."

Finally, Fred does sigh and say to me, "Ach, Charlie. It would be better if you could be a man." Klunk. Thanks, Unc, I think. I'm wishing now that I too could turn the clock back, at least five minutes. I'm sorry I told him.

The chicken is completely inedible. It's as tough as a basketball, and the meat is still red from the blood that apparently didn't drain out. Luckily there's stuffing and wild rice and Fred's traditional mince pie for dessert. We eat this shabby buffet around the living room. A fire crackles in the fireplace. Father and Fred, both pretty far gone by now, blame each other.

Fred goes first. "You killed this bird instantly, didn't you? That's very important, you know. Otherwise the adrenalin from its fear will ruin the meat. Then you have to drain all the blood out."

Father barks back. "It would have been fine if it had been cooked properly, Fred. You're losing your touch."

"Why don't we open some presents?" Mother says. She hands all three of us "children" an envelope. We know what's in it: Fred's traditional $25 check.

"I know that toughness," Fred goes on, standing shakily next to the tree, his voice rising. "My father used to hunt, too,

you know. You didn't kill it instantly."
Then Barney, who rarely says a word,
pipes up, "That's right, he ran around with
his head half off."
"You don't know what you're talking
about," Father screams at poor Barney.
"And, damn it, Fred, you're too damn drunk
to cook instant oatmeal."
"Ha!" Fred yells. "And you, Robert, have
turned your own son into a sissy!" He looks
right at me and says the word "sissy" with
an obscene drawl.
Father lunges at Fred. Fred falls right
into the tree. The tree falls over against
the curtains, Mother's block-printed
curtains. The curtains catch on fire from
the candles. Everybody screams.
Father shouts, "Oh shit, now you did
it!" with transparent delight in his voice,
like it's Fred's fault. Mother stands
paralyzed in the center of the room. Barney
starts moving the presents from under the
tree as if to save them. I start to help
Fred up and then remember how he betrayed
me, so I freeze up myself. The dog Herzie
starts to bark. If it weren't for good old
Pookie, the house would have burned up, and
us with it. She grabs the big bowl of
eggnog from the sideboard and dumps it all
over the flaming curtains, the tree, and
the presents, and then stomps any candles
still smoldering on the rug. It makes a
gooey mess, but the fire goes right out.
Myself, I'm praying with all my soul
that the next minute does not come, that
the world ends right here, right now. I

hold my breath waiting for Father's, and
Mother's, reaction to what Fred has so
artlessly revealed. I think of the guns in
the bottom of the liquor cabinet—let me
just go blow my brains out now and save
everyone a lot of trouble. I glare at Fred,
still on the floor. No, I'd shoot him first.

Mother goes to help Fred up. He's not
hurt, unfortunately as far as I'm
concerned. Mother is clearly furious, but
more about the mess than anything, and she
quickly moves in with a bucket and rags to
get the eggnog off the floor.

The antique clock ticks, and I think of
"The Pit and the Pendulum." But, suddenly,
everyone is as sheepish as a herd of lambs.
Father looks right at Fred and laughs. He
shrugs his shoulders. "Well, Fred, Merry
Christmas." It's as if Fred's words were
never uttered. As though the clock had
turned back.

Fred looks at Father, smiles. "OK,
Robert," he says.

Not content with merely saving the house
from burning down, Pookie, dear, sweet
Pookie, whom I may have maligned at one
time and for which I am truly repentant,
moves in to save the evening, too. Just
when it looks as if the Christmas Eve will
be a total disaster family-wise, perhaps
the most enduring tradition of all, good
old Pookie sits down at the piano and
starts to play. She's no virtuoso, but we
recognize the tune. We all sing along.

God rest ye merry gentlemen,
Let nothing you dismay . . .

On and on into the silent night we go,
singing every carol we know, until we're
all exhausted. Fred heads his Mercedes
toward Milwaukee (I'm hoping he'll crash),
and the rest of us head for bed. Except for
Mrs. Santa, of course, who stays behind to
clean up some more and stuff our stockings
(at our age!).

When we reach Pookie's room, I tell her,
"Thanks, kid, you saved the day."

She kisses me on the cheek, then gives
me a knowing look, filled with anguish.
"Are you going to call Mike tomorrow?" she
asks. I remember when she called me in
Boston and you answered the phone, all
embarrassed. She knows. She may think it's
disgusting, but she accepts it. This means
more to me than anything. Next thing I know
we're hugging in a way my family never hugs
and we're both blubbering into each other's
shoulders.

One thing I decide lying in bed that
night is that there just isn't any pleasing
Father. It can't be done. He will be
dissatisfied with me—and everyone else too
until kingdom come. So I give up. I'm just
not going to try any more.

It snows during the night. The next
morning, the sun shines on the new-fallen
snow, and it's just sublime.

Love,

XXX

Charlie

TWELVE

MY SUMMER VACATION

— 1 —

*H*erzie, I think I'm in love," I said to my dog, Herziger von Sausage, a dachshund about fifty in dog years, hair graying along his snout. I was sixteen in human years, home from a catastrophic first year at my all-boys boarding school. We sat on the floor in my knotty pine bedroom. I loved to rub my cheek against his fuzzy neck. It was late afternoon. We were waiting for our dinners.

"Maggie. You remember her? She smells like flowers, her hairspray, VO5 I think. You're the only one I can talk to, Herzie." I knew he understood me, maybe not all the words, but the feelings. I remembered when Mother ran over Tootsie. I could see the sadness in his eyes.

"I'm horny as a dog—is that disrespectful?—sorry, horny as a toad. And I love this girl. But she doesn't know it. I need to tell her, but I am sooo scared,

Herzie." I hold him tight. He knows. He doesn't pull away. He looks at me with wise eyes. He knows a fuck of a lot more than we give him credit for.

"What if she says no? Who the hell would want *me*? My face is covered with zits. Look at this one!" I point to the purple swelling on the side of my nose the size of a large dung beetle. "And I collect bugs. How uncool is that? I'm a complete spaz at sports, even sailing where I used to win until the boats got too big for me. I used to think I was smart until I went to that elite school and got a D in *David Copperfield* because the book had too many words in it. *I* wouldn't want to be my friend. Why should anyone else want to be? Especially a girlfriend? I've never even kissed a girl.

"I'm funny. That's about all I have going for me. That should be enough. She—Maggie's—no beauty queen. She has big legs. She wears blue teardrop glasses like a housewife. She's not super-bright.

"But she's funny, too. I'm going to tell her tomorrow."

— 2 —

I hate to admit that I missed Hmmm while he was away at boarding school. It sounds like the boarding kennel where they put us when they go on one of their trips. I try to stay unattached to my humans, or distant, but Hmmm and I have had a special relationship. He pays pretty good attention to me. I can feel his love. At some point after Mama was murdered, I decided to let him love me.

He's an odd kid, keeps to himself. Lonely as anything. Not much of a pack to hang out with.

This summer he has paid more attention to the other kids around the lake than me. I could feel him clawing his way into the in-crowd, and I'm rooting for him. He doesn't know I've been watching, but I've been seeing him go to the basement and come up with bottle after bottle of that foul-smelling stuff they call liquor. Different colors. Brown, clear, yellowish. You know I'm partially colorblind, can't see red, but I can see blues, yellows, and other shades. He would hide the bottle in his shirt as he ran down to the lake in the evening and hop on a boat with his pack.

I knew he was buying their friendship with drink, but hey, whatever works. You have to do what you have to do to be wanted in this world.

I could vaguely see the lights of the boat as it putted and drifted around the lake.

When he would finally come home, I could see that he was unsteady on his feet to say the least and smelled the way the place where they made the liquor must've stunk. I'd follow him into his bedroom. Sometimes he stopped in the bathroom and puked his guts out. That smell is not pleasant, especially for someone with as sensitive a sniffer as me.

Then he'd roll all over the rug with me, slobbering me with a drink-enhanced flood of affection that was, well, mostly embarrassing.

"Oh, Herzie, you're the best dog, Herzie, Herzie, Herzie . . ."

I'd squirm away and give him my "back-off buddy" glance. I like the kid OK, but I don't like to be smothered, especially with the insincerity of alcohol.

— 3 —

We ate our dinner in the breakfast nook in silence, thank God. No pontificating from Father. It was Monday night, hot and muggy as hell, and he had to operate on some people's eyes in the morning, so he didn't drink. One or two days a week he didn't drink. He moped in silence instead.

Even Pookie was quiet. A college sophisticate visiting for the summer from Colorado, she wasn't the brat she used to be. I kind of liked her, which was tough to admit after so many years of sibling squabbling. She would probably understand my predicament with Maggie, but I could never admit how terrified I was to pick up the damn phone.

I poked at my roast chicken, rice, and barely thawed peas, not hungry in the least. One of the many embarrassing abnormalities of this family is that we keep the phone in the half-bath just off the breakfast nook. I couldn't see it, but it loomed there like the odor of someone's large dump, daring me to pick it up and call her. My stomach felt like one of those concoctions I liked to make in my basement laboratory, hydrochloric acid and zinc, filling up a balloon with hydrogen, which I would ignite in a satisfying explosion. The boys at school talk about igniting your farts like that, but it probably wouldn't work.

After dinner, with no more excuses, I retreated to the toilet and released some of that gas. But I couldn't do it. I couldn't pick up the damn phone and dial her number.

I shuffled to the playroom and sulked in front of the black-and-white TV. The news showed the sit-ins sweeping lunch counters across the south.

I patted my lap for Herzie, and we watched Huckleberry Hound together. I don't know how much he understood.

That night, I pilfered a needle from my mother's antique sewing table. I locked the bathroom door. I burned the tip with a match and poked the needle into the middle of that purple boil on the side of my nose. It exploded in a volcanic eruption of blood and puss. As satisfying as an orgasm.

With Herzie curled at the foot of my bed, I listened to WLAC out of Memphis, fifty thousand watts, Howlin' Wolf, Muddy Waters, blues, on my fancy Sherwood tuner with the Altec-Lansing speaker. All I'd wanted was a portable record changer, but my father shopped for the best. Together we built the massive speaker cabinet that I had to Railway Express back and forth from boarding school.

I listened to my Nina Simone record, "Don't Smoke in Bed." I listened to Billie Holiday, "Don't Explain." I was feeling the broken heart I was fairly sure Maggie would leave me with.

I read from *Lady Sings the Blues: The Billie Holiday Story* that Charlie had given me for Christmas a couple years ago. "Mom and Pop were just a couple of kids when they got married. He was eighteen, she was seventeen, and I was three."

Next morning, I was perusing the newspaper at breakfast, reading the headlines. *The Milwaukee Sentinel.* A letter to the editor caught my eye, titled, "The Pike Lake Snob Curtain."

"Listen to this," I said to my mother who was serving me fried eggs and bacon. I read it aloud:

My buddy and I were fishing on Pike Lake in Waukesha County where they have all these fine homes. When I was casting, the hook accidentally caught in my buddy's eye. I hurried the boat to the nearest house, a big mansion with a lawn the size of a golf course. I knocked on the door. Some maid answered, but she wouldn't let us in to use the phone even when I told her the problem. I tried two more swell places and got the same cold shoulder. At the last place, the rich housewife herself answered the door and looked right at my buddy with the blood streaming down his face. "Oh, dear, you'll get blood all over my carpet. I'll call the ambulance for you. You go wait up on the road." I'm telling you, it's like there's a snob curtain around that lake. I've never in my life come across such snobbery!

Jack Kowalski
West Allis

"Wow," my mother said. "I wonder who those crude people were." I knew she would have let the fishermen in. I folded up that whole section of the paper and stuck it in the pocket of my jeans and left for work.

I had a real job, my first, in the maintenance department of my cousin's factory, half an hour away. I liked the job. The factory made counters—wheels of numbers like on car's odometer but for counting widgets or whatever. One of my coworkers, a muscular man in his thirties who fixed all the machines on the assembly line, was really smart. Not book smart necessarily, but he could fix anything. He used to tease me about "all the little cunts running around in my brain," and I couldn't deny he was right about that, though he made me blush.

I drove to work as usual. My father had bought the used Jeep, a blue CJ-5, while I was at school. He said he bought it to haul our boats around and for dealing with the snow. But in the summer, I was the one to drive it, a wide-open car with all of the canvas cab removed, a perfect car for the likes of me. He never "gave" it to me, perhaps afraid of "spoiling" me, but he must've bought it with me in mind, and I did appreciate it. I drove it everywhere, often with Herzie sitting in the seat beside me.

— 4 —

You know that stereotype of the dog in the car with his head out the window, his ears blowing in the wind? That was me with Hmmm in that Jeep, only there were no windows, just the wind. I'd sit in the seat next to him while he drove all over the place, past the wondrous manure smells of the dairy farms that populated "America's Dairyland," as Hmmm told me the license plates called it.

Let me explain (dogsplain) something to you humans. We are not focused on understanding the whole shebang like you are. We are more focused on enjoying our being. You have to understand that we hear twice as much and smell fifty times as much as you do. While you are lecturing us about peeing on your precious carpet, we are noting the tempo of the cricket chirps, the roar of the wind, the cacophony of birdsong. What we mostly do is create this symphony as we bounce our attention between the insects and the birds. One of your philosophers spoke of the "music of the spheres." (Don't ask how I know this.) It's not about no spheres, buddy. It's about the song of life. If that weren't enough, we get to smell everything, and I do mean *everything*! Again, we don't try to identify each smell, unless it's the fear smell of a predator. So we nod our heads to the "music." I put that in quotes because it's nothing like your music, so limited in its permissible tones. Our music is multi-tonic, utilizing every note in our incredibly broad spectrum of sounds and smells. It's a little like the programs you watch on your TV, but so much more sophisticated. With an imperceptible nod of our head, we are directing a wondrous abstract—you would say—film only with the fifth dimension of smell. The smells we take from the present, but we can also access the spiral of memory to spice up the tornado of consciousness, if you want to call it that.

So, when you humans see us "sleeping" sixteen hours a day, you have no idea what amazing visions we are swimming through. We hear all the birdsong you can imagine. We hear the buzzing of millions of insects. We hear the howl of the wind. We hear thousands of dogs barking around the countryside. We hear your trains, your cars. We hear frogs croaking, for god's sake.

And the smells! As I said, this is manure country, and we get a lot of that. Luckily, we love it. We smell every flower, every tree, every puddle of piss from every animal within a square mile. It reminds us of the abundance of the natural world. We have no choice but to simply fucking enjoy it. And we do, we do.

— 5 —

*A*fter dinner, I snuck into the basement and fetched a bottle of Smirnoff vodka and Rose's lime juice. Herzie and I waited on the pier and watched the pale streak of the sunset die in the west. The dog wagged his tail and looked at me inquisitively. The sky had cleared some, though it was still scarred with dark wintry clouds—cirrostratus, I happened to know.

A couple of fishermen wearing Milwaukee Braves baseball caps trolled by in a rundown old boat. I thought of the letter. I remembered a long time ago when I was stranded on the island after a sailboat race because I was too shy to tell the people I was with I didn't have a ride home. Some fishermen happened by and gave me a lift in their smelly old boat.

I spotted the speck of a boat with its white-water rooster tail approaching, and I said to the dog, "I will tell Maggie that I love her tonight, no matter how drunk I have to get. And that's a promise."

I jumped on the bow of Brad's red-and-white fiberglass boat, a water-jet-propelled inboard. The dog gave a wistful bark. Brad gunned the motor. I fell on my ass, nearly into the lake. I grabbed the windshield awkwardly, trying not to look scared. "Hey, the vodka!" I yelled.

Brad slowed the boat and let me climb inside. Brad and his girlfriend, Susan, sat in the front. Carl sat in back.

Brad was everything I wasn't: blue-eyed handsome with curly blond hair, naturally athletic, captain of the football team at his country day school, socially at ease, every girl's heart throb, rich. His only deficiency was in the academic realm, where I used to excel, and this, I had always presumed, was why Brad befriended me. That, and the alcohol.

I passed the vodka around, and each of them poured

it in a paper cup with the lime juice, even little Susan,
snuggled next to Brad. She had an upturned button nose
and a streak of bleached blond in her short ducktail.

The gimlet burned my throat, soothed my anxiety,
and settled uneasily in my stomach.

Maggie was waiting for us on her pier in Turtle Bay
at the north end of the lake.

"Hi, Barney," she said sweetly. Terror rippled through
my body, but I smiled back and said "Hi!" a little too
fast and a little too loud.

She sat between Carl and me in the back seat. She
was dressed in Black Watch plaid Bermudas with a
frilly top, through which I could see her bra. She had an
engaging smile and laughing blue eyes. She too had
blond streaks in her brown pageboy.

She and Carl giggled and gossiped together a lot, but
Carl was an odd fish, blond and handsome in an effemi-
nate sort of way, a member of an old family, but apparently uninterested in romance.

In the middle of the lake, Brad stopped the boat.
The north-wind-impelled waves lapped the sides as we
drifted. It was not a large lake, three miles by one mile,
average sized for your Wisconsin inland lake, surrounded
by oak and pine forests and grand homes, not a single
commercial establishment. The sky was dark now, and
the moon was nearly full. When the streaks of clouds let
them through, moonbeams danced off the water. The
uninhabited island near the center of the lake loomed
over us, a dark presence. The bottle continued to circu-
late. Hoping to impress Maggie, I pulled out the news-

paper from my back pocket and read the snob curtain letter aloud.

"What a scream!" Carl squealed. "How petty can you get?" Then he said, "You can't be too careful though. I wouldn't be surprised if that fisherman made up that story."

"I doubt it, Carl," Brad said. "It's disgusting how cold people are around here. We ought to do something."

"Like what?" Maggie asked.

"Burn their houses down," I declared in my extravagant mode.

"Come on, Barney," Carl whined. "We don't even know who it was."

"I know," Maggie said. She looked around. "But I can't tell."

"C'mon, Maggie," pled little Susan.

"Ve haf vays of making you to talk, Maggie," I clowned, handing Maggie the vodka.

"How about if we guess?" Carl suggested.

"Guess away," Maggie said. "You won't get it."

Brad said, "Don't underestimate Carl's knowledge of Pike Lake."

We hollered names, louder and louder as the evening wore on, identifying the residents of each successive house all the way around the lake. Carl did indeed know all the obscure families that Brad, Susan, and I would have missed. Maggie just shook her head at every name. "I'm getting dizzy," she said.

With horror, I suddenly glimpsed where this was

going. I tried to end the game. "Let's stop this, gang. This is boring," I said. But the others persisted. Finally there was only one house left, and everyone just stared at Maggie.

She hid her face in her hands. "I was there. It was my mother that complained about the blood. I was so mortified. I hid in my room for the rest of the day. You want to burn my house down? Did you bring any matches?"

"We've got to do somethin'," Brad slurred, a drunken swagger in his voice.

"Naw," I said, my neck bristling. "Let's forget it,"

Quiet little Susan was emboldened by the vodka, too. "We could just light little fires on their piers."

I thought quickly. "OK, we can do that. We can use the newspaper."

"Good, Barney," Brad enthused.

"We could skip your house, Maggie," I suggested. "I mean your mother did call the ambulance."

"People have the right not to open their doors to just anyone," Carl submitted.

The others glared at him. "Carl, really," Brad sneered.

"But let's not skip my house," Maggie said. "My mother was the worst."

Brad drove the boat as quietly as possible to the house two docks up from Maggie's.

I crumpled a full newspaper page and put it on the dock. Maggie lit it. A flame rose and quickly went out. We repeated this ritual at four more piers, including Maggie's, then retreated to the middle of the lake. Nothing happened. No one came out of their houses. No one noticed.

"Oh, well." I said. Now, I thought. I put my arm around the back of the seat behind Maggie. I pulled her toward me and kissed her.

She kissed me back full on the lips, a lover's kiss. I was in heaven.

— 6 —

*T*wo days passed with me walking two inches off the ground. Then after work, I took a shower and snuck into the basement for a bottle of Jim Beam. I went for a drive with Herzie. We went to the next county where I could pretend to be eighteen and buy beer. I bought a six-pack of Blatz—I liked to think of it as the family beer, and we were related, though distantly. "I'm from Milwaukee and I ought to know: It's draft-brewed Blatz wherever you go . . ."

The Jeep radio got only one station, the top 40 station. The Shirelles, "Will You Still Love Me Tomorrow."

I told Herzie, "It's boilermakers were having tonight, Puppykins." As we drove along, I took a swig from the Jim Beam and then from the beer, then another, and another, fortifying myself for this conversation I planned to have with Maggie.

Feeling good, I drove back onto our "street" I guess you'd call it, a narrow, vaguely paved road off Highway C called "Sauerkraut Road" for all the German families that lived on it, about a dozen houses, most of them larger than ours. Our house was a mile in, but to get to Maggie's house, you had to turn off on another road fifty feet from our driveway. It was called "Tannery Row," for the industry that generated most of the wealth of the families who lived on it, going back a ways to the days of harnesses, saddles, and beaver hats.

There was a gate made of cyclone fencing at the beginning of Tannery Row. It was usually open, but they closed it several days out of the year in order to keep the road private. Apparently, without the gate, the road would become public, heaven forbid, allowing the rabble to cruise along it day and night. Fortunately, it was open this night.

Maggie's house was the third driveway in through the woods. Her house was bigger than ours and uglier, though our house was no Frank Lloyd Wright. Her house was a white clapboard box that had, like our house, succumbed to the 1950s fad of picture windows on the lake side, all out of proportion.

Despite the boilermakers, my stomach was churning. Still I was determined. I rang the bell, and Maggie opened the door.

"Want to go for a drive?" I asked. "I got boilermakers."

She smiled at that. Like me, she loved to drink. She had such a sweet smile.

I felt this upwelling of feeling toward her. I wanted to embrace her fully, but instead gave her a perfunctory hug.

We were both wearing our madras Bermuda shorts, as was the fashion. She wore a pink blouse with the top two buttons undone—for me? I wore a baby blue Izod with the alligator on the chest.

She climbed up to sit in the passenger seat, Herzie's seat. He seemed to look at her challengingly, like this was *his* seat. "Herzie!" I commanded. "Get in back." With some reluctance, he finally jumped into the small truck bed in the back.

"I love this Jeep," she said, and my heart fluttered as if she had said she loved me. As we drove off, I handed her a Blatz and the Jim Beam. She swigged the bourbon and chased it with a sip of beer.

The radio played Elvis, "It's Now or Never."

I drove back to Sauerkraut Road. I knew I wanted to go someplace private, and I had just the place in mind. About a half mile out toward the highway, I turned onto a dirt road. At the end of the road was the dump.

"You brought me to the dump, Barney?" she laughed.

"It's private. We can drink in peace. And it doesn't smell."

"OK."

The dump was filled with old bed frames, rotten farm equipment, mattresses, dysfunctional toasters, rotting cardboard boxes.

We passed the bottle back and forth in silence, chasing our swigs of bourbon with slugs of beer. I was waiting for just the right moment. My palms got sweaty and my stomach roiled.

I tapped on the steering wheel to the Everly Brothers, "Cathy's Clown."

Herzie jumped out of the Jeep and rooted through the rummage, sniffing for treasures.

To break the silence, I asked her, "You went to mass on Sunday?"

"Of course," she answered, with slight annoyance in her tone. "I go every Sunday."

"What did you confess?"

"That's a secret, Barney."

"Oh, yeah. You know I'm an atheist. But if I were any religion, I'd be Catholic, because at least you guys take it seriously, you know what I mean? And you have that confession thing, where you can sin like all get out and then confess, and the sin gets, what do you call it, absolved?"

"You don't believe in God?"

"No. The world is too fucked up for there to be a God."

"Don't say that."

"What does the priest tell you to do when you confess a sin, like drinking these boilermakers?" I was really curious.

"Usually, he'll tell me to say some Hail Marys."

"Really? Like that pass at the end of a football game?"

"No, Stupid. It's a prayer. You say it with the rosary." The boilermakers were slurring her words.

"How does it go?"

"'Hail Mary, full of grace, the Lord is with thee;

blessed art thou amongst women, and blessed is the fruit of thy womb, Jesus. Holy Mary, Mother of God, pray for us sinners, now and at the hour of our death. Amen.'" She tipped her beer at me like a toast and started giggling. "God, it sounds so blasphemous when I say it to you!"

I took her laugh as some kind of cue and reached over to embrace her.

Etta James was singing "At Last."

She pulled away startled. "Barney! What are you doing?"

I'm thinking I fucked up, but I just blurted it out. "Maggie, I'm in love with you." Nervous as hell, I started fiddling with the gear shift on the floor between us.

"Oh, Barney." Pause. "I love you, too." Pause. "As a friend."

Those three words knocked the wind out of me. She might as well have said, "I hate you."

I slumped back in my seat. I took three swigs of bourbon and three slugs of Blatz. Maggie did the same, as if to keep up. We were pretty loaded by then.

"Let me drive your Jeep, Barney-Barn-Barn."

I didn't care much about anything anymore. My heart ached. But at least I'd finally fucking told her.

We switched seats. She started the engine and raced it.

"Do you know how to drive a stick?"

"How hard can it be?" She pulled on the shift and ground the gears.

"You have to depress the clutch first, that pedal on

the left, next to the brake, then shift, then slowly release the clutch."

She tried it twice, jerking the Jeep forward and killing the engine. On the third try, the transmission engaged, and the Jeep lurched forward about six feet before we heard a horrible squealing.

"Oh, no!" I screamed. "Herzie!" I jumped out of the car and looked. He was stuck under the right front wheel, yelping like hell. I went around and jumped in the driver's seat as Maggie jumped out and puked on an old mattress. I lurched the Jeep forward, jumped out again, and examined Herzie. His hind legs and much of his hindquarters were crushed. I tried to suppress the sobs, but they just heaved out of me like vomit. I found a flattened cardboard box and carefully nudged him onto it. I lifted him into the truck bed. I tried to drive gently home. Maggie was snuffling next to me. We couldn't look at each other. "I'm sorry, Barney," she said as I dropped her at the top of her driveway. I drove home.

— 7 —

$\mathcal{S}$ hit! My fucking legs! I think I'm dead now. If I don't die on my own, they'll kill me for sure, just like they did Mama. I didn't like Maggie before, her flowery smell. Now I hated her, for what she did to Hmmm and to me.

The pain in my rear end is intolerable. I discover that if I squinch my eyes shut, I can leave my body and the pain behind and hover in some kind of dream world.

I'm really scared. I think they will murder me like they did Mama after they ran over her, motherfuckers. Motherkillers. And this was Hmmm's beloved who killed me. You better break the shit up with her whatever you do.

I'm trying to focus on the cacophonic symphony, but the pain is great, and the smell of the vet is overwhelming. The smell of sick dogs and cats is grating on the nose. Plus all those chemicals. And fear! There must be a dozen other animals here fearfully waiting to die.

The gas chamber where they murdered Mama is right next door. It's most likely they'll do the same to me. I can smell death. It smells like dust. They don't want to be bothered by any crippled dog. But I want to live as long as I can. I think that's kind of normal.

But I'll probably be killed today. "Put to sleep." You gotta love humans. They can make the cruelest of acts to sound like a favor to the victim. I'll be overpowered with smell. I remember smelling it when they murdered my mother. The smell of death is nothing if not inimitable.

So what the fuck do I have to look forward to? Nothing? Nothing? Nothing? For like, *ever?* Maybe you stop going forward in time. But that doesn't mean you can't go back. Time is like a mountain. The present is that little point right at the top. The past is all the rest of it. But it's not like it doesn't exist. Time is not nearly that simple.

I can hope for some lingering awareness, I guess.

Have faith. And if it's all for nothing, so be it. Nothing feels no pain.

And yet I can smell Mama!

— 8 —

W ell, we'll have to put him to sleep." The first thing my father said when I told him Herzie had been hit.

"Can we take him to the vet?" I asked.

"Sure, but they'll want to put him to sleep and charge a fortune. We could do it ourselves and save the trouble."

I looked at him with every muscle clenched against bursting into tears. I remembered him forcing me to drown a cat a few years ago.

"We'll take him to the vet," my father conceded.

I drove the Jeep, my father beside me, Herzie in the back with a blanket over him. Wheezing. Ever so quietly whimpering.

We waited at the vet. My father said, "I know you really liked that dog. Was it you that hit it?"

"No."

"Who then?"

"Maggie Gerber."

"I should call her father."

"No!" I screamed. He looked at me, not unsympathetically.

After about forty-five minutes, the vet came out, a young gray-haired man with a mustache. "There's not much we can do for him. I hate to say this, but the humane thing to do is put him to sleep. He's in a lot of pain."

My father said, "Yes, well, that's what we'll do then."

"No!" I yelled again. My father and the vet both looked shocked.

"I'm sorry, Barney," my father said. "You heard the vet."

"No!" I screamed as loud as I could.

My father looked hopelessly at the vet.

The vet said, "Well, we can bandage his hindquarters so he's not bleeding. He won't be able to walk. And his internal organs are damaged. I don't know how long he'll survive."

I glared at my father with an intensity I doubt he had ever seen from me.

My father said, "Do what you can, Doc. We'll take him home and nurse him as best we can."

It was past midnight when we got out of the vet's office with Herzie panting in a box, his entire lower half wrapped in adhesive tape. He looked at me with a sad look.

My father fetched a syringe and needle from his medical supplies. "Can you give him a shot, Barney?" he asked. "Morphine. I'm not supposed to have it, but I do. "He showed me how to stick it quick into Herzie's left shoulder. "If we did three doses, it would put him all the way out of his misery."

I glared at him and shook my head. "The least we can do is let him die naturally," I said. "If he has to die."

— 9 —

I heard Hmmm's scream of "No!" and I knew it had saved my life. I appreciated it. He so rarely stood up to his bully of a father. But I'm not sure it was worth it. I couldn't really eat. There was something wrong with my pee and my shit. Like my rear end wasn't working any more.

Still, Hmmm was nice to me. He fed me milk through a baby bottle. He talked to me. I didn't understand half of what he said, but the part I did understand was that he loved me. That's worth something.

This death thing. The smell of death is, well, fecund—the soil for new life. We dogs don't know any more than you do about consciousness. I'll keep a piece of it or I won't. That I most likely won't is sad to me, having struggled through life; many dogs had it worse, but still to just disappear? That seems wasteful. But life thrives on waste.

If we don't get to keep just a kibble of consciousness, I guess our experience will revert to what it was before we were born. That wasn't so bad. What if nothing is really everything? Nothing has its role. Without nothing there'd be no something. Nothing created something, I suppose because it was lonely.

— 10 —

*H*erzie lasted about two weeks. Except when I was at work, I spent all my time with him, lying on the day bed in the playroom. I even slept down there. He was getting progressively weaker. When he started to whimper with pain, I injected him with morphine and talked to him.

"You're my best friend, Herzie. I know you're on your way out of here. If I believed, I would pray for you. How did that go? 'Hail Mary, full of grace, the Lord is with thee . . .' For you now, it's like that end-of-game football pass."

The summer raced toward its end. It was just after dinner the night he died. I was lying next to him. He started to whimper. I reached for the morphine, but by the time I filled the syringe, he was quiet. "Herzie?" I yelled. His breathing had stopped. His eyes stared out empty. "Herzie!" I called. I shook him. I squeezed his chest to get him to breathe.

I called my father. "Dad!" I never called him Dad.

He came and poked at the carcass. He looked at me. "He's gone, Son."

I cried. My father left me to my tears.

I went to the basement and grabbed a bottle of Myers's rum. I went to my laboratory. I drank the sweet rum.

Carelessly I mixed half a bottle of ferrous oxide and powdered aluminum in a silvery-orange mountain on the floor, under the old wooden table. Thermite, the guts of the incendiary bombs of World War II. I stuck a piece of magnesium ribbon in the mountain peak. I lit the ribbon.

Kabloom! It made a huge flash. The black paint on the bottom of the table caught fire. For all the "safety first" signs and "acid to water" warnings I'd posted to make the lab look authentic and dangerous, there was no fire extinguisher. But a bottle of water from the sink did the trick. I saved the house from burning down.

In the ruins of the chemical mountain, there was a globular hunk of metallic iron an inch in irregular diameter. There was small hole in the center. I cut a length from a ball of string that was in the drawer.

For Maggie, I thought. The next thought crept up on me. I needed to tell her about Herzie! Maybe she'll feel sorry for me and . . .

I staggered out through the root cellar, a tunnel with a wooden flap of a door that opened into the woods.

I jumped into the Jeep and took off down the road. I got to the gate. It was locked! I stared at it.

"The goddamn Pike Lake snob curtain!" I shouted out loud as I backed up the Jeep for a running start and slammed into the gate. It bent at enough of an angle for it to pop open. With exhilaration overcoming my grief for Herzie, I sped to Maggie's house.

She came out when I rang the bell.

"You're drunk," she said.

Standing in the doorway, I gave her the thermite necklace.

"What's this?"

SQUIRRELS IN THE WALL

"I made it for you."

"Really?" she said, unimpressed. "You think I would wear a hunk of metal?"

I was surprised by the stridency of her tone.

"Herzie died."

"Oh, no, Barney. I'm so sorry." She hugged me.

"And I smashed the Pike Lake snob curtain."

"What?"

"The gate to Tannery Row."

"No!"

"Yes."

"Wow, that's pretty cool, Barney. But you better go home now. If my father finds out . . ."

So much for my pity-sex fantasy. I went home, still proud of myself.

The next morning, my mother woke me. "The police are here for you, Barney. What did you do?"

"N-nothing."

I jumped into my shorts and went downstairs to confront the waiting Captain Lutz. The Village of Pike Lake has four hundred residents and a full-time police force, making it among the communities with highest ratio of police to residents in the country.

Fat, gray, and intimidating, the captain asked, "Barney, did you crash the Tannery Row gate?"

"No."

"It looks like it might have been done with a Jeep. Can you drive the Jeep to the gate please?"

I looked at my father, who scowled at me. "OK," I said.

We drove to the crime scene. Sure enough, the front of the Jeep with its red hydraulic prong in front fit the damage perfectly. There was even some matching red paint on the diamond-shaped wires of the gate.

"Well, we can investigate further, I suppose," Lutz said.

"That's OK," I said. "I did it."

My father blurted, "Why did you lie?" Then he turned to the cop and said, "Whatever you need to do, Captain."

"We'll leave it your hands, Dr. Blatz."

"OK. You know these kids have been experimenting with alcohol."

That was his defense. He might have mentioned the dog.

I was grounded for the rest of the summer, about a week. My father didn't forgive me for years, not because of the vandalism, but because I lied about it.

I couldn't wait to get back to my hated boarding school.

THIRTEEN

THIS IS THE WEEK
THAT WAS

THERE WAS THIS GUY, BARNEY BLATZ, SEE. LONELY
guy you might say. College dropout. Wandered the
South with his best friend, Brad, for a summer, selling
hot tamales on the street in New Orleans, trying to be a
bum, which seemed like the most authentic thing to be
in that day and age. He wrote in his notebook things
like "not caring is a positive thing," Buddhistically on
the one hand, but cold as hell on the other.

He wasn't a stupid guy, though he felt like it most of
the time. He'd gone to the best schools—Devon Acad-
emy, Columbia—and at the start of our story, he'd just
been admitted to Berkeley. He wasn't political, at least
not yet, but he knew there was something wrong with
Columbia, a pretend Ivy League school in the middle of
Harlem. We're talking 1963, so civil rights were in the
air. He did remember that he got home from that failed
bum trip in time to hear the "I Have a Dream" speech.
Cried his eyes out.

The biggest event of late 1963 wasn't the assassination. It was our guy discovering marijuana and peyote. The first time he smoked, he said to his friend and roommate Matt and their dealer, Count Odin Bylonski, a squat man with a full black beard and a rat's nest of curly hair, "I don't feel anything."

"Me neither," Matt said.

"Wait," the Count said. "That's the word Kafka had posted above his desk. Wait."

"Woof," our guy said.

"Meow," Matt said.

"Moo," our guy said.

Then they all laughed for an hour.

Not that the assassination didn't loom large. That kind of thing was not supposed to happen in the United States of America where everything was peachy keen.

Our guy was working as a copyboy at the Oakland *Tribune,* a far right rag run by William Knowland, ex-senator from Formosa, as they called him at Berkeley.

Our guy was in the newsroom by himself on that Sunday, manning the phones, watching the wire. When the Jack Ruby thing went down, he thought he might be one of the first in the country to know this huge piece of news as it clacked out of the teletype machine. He called the city editor to see if he wanted to do a special edition. The city editor laughed. "Don't you know the entire country watched the whole thing on TV? It's not exactly news anymore."

Toward the holidays, our guy was like: Work? School? He weighed the pros and cons. Work got you money and was sort of interesting. School gave you much more free time, he knew how to fake it, and after sorting through the bullshit, it might be sort of interesting.

On the first day of his creative writing class, he was introduced to the teaching assistant, Zelda Weissman. Straight jet-black hair down to her shoulders, bangs cut across her forehead like a helmet. Huge vulnerable eyes. Creamy skin. A smile that forced one out of you.

He was smitten. He knew she was way out of his league. A fucking graduate student, what, at least four years older than him? To say nothing of brilliant. A homey New York accent, even though she was from Philly.

But he also had a pattern of going for women who were out of his league. It made the rejection easier. If a woman was on his level—you know, a little clumsy, self-confidence in the toilet—it really stung when she said, "Let's be friends," or whatever.

Full disclosure. He wasn't a virgin. He'd lost that to a sensuous Harlem prostitute his first week at Columbia. And he'd had a Barnard girlfriend in the spring, a sweet sexual connection without much else going for it. He wasn't brokenhearted when she left to return to her native Argentina, but they made out like newlyweds on the deck of the freighter that was taking her home, to the point where the ship left the dock, and our guy had to be lowered onto one of the tugs to get back to shore.

In Berkeley, he roomed and hung with Matt who had lived down the hall in their Columbia dorm. He was an elven fellow, Matt, cute as all get-out, a shock of curly brown hair. That winter they'd found a sizable two-bedroom flat on Ashby just above Telegraph, bare sheetrock on the walls, mattresses on the floor, $75 a month. Their first pad.

Our guy was trying to write a novel about being on the bum with Brad in the south. He wrote: "On the Greyhound back home, having failed as a bum, Barney stared through the night as his own terrified image in the window as the bus bounced down the highway."

Zelda liked that. "Great image! Now you've got something. Keep going," she wrote on his onion skin paper.

She drove a blue Honda 50 motor scooter. What could be hipper than that?

Certain she would decline, he invited her to dinner after one of their conferences.

She said, "I'd love to!"

He scrambled to clean the apartment. At one point, at his instigation, they'd stopped doing the arduous labor of looking for ashtrays and just put their smokes out on the brown painted wooden floor. He swept up the butts and even washed the floor, though of course he couldn't remove all the burn marks.

At the Berkeley Co-op just up the street, he bought a top sirloin, two artichokes, two baking potatoes, butter, sour cream. Wine. Our guy was into sour wines then, Chianti in those basket-wrapped bottles.

Was he excited about this date? You betcha. He arranged for Matt to hang out elsewhere. At five in the afternoon, he put the potatoes in the filthy gas oven. He boiled the artichokes. He mixed the vinegar and oil dressing for the chokes. He broiled the steak, five minutes on a side.

She rang the bell at five after six. He nearly fell down the stairs rushing to open the door.

"Hi!" she smiled.

"Hi, back," he grinned.

They sat down to eat at the yellow Formica kitchen table. She already knew about him from his writing.

She had graduated from Bryn Mawr. "I won a prize for a story I wrote about a girl who makes love to her cat," she said.

He shook that image out of his mind. He confessed to her. "I get the feeling it's all fucked up. All of it. The whole thing."

She looked at him with bottomless sympathy. "Oh, Barney," she said.

They went to the living room. He put Miles Davis, "Some Day My Prince Will Come," on the stereo.

"This is my song," she said.

"There is something sweetly Disney about you," he said.

"Thank you, I think," she laughed. "Mostly I'm just scared."

"Me too, but I guess you knew that already."

She fell into his arms.

Finally, he thought.

They kissed and bumped around like teenagers for a while, and then, get this, our guy, totally out of character, picked her up and carried her into the bedroom. He took off her clothes and then his own. They held each other against the impending apocalypse.

They made love slowly. Was he any good at it? Probably not. He was an amateur. Nevertheless when they awoke in the morning still entwined, she wrote on his palm with her finger. "I love you."

His eyes wet up. "I love you, too."

That was on Wednesday.

ON SATURDAY, MATT and our guy went around the corner from where they lived to the place above the Chinese restaurant where Count Odin and a bunch of others lived. The word was that LSD had hit town.

They'd been expecting it. They read the *Psychedelic Review* and knew all about Leary's experiments at Harvard.

It came in an innocent looking sugar cube. Could have been anything, but it wasn't. It was the real thing.

Odin took charge. "First, you'll want to relax. Take a deep breath. This may be intense." Our guy already knew that this was an understatement. "Here's what to expect, according to Leary. These are, like, the stages." He read from the *Psychedelic Review.*

"'Bodily pressure, earth-sinking-in-water.

"'Body disintegrating or blown to atoms, fire-sinking-into-water.

"'Pressure on head and ears, rocket-launching-into-space.

"'Tingling in extremities.

"'Feelings of body melting or flowing as if wax.

"'Trembling or shaking, beginning in pelvic regions and spreading to torso.'

"That's what *he* felt, anyway," Odin continued. "Everyone's experience is different. The important thing is to keep reminding yourself that it's the drug, you know?"

There was music playing, some obscure East Indian guy named Ravi Shankar, a frantic rambling through ever-changing rhythms.

The first thing our guy noticed from the drug was that his mouth was sort of puffing up inside and tasting of ether. Early hospital, appendicitis. Staring at a candle seemed to help. Yet he felt himself disintegrating. He knew it was the drug.

It's the drug. It's the drug.

He smoked a cigarette and stared into the volcanic glowing ash as if into the fires of hell. Colors were . . . hard to say what the fuck they were doing. He was way beyond the restrictive universe of words.

Time was the next sense to go haywire. Minutes would pass that felt like hours. The events, the images, the hallucinations per second overwhelmed his internal clock. There was an ominous roar in the background as if something, *something*, was coming, something like death. A demonic *Om*. He'd read in the books that ego death isn't real death. It sure as hell felt like it.

He bobbed his head in time with the music, Charles Mingus, "Goodbye Pork Pie Hat." The strands of color danced to the rhythm of head bobbing.

His breath was shortening. Fear was rising.

He looked over at Matt, crumpled into his own little disintegrating world. Our guy asked him, "You OK?"

Pause. "I think so."

They laughed.

The roar grew louder. In the encroaching distance there was a . . . what? Words fail again. A billowing bubble? A mummy wrapped in multicolored ribbons? Some kind of undulating hornets' nest of dream-memories. Images are so fleeting, no sense in trying to identify them, the name that can be named is not a constant name. It worked for him to direct the symphony of colors by moving to the music.

The terror slithered up his legs like miniature snakes.

The ghosts of animals he'd helped kill—toads, bees, mice, cats, and Herzie the dog—swarmed over him, wrapping him in that ectoplasm that ghosts are made of, spinning around him with the speed of Sambo's butter churn. Each animal had its own quick View-Master show in this swirl of images; calling them hallucinations just didn't say it. *This is a thing. This is a motherfucker.*

The animals began chasing him. They wanted to devour him. A swarm of all the moths, butterflies, locusts, and insects our guy had pinned to foam board and mounted. They chased him toward an insectoid darkness, millions of insect corpses. On the other side of the wall of insects was Nothing. Where you go when you die—to Nothing.

Palpable, dense nothing, like uranium Jell-O.

"It's only your Ego, and it's supposed to die," says the vanishing voice of reason, the one informed by all the reading and talking to friends. *This thing does not want to die. And yet it's unraveling, the mummy-cloth ribbons.* He had a lot invested in his Ego, even if its price was on the low side about now. He was feeling and hearing something at the end of these ribbons. The color turned black, but like black hole black.

It's just the drug. I'm not going to die. It's just the drug. I'm not going to die.

He danced to the music, more Mingus, "Black Saint and the Sinner Lady," a wild romp in cacophonic catatonia. This puffy mummy of an unraveling cloud danced with him, mocking him, yes, but in an ever-so-slightly less threatening way. He breathed. The music soared through its rhythms, relativity full circle. The tempo crescendoing toward orgasm.

Suddenly: *Crash!*

Crash!

Crash!

The world ended.

He died.

Just like that.

THE NEEDLE HAD gotten stuck in the groove. Odin, red-faced, eyeball dilated, jiggled the arm. The music resumed.

Dead stillness. He wasn't dead. Some kind of weird mirror popped up from nowhere. He could see himself as Zelda saw him. He had that Buddha smile. There was calm in his heart. Radiance wallpapered the room.

"OK!" he said out loud to himself. In her loving him, he could love himself, something he wasn't used to. In general, he didn't like himself very much.

Until now.

This was a game changer.

He danced in the radiance. Matt and Count Odin joined him. He became the music. *Oh, the present*, he thought. *The present.* He still had words but no need for words; words were a prison of suppressed consciousness. Words were in the past.

He spoke to his friends in a deep prophetic voice: "Everything is all right!"

Matt asked him, "In what sense do you mean that?"

Pause. "I don't mean in senses," said our new sage.

The world was perfect, and it seemed like this state would last forever.

There was this light they talk about. Like the sun but not like the sun. Like the moon but not like the moon. A shimmering disk of energy, clearly in charge. Our guy could see how one might want to anthropomorphize this light into a humanoid deity, but why bother? It was powerful just as it was, beaming spiritual iridescence. Vibrant ether swept through the aura of this light and scattered joy about the universe as if planting apple trees. Above all, it was friendly, this light.

"Let's go for a ride," Count Odin said. The others looked at him skeptically. "Hey, I've done this a thousand times. I'm hardly even high. I could fly an airplane."

"Do you have one?" Matt asked. They laughed.

What he had was a green 1952 Hudson Hornet, built like a tank. They climbed into the plush seats and the ancient car smell, opposite of the new car smell. The street lamps glimmered like miniature stars. The moon itself loomed overhead and shocked him with its luminescence.

The car wound its way up into the Berkeley Hills, up Snake Road to Grizzly Peak. Odin parked the Hudson in one of the viewing areas, next to a group of necking teens.

Our boys got out of the car and walked to the edge of the cliff. They sat in the roots of an old cypress tree. They looked. They breathed.

After a while, our guy said, "Maybe it's not so bad."

He was looking at the world through Zelda's eyes as she saw him, or at least as he imagined she did.

The cities around the Bay shimmered like a dragon decorated for Christmas, twinkling lights as far as the eye could see. It—this creature—purred, white noise, noise made mostly by white people. It hummed with the sound of a beatific *Om*. The water of the Bay in the center beamed its own deep being. You could see the myriad lights of San Francisco, the two bridges, as well as Alcatraz and San Quentin. And then he thought of each light as a person and all the lights coming out of windows and all of the people living their poignant dramas. *What a big thing the present moment is.*

A squadron of fighter planes broke the silence like a small earthquake wrapped in a thunderstorm. The earth shook. The boys' euphoria was punctured for a minute.

Our guy in his prophetic voice declared: "There's going to be a war."

The other boys didn't contradict him.

"Follow me," Count Odin said. He led them across the street and into the fragrant eucalyptus woods, up a dirt road through darkness as dense as nothing, but nothing had won, and they were no longer afraid.

They had to climb around a gate to get to the fire lookout tower at the top of the hill, a redwood frame of three stories. The boys climbed the stairs.

At the top, the hush in the air was palpable. On one side of the tower was the transcendent Beautiful City, El Greco's "Toledo." On the other side was the lush countryside, newly green from the rainy season. Hills glowing in the moonlight, representing earth. Our mother. The silence was so deep it brought tears to his eyes.

Our guy, full of exuberance, shouted to the world, "Nothing and something are the same thing!"

Matt cocked his head at him. "Really?"

"I don't think so," Odin declared.

They started arguing.

IT WENT DOWNHILL from there, literally and figuratively. After a pancake breakfast at Sambo's the morning after their date—he had the Swedish—Zelda told him she was engaged and would be married next summer, and she was sorry she couldn't keep seeing him because she really liked him and all. He pined after her for months. More or less stalked her to her wedding in Atlantic City. It wasn't a pretty picture.

As for the enlightenment, that lasted until the following Monday when he had a midterm exam in experimental psychology where they torture rats. He couldn't remember who injected the rats with amphetamines and clocked the acceleration of their maze-running ability.

As for the timeless radiance overlooking the bay, it was easy to forget about an experience that doesn't fit into words.

Our guy was right about the war though.

FOURTEEN

GUNS ON THE WALL II

BARNEY, NOW BEARDED, BESPECTACLED, AND graying, gaped rudely at Jeffery, ghost from the ancient past. Barney was on a rare visit to his ancestral home from California, attempting, with mixed success, to reclaim his past. The afternoon was late-August cool and cloudy.

His long white hair streaming outside his leather aviator's skull cap, Jeffery said to Barney with a big smile, "How do you like my little trike?" He bowed toward a unique reddish-brown, three-wheeled vehicle, hybrid off-spring of a motorcycle front and a Volkswagen rear.

"Your creation, of course?" Barney said of the tricycle.

"Of course." Jeffery had white whiskers drooping from his upper lip like Rutherford B. Hayes and a leather jacket replete with gleaming buckles and snaps like Marlon Brando in *The Wild Ones*. Both Jeffery and Barney wore Levi's 501s with a black pocket T.

They shook hands warmly, resisting the urge to embrace. "Can you believe thirty years?" Barney said.

"I don't believe in years anymore," Jeffery answered cryptically. "It's all one time. See?" He raised his hand toward the house as if presenting it. "Nothing has changed." The house was the same white-and-green bungalow on Elk Lake Road where Barney had come for Cub Scout meetings.

On the way into the back of the house, the way they'd always gone in, Jeffery bowed once more. "Meet Bruno," he said. Bruno was a red metal brontosaurus who stood in the backyard about five feet high and eight feet long. "That's what I do now," Jeffery said. "I do art. Try to lift it."

Barney tried and failed.

"It weighs about half a ton. Solid steel. You know those wooden kits of dinosaurs? I just took the pieces from one of those and blew them up about ten times. You should have seen us trying to get it here. Took ten guys. I work in heavy metal. The heavier the better."

Barney, a man-of-the-world now who knew something about art, was impressed. Though the sculpture was just a model of a skeleton, the sadness in the eye sockets and the animated swish of the tail spoke of life.

Inside the house, Jeffery led Barney into the living room where his mother and father sat hollowly transfixed by *The Wheel of Fortune* on TV. "You remember Barney?" he said to them.

"Why Barney, how nice to see you," his mother spoke from a great distance, keeping one eye on the screen.

Barney shook each of their frail hands and followed Jeffery upstairs. "The old man had a triple bypass," Jeffery whispered. "Mom has cancer. It started in the breast, but it's spread all over now. They sit there like zombies all day long, waiting to die. It's so sad, seeing what we have to look forward to."

Jeffery was still a head taller than Barney and had to duck his head inside his room, its ceiling slanted with the rake of the roof. The walls were painted black and the room was as dark as a movie theater in the afternoon. Jeffery turned a switch, and a violet light emerged from the eyes of a human skull inside a hollow TV set. Another switch turned on a neon triangle advertising Blatz beer. "Your cousins," Jeffery said.

"My distant cousins," Barney corrected.

Another switch began the amoebic churning of a pink lava lamp. Another lit a Coleman lantern wick inside a clear globe, perched on top of an intricate tangle of wrought iron curlicues. Still another lit up the eyes of an antlered deer head above the door. "Have a seat," Jeffery said, bowing toward the bed.

Barney had to plot a path through the array of "stuff" that covered the floor and the walls and hung from the ceiling. Jeffery identified each thing Barney stumbled over. A 16mm shell, a found hunk of machinery that Jeffery had fashioned into a ruined Roman aqueduct ("I left it outside for a year and poured battery acid on it to get it the right color"), a working toy steam engine, an ancient tin of Nabisco saltines, an empty Corona beer bottle, a balsa-wood model Sopwith Camel biplane.

In the center of the room was a wooden trunk, stenciled on the side "Pvt. Jeffery Trapp," covered with a swatch of luminous violet silk. In the center of the trunk was another heavy metal sculpture, about the size of a breadbox: a phoenix with wings artfully twisted to suggest flames.

Jeffery peeled off his aviator's cap. His white hair hung off the top of his bald head like Benjamin Franklin's. "I collect things," he said.

"No kidding," Barney responded. "You were in the army?"

"Three years in Nam. You?"

"Conscientiously objected, as a Zen Buddhist. Combat?"

"No. I wanted to. I was itching for it, but they had me cooking and fixing the jeeps. I kept going AWOL."

"You wanted to?"

"Damn right. I was bored to death. Smoke?" Jeffery picked up a small pipe made of carburetor parts and lit it. Marijuana smoke tickled Barney's nose.

"I can't believe it. In rural Wisconsin?" Barney sucked in a huge toke.

"You remember Harold Petersen from grade school?"

"Harold Petersen. We used to call him 'Mr. Manure.'"

"He grows this on his farm."

"No shit?"

"No shit."

"How do you live, Jeffery?"

"You see how I live."

"I mean, how do you make a living?"

"I trade. I live outside the money economy. I have no use for money. It just gets in the way. My rent is cheap."

"You been married?" Barney asked.

"Married, divorced, one kid. A daughter, about to graduate from high school. She's great. I see her once a year. She's the reason I live off the underground economy, though. Her mother's got court orders coming out of her ears for child support."

Barney's feminist hackles rose. "Don't you feel guilty?"

"No."

"I pay my support," Barney said. "I've got two kids, a girl ten, a boy twelve. I do what I can for them, though I'm a poor working stiff myself." He heard himself bragging. "I make my living teaching preschool. What do you trade, mostly?"

"See anything you want?"

"Sure. Your phoenix."

"You like that little birdy, huh? I used this little creature painted on the Corona label as a model," he said, handing Barney the clear glass bottle showing a miniscule firebird as the logo.

"You turned that into this?" Barney exclaimed, indicating the heavy metal centerpiece of the room. "Amazing. How much you want for it?"

"I told you, I don't deal in money. Do you still have those guns you had in your room when we were kids?"

"They're still there, hanging in the same spot. You want them? I hate guns."

"Sure. It's a deal. That's what I deal in mostly, guns.

Here's my card." He handed Barney a card showing a Colt .45 emblazoned with the words, "Trader Trapp, New, Used, Antique Firearms." "I'll show you," Jeffery said, diving into a drawer. He pulled out a case of twin, pearl handled derringers. From under the bed, he extracted a German Luger, well-oiled and menacing. From a case in the corner, a sawed-off shot gun. "And look at these, my pièces de résistance."

From another corner, he pulled out two fierce looking automatic rifles. "The twin pillars of the world economy: a US M-16 and a Russian AK-47. Still automatic. Very illegal." His eyes glowed.

"I hate guns," Barney repeated. Tension bristled between them. "I spent two years working in a psychiatric halfway house because I hate guns. You ought to melt them all down and make more sculptures out of them."

"Guns are my life," Jeffery said. "Instead of banning guns the way you patsy-fists whine, they should issue one of these babies"—he rattled the M-16 in both his hands—"to everyone at birth. That way, there'd be no more crime."

An awful silence fell between them.

"I guess I should be going. I haven't always hated guns," he said as if to bridge the divide. "When I was a heavy-duty revolutionary, I had fantasies of going to the admin building of the school district with my Grandpa's .45 and arresting the top administrators."

Jeffery walked Barney out to Barney's father's gray Buick. "I'm having a surprise party for my birthday next Saturday," Jeffery said.

"You're having a surprise party?" Barney asked, smiling through his moral indignation.

"Yeah. I'll provide the surprise. I'll pick you up."

"Maybe, Jeffery. I don't know. We'll see."

ON SATURDAY, JEFFERY roared up to the barn-shaped front of the Blatz house on his "trike," with a wooden crate tied to the back seat. He lifted the Amelia Earhart goggles from his eyes with his big leather gloves as Barney came out to greet him.

"Hey, guy," Jeffery said, beaming. "Your phoenix." Inside the crate, like a caged bird, was the heavy metal phoenix from the center of Jeffery's room. "I packaged him so you can take him on the plane back to California."

"Oh." Barney looked away, embarrassed. He'd forgotten about the deal and the birthday party. "OK." The crate itself had rope handles and was as fine a piece of craftsmanship as the sculpture inside. He lugged it into the house. "C'mon. I'll get the guns."

He led Jeffery through the den, where his mother and father, now in their eighties, stared at the Pro-Am golf tournament on the TV. "Well, well, Jeffery," Barney's mother said abstractly. "How's your mother?"

"Dying," Jeffery said with characteristic candor, "but otherwise fine."

"Aren't we all?" Father said. "How've you been, young man? I guess you're not so young any more either, are you?"

"Me? Oh, I don't worry about anything," Jeffery answered.

Once in the bedroom, Jeffery observed, "I told you, Barney. Nothing changes. It's all one time. This room is exactly the same as it was when I was here last."

Barney rolled the same old desk chair up against the wall and stretched up to retrieve the three antique guns.

"Why don't you keep one?" Jeffery said. "That phoenix isn't worth all three."

"Don't undervalue your work, Jeffery."

"Don't undervalue your guns, Barney."

They laughed.

"OK, I'll keep the oldest," Barney said.

"They don't fire anyway, so they're not really guns," Jeffery added. "Let's go to the party."

"Um," Barney said.

"Come on!" Jeffery ordered.

Rifling through the files in his mind for excuses and finding none, Barney finally said, "OK."

The back seat of the trike was one of those 1950s modern fiberglass chairs shaped like an upside-down Nazi helmet. Barney wondered if the resemblance was intentional on Jeffery's part, more punk/heavy-metal fashion than political statement, Hell's Angels' kitsch. He couldn't ask. Instead, he blurted, "No seat belt?"

"No seat belt," Jeffery answered.

They zipped down the driveway, through the woods to the country highway, two lanes, twisting northward past corn fields, graveyards, and swaths of oak and maple forest, rolling over the hills that were known as the Kettle Moraine—rounded deposits of earth left by the receding glaciers ten thousand years ago. The warm summer wind blew Barney's hair and ruffled his anxiety as he clutched the seat, cradling the antique guns between his thighs.

They stopped at a bright purple house in the middle of nowhere, a dozen people gathered out front. "I used to live here," Jeffery said. "When I was married." The cycle was surrounded by well-wishers shouting "Surprise! Surprise! We want our surprise!"

Jeffery, a stranger to social convention, introduced Barney to no one. Barney introduced himself. There were about a dozen folks in all, including Harold Petersen—"Mr. Manure"—who looked the same, dressed in bib overalls and crew-cut hair, but at least he didn't smell. Some of the men wore ponytails and caps with "Caterpillar," written above the visor, or "Brewers." *Redneck hippies,* Barney thought, but then dismissed the thought in the name of open-mindedness. Some of the women held babies. There was a smattering of children of various sizes. The adults were all drinking Coors or Corona.

Harold passed a fat joint around.

"You remember me?" Barney asked him.

"Sure," Harold said. "The ticklish brain who couldn't play baseball for shit."

Barney laughed. "I remember when you tickled me in class that time so much that I burst out crying. God, that was humiliating."

"Sorry. I thought you were cute."

Jeffery yelled above the din, "The surprise is in here." He bowed toward a dilapidated shed behind the house. He opened the door.

"Ta-*da!*" he sang.

Inside was a yellow Volkswagen bug with no engine, three flat tires, and a body that appeared to have been rolled at least six times. The words "Modern Civilization" were spray-painted in black all the way around the bug.

"It's my latest sculpture," Jeffery declared with satiric pomp. "I call it 'Modern Civilization,' and today, my friends, we are going to destroy it. C'mon men!"

The men, including Barney, and one of the women, surrounded the car and lifted it easily off the ground. "To the middle of the field!" Jeffery commanded. "And sing!"

They sang, "Happy birthday to you . . ." followed by, "How old are you . . . ?" As they set the car down in the center of the field, Jeffery shouted, "Forty-four years and damn proud of it." The others cheered. "And now, for the rest of your surprise," Jeffery announced.

Excited, he ran back to the shed and rolled out of it something the size of a console television, covered with a tarp. "Drum roll, please!" he commanded.

Harold slapped his thighs in compliance.

"Ta-*da!*" Jeffery snapped off the tarp with a flourish.

The party let go a collective gasp.

It was a gleaming black cannon, on a carriage of varnished oak, with brass fittings, masterfully crafted.

Where the thirty-inch barrel pivoted on the carriage (the "trunnian" Jeffery called it) were two birds, one on each side, doves, actually, similar in design to the familiar peace button, but with the talons and fierce beady eyes of birds of prey.

"I finished it yesterday," Jeffery said. "It's a virgin, never been fired. You are witnessing history." In hushed silence, the party watched Jeffery jam the black powder down the cannon's muzzle, stuff in a paper wad, and load the projectile, a concrete-filled coffee can. He set the fuse in the breech and angled the barrel carefully toward "Modern Civilization."

"Barney," Jeffery declared, ceremoniously bowing and flourishing to him a yellow Bic lighter. "The honor is yours. Fire!"

"You do it, Jeffery. I'm not into this."

"I'm afraid I'll have to insist, Barney," Jeffery said.

"Oh, all right." His heart racing, Barney flicked the lighter under the wick. His hand shook. Finally, the wick sputtered. "Back, everyone!" Jeffery ordered.

Ker-bloom!

The projectile arched through the air and slammed onto the ground several yards shy of the Volkswagen. The sound filled Barney's mind, crowding out his other thoughts. Jeffery readjusted the angle the cannon loaded it again, and Barney nervously fired it off.

Ker-bloom!

This time the can landed way beyond the target.

"This is it," Jeffery said confidently as he sighted and loaded the cannon once more. "Barney?"

The awful noise had now obliterated all of Barney's will. With some eagerness this time, he lit the wick.

Ker-bloom!

The projectile arced perfectly through the air and crashed through the roof of the Bug with a resounding *thunk.*

Barney smiled as if he had just fallen in love.

The crowd cheered.

"And now, ladies and gentlemen," Jeffery pontificated. "Let the destruction of Modern Civilization commence."

He loaded the cannon again. The others in the party scattered and returned with all manner of weaponry. There was an odd .22 Gatling gun with six rotating barrels. A couple of M-16s. An Uzi. A mortar the size of a bowling ball that Jeffery had also forged. A .44 magnum revolver. A Colt .45 classic six-shooter. A double-barreled 12-gauge shotgun with buckshot loads that obliterated the side window of the VW in one shot. Barney shot everything at least once. The countryside echoed with the sounds of a Civil War battlefield.

By the time the dusk settled softly onto the field, all that remained of "Modern Civilization" were a few hunks of twisted metal, and Barney's ears rang with a strange exaltation, as though there were nothing left to worry about.

FIFTEEN

TURTLE BAY

— 1 —

*T*he collapse of your second marriage has left you feeling numb, wandering around in a fog, unable to think, or feel, or do much of anything. You left her, so you don't really have a place to stay. You impose upon your friend Matt for a while, but it's clear you're in the way of *his* complicated marriage. You decide to leave the Bay Area and head back east.

You collect some supplies and hole up inside your Toyota camper, hauling your camper shell on your back, complete with bed, refrigerator, stove, stereo, library. You wear nothing but turtleneck sweaters, even though it's summer. You drive, slowly—very slowly—out of California, across the country, stopping only every other day or so when the white line begins to blur, camping by the side of the road, all the way to Pike Lake, your ancestral home in rural Wisconsin.

You allow yourself two months to recuperate before

you will have to return to your job as a writer for an environmental magazine. After a brief tour of the place to find your old haunts—the boathouse, your shack of a hideout, your dank mad-scientist laboratory in the basement—you hibernate in your childhood room, with the walls and ceiling of manly knotty pine.

You expect your father to be mad like he was the first time, when you left your first wife, the mother of your children, ten years ago. He said to you over the phone: "Divorce, revolution, suicide, it's all the same thing." This time he says, "Your generation is more honest than ours was. I don't know of too many of us who were completely monogamous."

You don't want to know more. You clam up. You do feel like a clam, a shell-shocked shell of a man, a clam whose body has been sucked up clean out of its shell by carnivorous parasites. There are traces of your ex everywhere in your old room, left from your visits here as a couple: ceramic elephants on the windowsill, Victoria Holt novels on the bookshelves.

You expect to crash, to freefall into the abyss of despair, and you are prepared for this, you look forward to crying it all out, but the tears don't come. Instead, there is just a sublime peace, an exhilarating sense of freedom, and a clammy emptiness.

— 2 —

Y ou sleep for days. No one bothers you. When you finally do emerge from hibernation, you resemble a zombie from one of those "living dead" movies. You can't feel a thing. It frightens you. To get out of the house one calm evening when the forests surrounding the lake glow yellow in the sunset, you take your father's old handmade lapstrake rowboat (he once gave it to you, but you still think of it as his). You row all the way to the north end of the lake, Turtle Bay. The boat fills with water up to your lower calves. You see that the bay looks different. The oak forests between the lake and the newish superhighway have been cut down. There is a monstrous barge anchored in the center of the bay, piled high with weeds and mud.

When you get back to the house, you ask your father what is going on.

"Oh, you're talking about a big brouhaha there," he says. "Old man Melieren thinks he's developing a fancy sport-fishing resort on his property. The village fathers, you know they've spent their lives insuring the exclusivity of their domain on this lake, are not pleased. He challenged their ordinance against commercial development on the lake in court. He won."

"That's it? Isn't anyone doing anything?"

"There've been appeals, but he's got a lot of money and some powerful allies."

You remember the rumors. Your friend Carl used to help spread them. Melieren was a reclusive old German who owned a blender manufacturing company in Milwaukee that was reputed to have built some of Hitler's gas ovens during the war. There was also talk of Chicago gangland connections, and you remember as a child seeing bullet holes after a shooting in one of the houses on his vast estate.

You learn that the alignment of forces in this present battle is far from simple. The working-class fishing interests who want more public access to the lake and the unions who want the jobs and hate all Pike Lakers—Milwaukee's power elite—equally, are pushing for the resort. The powerful state Department of Natural Resources (DNR) at first went to bat for the resort advocates, until an enterprising naturalist discovered a rare spotted turtle (*clemmys guttata*), an endangered species, in the marshes around the edge of the bay.

Your father tells you that the DNR has called a hearing on the issue that will take place the first week you are here, but Melieren has already started dredging the bay, apparently so he can have a *fait accompli* before the hearing has a chance to rule. This is the barge you saw, a dredge.

With nothing better to do, you go with your father to the hearing. Personally, you are torn. You certainly sympathize with the turtles, but the exclusivity of the Pike Lake snobs turns your stomach. This latter group uses the turtle issue, but they kill these same turtles elsewhere in the lake when they spray the weeds with defoliants to improve the swimming near their own lake frontages.

At the meeting, you see childhood acquaintances

now grown, playing out their roles. You've seen none of these people for years. Ted is here, balding, a high-powered lawyer, representing the village. Your old heart-throb Maggie—Ted's sister—now fat and domestic, has organized a contingent of residents.

"Well, hello, Barney," she says.

Her voice is chilly, as is that of the others. You have learned to recognize the tone, something like: "How could you marry a black woman and embarrass your family so."

You don't go out of your way to tell any of them you've separated. They'd be too obviously pleased.

Your father surprises you by speaking at the meeting. He actually gives voice to reason.

"As an old fisherman myself, I can understand the need for lake access. But a resort is likely to bring the powerboats and the jet skis, which won't help the fishing at all. May I suggest a compromise, a smaller scale public access, without the controversial resort?"

From the silence of the crowd, it is clear that this viewpoint has pleased no one.

The hearing issues a weak decision, which gives Melieren ten days to cease and desist his dredging operation, plenty of time to complete the job.

On the way home that night, silence once more prevails between your father and you. On the superhighway, right where you can see Turtle Bay through the newly thinned trees, you spot a small animal in your headlights, a turtle, laboriously crossing the road. You brake and swerve to miss it, but you fail, and it squishes against the tire of your camper truck. You feel something jump into your ear.

— 3 —

*A*ll night long, your ear itches.

In the morning, you hear the voice for the first time.

"Hello, Barney."

You twist around in your bed looking for the source of the voice.

"My name is Slrp. I will be your teacher."

Oh-oh, you think. You stay in bed that day, knowing that you are losing your grip, and that there's nothing you can do about it.

"I am a turtle who has left my body, the very body that you yourself smeared all over the road with your truck. To be fair, we planned this assault on your kind. Our situation is exceedingly desperate, and we need your help. I'm afraid you will have to help us whether you want to or not. No more passivity for the likes of you."

You see that your family is concerned. When they come to check on you, you can show them only your empty shell. In order not to reveal you have been possessed by something you don't think they'll understand, you show only your emptiness. You don't speak in their presence. You see them hover over you, and you clam up some more. A plexiglass wall of estrangement has come between you and all other humans.

They bring doctors. You speak to them only enough to confuse them, to protect yourself from them carting you off some place. When they ask how you are, you say, "Fine, thank you," and smile wanly. "Just a little under the weather." They check you for mononucleosis and Epstein-Barr. They give you Rorschach tests, but you know the right answers. You see in the inkblots flowers, futuristic automobiles, genitalia, normal stuff like that, and you don't tell them about the raging flames or the delicious-looking planaria. The collective decision from the assembled experts and family members is to leave you alone and see what happens.

The voice of Slrp tells you to go for a morning row in your father's rowboat. He tells you to take off your clothes, jump in the lake, and swim naked in the reedy waters of Turtle Bay. The water is icy cold, but your body seems to be just as cold itself, so you don't feel it. You don't seem to mind the mucky bottom, the slithery clumps of algae, or the lily pads scratching your underside.

Even though you grew up on this lake and in the summer went swimming every day, you were a lousy swimmer. You were afraid of drowning. When you were five, the neighbor's maid's toddler stepped off the pier and into the drink. He drowned. You remember watching with a gathering of neighbors as the mother bawled her heart out.

But now swimming comes as second nature to you.

Slrp introduces you to the others. "This is Barney," he tells them from his perch inside your skull in some kind of silent language that you seem to understand. You notice that Slrp has penetrated deeper into your mind. "He will be saving us," Slrp tells the others. "We haven't much time."

You meet the oldest turtles first. Sis, the matriarch, gazes at you with the wisdom of her hundred winters, or "sleeps," as they're called. She sits on a rock and cocks her head from side to side as she checks you out. She has a leathery face with yellow speckles on it, a perpetual frown, just like your father, and yellow spots all over her carapace, quite a few more than her male counterparts. You are stretched out in the shallow water next to her, with just your head sticking up. The sadness she expresses to you weighs you down like the shell on your back. She communicates not in words, but in something your mind calls "quanta of feeling states," without thinking about it, little units of odd feeling that enter your ear and fill up the cavity Slrp seems to be digging in your mind, as if looking for a place to bury his eggs.

Slrp tells you a long-winded story that explains how what is happening to you is, in fact, happening to you, even though it is, of course, impossible.

"Once upon a time, this lake was named Turtle Lake, and turtles reigned supreme. We thought we had invented a perfect world. Our ancestors, who looked like flat, rounded lizards, decided to grow these shells on our backs so that we would always be safe. We became one of the most invulnerable people on earth, by using our brains to alter our own biochemical evolution. Our

ancestors got together and imagined these shells we
wear. We learned to live a long time. But we hadn't figured on humans coming along and mucking up the
works. We know as well as you do that, unless we take
drastic action, our days as a people are numbered.

"You are a part of our desperate effort to save ourselves," he says.

You meet the others of the turtle clan who swim
around you in curiosity. There's Sri, a young renegade,
perhaps your own age of forty-two (you can tell their
age by counting the rims around the scales that make up
their shells), who glares at you and regards this whole
scheme of his elders to be harebrained. "Not all of us
want you here," he images to you. He has a frightening
yellow streak across his beak. "Some of us want to mi-
grate to calmer waters, to another lake that legend tells
us is not far away."

"It's called Mud Lake," you tell him, and then you
realize your mistake. "That is, humans call it Mud Lake.
It's small. There are a lot of turtles there."

"Not a lot. We know better. There are not a lot of
turtles anywhere anymore," Sri groans.

You see that there are many depressed spirits among
the turtle-people, as you are coming to think of them.
But even so, you find yourself arguing, "Sooner or later
the humans will unleash their poisons on Mud Lake, too.
You can't keep moving forever. Sometimes you have to
take a stand."

"That's easy for you to say," Sri hisses.

You haven't convinced him, but you think you have

impressed him enough to gain his grudging tolerance, if not acceptance.

And then you wonder what you are arguing for, and you realize that Slrp is taking over more and more of your synapses. More and more, you are seeing things from his point of view. That night in your bed, you fight him.

"What right do you have to come in here and invade my mind?" you demand of him.

"You weren't using it," Slrp answers wryly.

"Anyway, I know this isn't really happening. It's just a rather vivid dream. I've lost my way, that's all."

"Who's to say, Barney?" he answers you. "You think of humans as an anomalous species, accomplishing wondrous things that no other species in the known universe has even imagined itself capable of doing. Walking erect, making tools, harnessing fire, developing a symbolic system of language, both spoken and written. Music. Art. Self-awareness. To say nothing of cars, submarines, television, atomic bombs, and tortoiseshell spectacles. Doesn't it strike your limited imagination that other species might all this time be achieving things equally anomalous, but in an entirely different direction, a spiritual direction, for which there just wouldn't be all that material flotsam to give us away?"

"Wait a minute, lizard-brain," you argue. Desperation creeps into your voice as you feel your resources gradually diminishing. Slrp expands his territory with something less than the speed of a rabbit, but with all the determination of that proverbial testudinate. "How can you possibly know all this stuff about atom bombs and shit, huh? You're going to tell me you read *The New York Times*?"

"No, but I can read it all in your mind right now. You underestimate us. You must understand that our consciousness has been evolving in a continuous fashion since the time of the dinosaurs. Inside our shells, over the millennia, we have learned techniques of meditation that have connected us to the primary forces of nature. It's a—how would you say? —'fringe benefit' of courting extinction. We watched what happened to our dinosaur cousins. We developed a life for ourselves of uncommon safety, from which it has been possible to imagine almost anything, as you can see."

You go to sleep with his voice, his cinematic clip of images, a Mobius strip of thought, cycling through your brain.

— **4** —

The next morning, you pull the covers all the way over your carapace so no one can see what has become of you. You peek your head out and stare at the knots on the ceiling. They look like delicious insects. You see a real fly in the air and follow it with your eyes. You feel sluggish but at the same time restless from the heat. You're incredibly thirsty. By the whisper of light creeping in the big picture window, you judge it is still early enough, the humans will still be sleeping.

You lumber to the edge of the bed. You dart your head out quickly and judge the distance to the floor. It's about half the length of your shell. *Oh-oh,* you think. It's too far, but your craving for water overrules your inveterate caution. You close your eyes and crawl all the way over the edge of the bed until your center of gravity sends you crashing to the floor—very unfortunately, on your back. By stretching your long, greenish brown neck out as far as it can go, and pushing with all your might against the floor with your webbed feet, you're are able to turn yourself onto your orangeish hypoplastron with another resounding crash, except this time you hardly hear a thing, deaf as a turtle.

You retract everything deep inside your shell and wait. When you detect no vibrations or, for that matter, psychic impulses, you begin to gradually crawl down the stairs and out of this unnatural outer shell of a house you find yourself in and amble laboriously—though it actually feels quick to you—down the hill to the lake.

At the water's edge, you balk at the notion of slipping in and swimming all the way to Turtle Bay and instead decide, despite the awkwardness, to row most of the way over there. After a quick dip off the rocks at the shore to quench the dehydration, you crawl into the rowboat and sit upright on the center seat, with your large shell hanging over the edge of the plank. Once you reach the bay, you beach the boat in the cattails and slip back into the water, feeling yourself again.

The water strokes you delectably. You flip and flop

and frolic beneath the surface for what seems like hours at a time. The other turtles greet you, swimming around you in an erotic dance.

There's one called Drusilla who swims around your tail and wags her head at you from below. *Drusilla? Come on. A human name?*

"I took it for you, Barney," she tells you. "Don't you have a human name?"

"Yes, but . . ."

"You forget. We know everything you know."

"And I know everything you know?"

"Of course."

Your carapace is beginning to ache. This is truly confusing.

"Will you stay with us now?" Drusilla asks.

Now you notice the dazzling galaxies of yellow light from the spots on her shell, a mirror to the night sky. "Of course," you say with assurance. You can't imagine ever leaving the water again. Or her for that matter. You've found your home.

She brings you a juicy dragonfly in her beak. You snap into its abdomen with your powerful jaws. Your mouth fills with the sweetness a bee must feel eating its own honey. She chomps on the dragonfly's head, and your jaws meet in the center of its thorax. You bump olfactory orifices.

Suddenly, the water vibrates and splashes you in the face. Drusilla and you both retract into your shells and then dive. Underwater, you can hear a faint groan that seems to be gradually growing louder. You look at

Drusilla questioningly. "It's the voice of doom," she says sadly. "The end of the world."

"I want to see it. Can you take me there?"

She beckons you to follow her by cocking her head. You swim after her, easily keeping up with her plodding stroke. When you come to the edge of the reeds, you poke your head out of the water. A giant, brown, rectangular monster with humans riding on its back is gobbling up the bottom of the marsh with its rolling, endless tongue.

You spend the afternoon gamboling in the muck with Drusilla. You watch the other turtles fucking. She shows you where she's hidden her eggs, and you stroke her neck consolingly when she breaks down at the thought of their future. You glimpse the beauty of this bay with a manic intensity that comes from the imminence of doom. You feel you can stay here forever, and that that's not a very long time at all.

But Slrp has other plans for you. As the light fades toward evening, you find yourself feeling a chill. "Whoa, Turtleman," Slrp images. "Let's not get carried away. You are useful to us as a human, less so as a turtle. The others don't understand this. They want you to be one of them, and they have their mental prowess, as you have seen. But I'm going to reconnect some of your synapses here, so at least you don't die of exposure."

Drained to your emptiest shell, you slither back into the rowboat. You see the silhouette of the dredge against the fading light of day. You row toward it, now abandoned at anchor. You see that it has a long conveyer belt with scoops fastened onto it so that it spoons the muck from the lake bottom and dumps it in a pile in the center of the barge. It occurs to you that they probably dump this muck in the deep parts of the lake. A big engine with a large external gas tank drives the mechanism.

With your stubby limbs, you awkwardly row back to the nest of humans. They greet you with alarm, but you are relieved that they can't seem to see the great carapace covering your body or the yellow tear drops spotting your face. "Where have you been?" the female human says. You forgot to wash the muck out of your hair.

"Fishing. Swimming," you answer. Suddenly embarrassed by your nakedness, you discover that you have absently picked up a towel at the boathouse and covered yourself in the frontal abdominal region, your most vulnerable spot.

You manage to dress yourself and pretend to be human for an hour or so. You sit with them at dinner, though you are full from eating earlier and you find their cow meat unappetizing. You carry on a conversation of sorts.

"It's taking me awhile to get over my breakup," you manage to mumble in human language. "It feels like an explosion!" You say this last word too loud and spit when you say it. But it gives you an idea. You clam up. They ignore you, just as they always have. You are uncommonly grateful.

After dinner, while the others watch Jacques Cousteau on television, you slither down into your old laboratory to see what you can scavenge. You find practically full pound bottles of sodium nitrate and sulfur, covered with spider webs. You remember what to do. Laboriously, awkwardly with your stubby webbed limbs, you burn up a full box of wooden matches, ten at a time, and then you grind the resulting charcoal in the spider-webbed mortar and pestle.

You keep forgetting what you are doing. You keep wanting to just crawl into your shell, but Slrp encourages you. "You know what you have to do, Son," he says, as if he were your real father. You find a loose piece of PVC drain pipe, three inches long, two inches in diameter, next to the water pump in the basement. You mix your gunpowder.

In the kitchen, you cook with an obsessive frenzy that you know must be frightening your parents, but you can't help it. Someone asks what you are doing. "Baking cookies," you snap.

"Isn't that a lot of salt?"

"I know what I'm doing," you shrill.

What you are really doing is making baker's dough, half flour, half salt, to plug the ends of the pipe. When you are finished with the dough, you take it into the dank basement again and pack the gunpowder into the pipe, sealing the ends with the baker's dough. You leave a small hole in one end. You realize that the baker's dough won't have a chance to dry, so you top it off with some quick-drying silicone sealant that you find in a caulking gun in the playroom. You have no fuse, but you do have a can of sodium peroxide. You remember how this stuff flares into yellow flame when it comes in contact with water.

You pack your stuff in a paper bag and leave the house by the tunnel that leads out of your laboratory to the middle of the woods by the shore of the lake. At the end of the tunnel is a door hinged at the top like the storm cellar door on Dorothy's house in *The Wizard of Oz*. It's a quiet night. The water is calm and reflects the three-quarter moon, as well as the mansion lights from the shore. You row quietly and determinedly to Turtle Bay.

"Don't be afraid, Turtleman," Slrp comforts you. "We will protect you. You are our friend."

Turtleman. That's you all right.

When you come up alongside the dredge, you see three dark heads poking out of the water. You recognize Sis, the matriarch.

"We have come to give you moral support," she images to you.

You see Sri. "I'm surprised to see you," you tell him.

"I admire your courage," he says. "Your plan might work."

"How do you know what I'm up to," you whine, somewhat peevishly, as if your privacy has been invaded again.

"We know what you know," the soft musical image of Drusilla intones.

"Hello, Drusilla," you say. Your chest constricts inside your shell. "You guys watch out now. This could make a big mess."

You slip the rowboat around to the gas tank of the dredge. You open the cap on the tank. You shake a line of gunpowder out of your pipe like salt from a saltshaker along the edge of the barge. You put the pipe filled with gunpowder next to the spout of the gas tank, with the gunpowder trail leading into the hole in the baker's dough seal. At the other end of this trail, you make a mountain of sodium peroxide.

Suddenly a wave from a passing motorboat rocks the barge and splashes water on the sodium peroxide, which ignites with a brilliant yellow glow. The barge pitches enough to spill some of the gas from the full tank. Oh-oh, you think. The gas catches fire and lights the pipe bomb prematurely which explodes with a blinding flash in your face. It ignites your beard and hair and knocks you out of the boat and into the water. You hit your head on a cattail root.

Stunned, you dog-paddle to the shore. You see your friends Sis, Sri, and Drusilla, all belly up dead in the muck. Your chest constricts again. The whole lake is on fire. You are dead too.

— 5 —

You find yourself wandering along the edge of the su-perhighway, an empty shell of a man. You see that a crowd has gathered to watch the fire and the efforts of the firefighters to put it out with long hoses from a truck on the shore. You immediately cause some stir in the crowd, perhaps because you are naked, perhaps because your hair and beard have burnt to a ghostly ash and your eyes are alight with mischief. The crowd opens a swath for you, which leads you directly into the hands of the village police, Captain Lutz, now old as Methuselah.

"Well, Barney Blatz. Fancy meeting you here. Did you have anything to do with this?"

You shout in a very loud voice, "I was trying to save the turtles."

He looks at you with a mixture of pity and scorn. "We'll try to get you some help," he says as he snaps the handcuffs roughly on your wrists behind your back.

He throws a blanket on you and takes you to the basement of a red brick Victorian hospital in Waukesha. They put you in two-point restraints, a bench with leather straps buckled on one arm and one ankle. You sleep for a long time.

When you wake up, you feel your flesh tingle. You smile to welcome your body back. You haven't felt this warm in years. You check your back: no shell. You check the mirror when they finally let you use the bathroom. No yellow blotches on your skin, which is now pinko-gray, not green.

You know how to handle the doctors. But you are in no hurry. You tell no one anything. You clam up. You sleep. You enjoy the emptiness. You wallow in it like the muck. You are grateful for the rest. You also figure things will die down in time. There's no point in tempting the legal establishment by showing anything remotely re-sembling presence of mind.

They move you to a place you're familiar with from other friends who have lost their marbles at times, Oconomowoc Memorial, a rich people's nut house, not a lobotomy factory. You make friends with a young girl who carries an old Bible around wrapped in a towel and a guy who stabbed his brother with a barbecue fork in a fit of rage.

At group one day, you start to say, "A few weeks ago, I was a turtle . . ." but the doctor sighs with a look of exasperation on her face, so you figure this is not the way to get released.

The next day, you try, "I've been having trouble with my feelings lately, after breaking up with my wife. For a while, I was suffering delusions, but I think I was running away from the reality of the pain caused by the breakup. I can feel the pain now. It's hard, but I'm doing it, and I'm doing much better."

Was that true? Not really. You didn't feel the pain until about a week later. On your first afternoon back in that house on the hill overlooking the lake, you retreat to your room. No one bothers you. You know they're afraid of you, but that's OK.

You lie on your human belly on the bed and sob your guts out: for the turtles, for the planet, for yourself, for your ex, for your children, for your bizarre family, for the fucking tragedy of the human/animal condition.

You bawl your ass off for at least three days, with breaks for sustenance, quick sandwiches.

They treat you just as though nothing has happened, as though you have just arrived from California, and you decide to act the same. They don't mention it, but you learn through the papers the explosion caused a big oil slick that almost wiped out the turtle population of Turtle Bay, but that all dredging has stopped, and Melieren has agreed to provide a sanctuary for the turtles in his greatly scaled-down plans for a public access with a small campground on his land.

In another week, you leave your camper shell behind and board a plane to California, only a month behind schedule, to resume your life, such as it is.

SIXTEEN

DRESS REHEARSAL

— 1 —

O n my first night home, my father says, "I've decided I'm going to commit suicide next spring. On April twenty-sixth." It is a warm night in July. We are eating dinner on the porch. The crickets chirp in the muggy dusk.

I laugh. "Why April twenty-sixth?" I ask.

He scratches at the eczema on his scalp. "That's the first real day of spring around here, when all the ice on the lake is melted, when the scilla and the hepatica start to bloom. I've stockpiled the Seconal. Seconal and bourbon, that's what I'll use." He toasts the idea with the bourbon he is drinking.

I laugh again. I don't believe he is serious, but then he is eighty-four years old. He has long enjoyed shocking people, especially his children. I sympathize with him for not wanting to lose control of his mind, his life, his bowels—as he's watched so many of his friends do. I also know enough about psychology to take any suicide threat seriously.

My mother, who has just turned eighty herself, says, "When you get as old as we are, you have to wonder if you haven't lived too long. It's awful to be a burden on people. I think it's worth considering."

I look at her. She's encouraging this fantasy? I wonder at her motives, but then she never was one to stand up to him.

I say to my father cautiously, "I can understand how you feel, but don't you think the message your suicide would send your grandchildren would be a little pessimistic?"

I'm not cautious enough. "Pessimistic?" he bristles. "I don't see how you can call someone who founded the first Society for the Prevention of Blindness in the state of Wisconsin pessimistic."

That's a non sequitur, Pops, I want to say. That was thirty years ago. We know you were tops in your field. We also know that you hated it, that you don't like people much, that you would have been an engineer if you hadn't flunked calculus. You are also known, by your children, if no one else, for having the gloomiest disposition in the state of Wisconsin, one of the reasons your oldest son and daughter live in New York and I live in San Francisco.

But I have learned not to argue, especially when he's been drinking, which is every night about this time. To be able to claim that he isn't an alcoholic, my father broods through the day without touching a drop until the sun crosses the yardarm. Then, at five o'clock sharp he starts to slug away about six bourbons an hour. By seven, he is ready for bed or an ugly scene, whichever comes first. We have learned to let him go to bed.

In my old bed that night, my annual pilgrimage home which isn't home, half my father's age now, I stare at the knots in the ceiling, oozing and leering at me as always, the eyes of hideous snakes, monstrous blobs of breathing protoplasm, snorting at me with the faint spurts of my father's snores from across the distance, miles and centuries away at the other end of the house. The knots remind me of the most fearful thing I can imagine, but I can't remember what it is. Out of the picture windows, it's country quiet and country dark, and I yearn for the street lamps and the noise of traffic—anything other than the fearful snores to remind me that I am not utterly alone.

Sweat pours out of me and drenches the sheet. I want the security of a blanket over me, but it's too hot. This is the second time I've been alone in this bed since my second marriage ended two years ago. Exploded is more like it. I got in big trouble for blowing up that barge on the lake. I went crazy, spent some time in the loony bin.

— 2 —

The next night the three of us are sipping our first drinks in front of the evening news. South Africa is exploding all over the screen. At the furniture warehouse commercial, my father clicks the mute button on the remote and asks, "Is this a homosexual relationship?"

I sink in my chair, wishing for invisibility. I hesitate too long. "I don't know," I say, giving it away.

Our parents don't know?

He hasn't told them?

He's talking about my brother Charlie, who will arrive the next morning with Mike, his live-in lover of several years. They spent a month here in the cottage last summer.

That night, the fear oozes out of me like toxic fumes from my decaying body, and paints my ceiling with dancing demons. I figure I'm losing it again, that it's me who is dying, not him, that I'm choking on him, that he's dumped his dying on me.

— 3 —

On the third day of my summer vacation, my brother Charlie arrives from New York. Charlie is thinking about taking early retirement from his job as a computer systems analyst—he is just fifty-five—and moving back to Wisconsin with his "friend" Mike to set up a consulting business and see after the aging folks' affairs.

Mike is coming the next day, Charlie says. He has stayed behind for some tests. I assume he means at the college where Mike teaches English to subsidize his poetry.

My brother has been more of a father to me than my father, and yet better, because he used to sign me out of boarding school and let me adventure out by myself in the nether worlds of Boston. I bask in his intellect. He knows just about everything about computers—and most everything else, too. He wears round, real tortoiseshell glasses and usually has the sprightliest smile of anyone in our family—a family, with the exception of Charlie and Pookie, not noted for its facial versatility.

When we have a private moment after the initial greetings, I tell him about our father's suicide plans, as Charlie puts his stuff away in his room.

"He loves to be dramatic, doesn't he?" Charlie says. "I don't think it's a real threat." He tells me all about Eliza as he pulls out his laptop computer. "Eliza is an artificial intelligence programmed to act like a Rogerian nondirective psychotherapist. It's sort of a party game, but it sometimes produces some insights." He loads the program.

"How do you do? Please tell me your problem," the prompt reads faintly on the screen.

My brother continues. "Last year, I showed this thing to Father. I left him alone with it. Five minutes later, he called me back, asking how to turn the thing off. 'You can read it if you want,' he told me. After the prompt, he'd written, 'I fear death.' Eliza returned with one of her stock responses, 'Why do you need to tell me you fear death?'

"Father had typed, 'I fear death because I don't believe in an afterworld.' So he's too scared to actually follow through with his threat," my brother says.

"I hope you're right, Charlie." I'm not so sure.

BOTH MY BROTHER and my father seem more anxious than usual that night as we swill our bourbons in front of the Evening News. Rock Hudson's cadaverous face flickers on the screen to tell the world that he has AIDS.

Absently my father pushes the mute button, though we all want to hear. Lapsing into his pontifical voice, he says, "This AIDS is just one more of nature's ways of controlling the population."

I know he's baiting Charlie.

Don't bite, Charlie, I silently urge.

He bites.

"How can you say that? Jesus, Father, how can you be that callous? These are real people. Maybe you never see any real people any more. You sound like Jerry Falwell. AIDS as punishment for sin? Maybe you always hated people, but Christ, that's your problem."

"Hate people? Me? You forget who struggled to treat their blindness for forty years, young man, while you diddled around with your machines and who knows what else."

"You're the one who's blind," my brother shoots back. He is shaking.

My mother and I look helplessly at each other. She escapes to the kitchen. This is not a new scene. Such family storms are periodic if not common.

"Someone has to worry about the goddamn population," Father yells.

"It's a problem of unequal distribution," I foolishly

reason. "If the wealth were evenly distributed in the world, there'd be plenty for everybody."

"Sure, and all you need to do that is one of your world totalitarian communistic governments," Father retorted. "I hope I don't live to see how *they* divide it up."

My mother, no doubt hopeful to derail the discussion, calls from the kitchen, "Dinner!"

Charlie, my mother, and I go to the porch and pick at our food while Father grouses about the house, stripped down to his boxer shorts in the summer heat, pouring himself one drink after another. Outside the air is sultry, full of the electric smell of ozone, ready to storm.

Father sticks his head in the doorway. "Goodnight, and goodbye, all. I'm moving the date up to tonight."

It takes a moment for the words to sink in. No one else seems to grasp the import of what he's saying.

"Hey," I say. "Did you hear him? He said he's killing himself tonight."

"No," my mother says, with more incredulity than denial. "Are you sure?"

"That's sure what it sounded like."

We all look at each other. "I guess I better go check," my mother says.

My brother and I follow her up the stairs. My father stands before his bureau, struggling to get the childproof cap off the Seconal bottle, his eyes lit with childlike glee.

"Robert!" Mother calls to him in her severest voice, as if he were a toddler about to break a favorite vase.

"Let me have it." She grabs the bottle out of his hand. He swings his arm at her, but he is too drunk to fight, and he careens to the floor. "Get to bed, Robert," she says, the firmness battling with the quaver in her voice. He doesn't move. He lies still on the floor, hopefully passed out.

The three of us go back downstairs again. "He's such a baby sometimes," my mother says, her eyes filling with tears.

I hunch around the hollow in my own chest, less from the drunken father spectacle than from seeing my mother cry. I have never seen her cry before. Ours is not an emotionally expressive family as a rule, Father's outbursts of anger being the exception that proves it.

There are crashing sounds in the upper regions. Thunder cracks in the sky, and my father is flopping about. He drags himself down the stairs again. We suck in our breath between our teeth. He slumps into a wicker porch chair. "I don't understand," he slurs. "Why are my children so fucking antagonistic?" He starts to blubber. I've seen him cry once or twice before.

I look at my brother, and his eyes too are wet. I envy them. My eyes are as dry as dust. Thunder shakes the house. Rain pours from the sky and all the eyes of my family but mine. My feelings sit like a rock in the pit of my stomach.

My father goes for another drink. I catch him on the way. "C'mon, Pops, you've had enough. Bedtime."

"Don't call me that!" he seethes at me.

I steer him to the top of the stairs. Just inside his

room, he slips from my grasp and crashes on top of my mother's antique sewing table, splintering table legs and splattering buttons, thimbles, spools of thread all over the floor.

"You!" he spits at me as if I'm the one who broke the table. "Which one are you? Oh, Barney, my youngest son."

Then he says, "I guess we never did like each other very much, did we?"

I reel back at his words. I'm unprepared for this indictment. "Speak for yourself," I spit back at him, but my voice cracks. The rock in my stomach jumps to my throat. The last holdout, I almost join the torrent of tears. Not quite, though. What hurts most of all is that he has spoken the truth.

— 4 —

The following day, for the first time in the known history of this household, no one arises. It is as if an entire day has been surgically excised from the tissue of time.

— 5 —

Early the next morning, I wake up so full of rage I fear I'm going to lose it again. I pound my mattress and roar into my pillow to ease the tension. I sneak out of the house without anyone seeing me and steal one of the cars like I used to. The sun is bright, and the air is clean from the storm. I drive some two miles away to another little lake and find a place in the bushes on the shore where there is no evidence of humans. I stare into the mirror surface of the water right at the spot where my father and I had lugged a green rowboat at five in the morning to fish, even though we had a perfectly good lake right outside our front door. The sun had risen, and the mosquitoes were biting but not the fish. My father had been trying to be a good daddy hanging out with his son, and as I looked at him, I just hated him, utterly, without reservation.

A fat toad galumphs out of the woods and puzzles at me lying in his path. It was strange to see a nocturnal toad in the daytime. I pick him up and look at him straight in the eye. His slimy fear oozes from his skin. I consider taking him back to my son in California, but then think he was meant to live free and let him go.

I return to the house calmer. I march to where I know Father is, in his office, listening to his ham radio. He can't communicate with those closest to him, so he covers his ears with headphones and communicates with people at the farthest reaches of the planet. I walk right up to where he's sitting at the desk, my jaw clenched in determination. He sheepishly looks up at me.

"Father," I say in a deep authoritative voice. He removes his headphones. "I just want to tell you." I pause for breath. "You can be awfully careless with other people's feelings." My eyes glare into his like one of his optical lasers.

He pouts his lips at me, blinks, and looks away. He doesn't say anything. He puts his headphones back on.

I turn sharply and leave the room, giddy. I had expected him to apologize or something. And yet, even though he hardly reacted at all, just by my standing up to him, something has changed between us. A deep serenity settles over me. For the first time in a very long time I think maybe I'm not going to lose it after all.

That afternoon, Charlie drives to the airport to pick up Mike, but returns to the house alone, pale, and tense.

"What happened?" I ask.

"I don't know. I called the apartment. No answer."

"Mike always was kind of irresponsible," I submit by way of encouragement.

Mike finally answers the phone at about five o'clock. When he hangs up, Charlie looks sick, and runs out of the house. He returns for dinner, but he doesn't look any better. He's obviously been crying.

"What's wrong, Charlie?" Mother asks when we are seated at the dinner table.

"My friend Mike is very sick. Lymphoma. It's a kind of cancer. He probably won't live very long."

AIDS, I think.

"AIDS," my father, the doctor, says.

"I'm going back to New York tomorrow," Charlie says.

No one says anything for the rest of that meal. Time usually passes slowly at the lake, but now it has slowed to an excruciating creep.

— 6 —

*T*he next day, my father has a stroke. He is stricken on the way to pick up the mail, a quarter mile down the road.

Mother finds him within an hour, unconscious in the road, on the way to her garden for fresh tomatoes. The tomatoes are especially ripe and succulent this year.

She runs to find Charlie and me, and we manage to wake him up and drag him back to the house. He can't move his left arm. We call the ambulance.

We follow the ambulance in the car to the local hospital about ten miles away.

They put him in intensive care, but the doctor says it's just a precaution. The stroke seems to be minor.

We hunch around the waiting room not saying much. Finally, my mother says to us in a cracking voice, "He's a good man, you know. He worked hard for you kids. I don't know why he won't reach out to you boys."

"He's scared, I guess," I say.

When the doctor confirms he's had a stroke, my first thought is, *I hope he doesn't become a vegetable.* My second thought is, *I hope it's not nursing home time, what an expense that would be.* Only then do I start to feel anything.

"Remember that camping trip we took in the marsh when everything went wrong?" Charlie says. "We had that green putt-putt, and it almost sank when we loaded all our stuff. Then after we'd gone about ten miles, they told us we couldn't have a boat there, and we had to unload the boat and find a local to haul us downriver in his truck. Then we spent the night on this farmer's field with the cows, and in the morning the farmer came and chased us off with a shotgun." He and Mother laugh.

I don't say anything. I'm thinking of a time he was nice to me, after I broke my leg.

— 7 —

I don't know what to say to Charlie. He's had to postpone his return to New York because of Father. The next morning, I finally get up the nerve to tell him that they know about him and Mike. I tell him that Father asked me point blank, and I hesitated too long.

"I'm sorry," I say.

"What could you say? It doesn't matter now anyway. I figured he knew when he diagnosed the AIDS."

"Does this mean you'll get it, too?"

"Probably. It might take a long time. No one seems to know."

"I guess this means you won't be moving here after all."

"Probably not."

I want to hug him and cry in his arms. But I'm afraid too of overreacting. All I can offer is, "It's all fucked up, isn't it, Charlie?"

"It's all fucked up, Barney."

Pookie in her new-wave haircut, short on top and long at the back, and mismatched earrings, dances in from New York that afternoon and spreads her good will like Tinker Bell. How she has managed to survive this family with such inveterate cheer is a mystery to me. She jokes with Mother.

"It's kind of nice not to have the old grouch around, isn't it?"

She tells Charlie, "I talked to Mike. He says for me to tell you it's not as bad as it sounds, there's worse ways to go, like what about being drawn-and-quartered?"

To me, she says, "Gee, Barney, that breakdown must have been good for you. You look better than ever."

I don't know whether it's her pixie dust or what, but Father is downright cheerful himself when we troop in to visit him, now in the general ward at the hospital, out of intensive care. "My brain seems to work OK," he says. "It's just my left arm and leg paralyzed. Too bad I'm left handed. Oh well, I kind of look forward to the challenge of walking again.

"And listen. Death isn't so bad, that's the real good news. I was right there. I could taste it. But here's what I learned. You don't really die. You just get closer and closer, fading more and more, but time slows down, too. So you keep your memories. Even the good ones. I'd forgotten how many good ones there are."

When it comes time to leave, Pookie sets the tone by embracing the old man long and hard and just letting her tears flow. He's crying again, too.

The others bawl up a storm, too. I wait to be last. There's stuff I want to tell him, stuff I got from him I want to thank him for, that in some ways I've lived my life in a philosophical dialectic with him, that I, too, yearn to resolve the contradictions between man and nature that caused him to live here in the first place, in the country, but I can't say these things now and maybe I never will. It is enough to have my feelings. I'm afraid my feelings will catch in my throat again, but they don't. Finally, my eyes mist up and drool all over the old bastard. I cry like a goddamn baby. I feel like I can breathe again.

SEVENTEEN

BLUE BABY

I WAS NEW TO CO-COUNSELING, A PROCESS WHERE two ordinary people take turns listening to each other for fifty minutes, like therapy, but not therapy because it's mutual. Also, there's nothing wrong with us. We were hurt, all of us. We all need to heal from the early hurts. Kate and I were in a class, learning techniques to draw each other out, to share early memories that might be at the root of our current emotional challenges. We were encouraged to cry, laugh, shake, and rage to release the tension that lingered from those early traumas.

I was working on the chronic voice in my head that said, "I wish I were dead." It was an odd voice that came up once or twice a day, without much emotion attached to it. I was reluctant to talk about it for fear of triggering the "take all suicide talk seriously" rule. It wasn't serious, my death wish, just annoying.

We sat on Kate's bed atop her Indian Madras bedspread, holding hands, a co-counseling ritual. She was a warm soul, with lively curls and an empathetic manner, early forties, like me. I was attracted to her, but, fortunately, co-counseling had rules against socializing with other co-counselors. Smiling, she said, "So you wish you were dead?" in a light-hearted tone.

That worked. I started to cry. But as often happened when the crying began, I began to choke, and the blood rushed out of my head the way it does when one stands up too fast. I went into a brief faint where everything went blank.

"Oh. I died there for a second. A little death," I told Kate.

"Glad it was just a second," Kate said, expertly draining the heaviness from the feelings, as we'd been taught to do. "What's your earliest memory of a little death?"

The memory flooded back to me. "I was about two. My sister Pookie and I were playing in the living room of our Grandma's house. Pookie would've been about five. She and Grandma had set up a card table and covered it with a blanket."

"Take your time, Barney. Stay with the feelings."

I breathed. "A hideyhole, Pookie called it. We were both inside while my grandma sat nearby in an armchair reading *Readers' Digest*. Pookie cuddled me, as she liked to do, treating me like one of her dolls."

"Stay there. What happened?" Kate asked.

I started shaking. Some tears oozed out. "I stopped breathing."

"You stopped breathing."

I stopped breathing again there too on Kate's bed. I

shook and heaved forth giant sobs. "It was *deliberate*," I said to Kate in a small voice.

"Deliberate?"

"Yeah. I don't know why, but at two years old, I'd had enough, I wanted to die, and somehow I understood I could make that happen if I stopped breathing."

"Stay there."

I cried for several minutes. "I guess what happened then is that Pookie called for Grandma, and Grandma picked me up and swatted me on the behind like a newborn to get me breathing again. It worked."

"Thank goodness."

"Thank goodness," I said. "This incident is historical in the sense that my sister has told me about it. I think she first told me years later when we were reading a story in a *Real Heroes* comic about a babysitter who saved a 'blue baby.' I remember the baby in the comic was a vivid blue."

"A vivid blue."

"But this—today—was the first time I had an inkling that my stopping breathing had been deliberate. What could have happened to me to make me want to check out at such a tender age?"

Soon the timer went off and Kate gave me an "attention-out" to bring me back to the present. "So, what three things wouldn't you like to have on a pizza?"

"Pineapple, coconut, motor oil."

THAT WOULD HAVE been in July. A month later, I was back at my parents' house on Pike Lake. It was a hot and muggy day, and the house wasn't air conditioned. It was so hot during the day that Pookie—who was also visiting—and I drove around through the nearby sylvan Kettle Moraine region in our father's air-conditioned Chevrolet just to stay cool.

We drove along two-lane roads winding between the rolling hills left by the glaciers some thousands of years ago. Pookie was a New York fabric artist now, knitting wearable art, coats with images of animals on them—tigers, lizards, turtles. She knitted a wall hanging of the view of Pike Lake from our lawn. Her short, blondish hair sported a fashionable razor cut.

"He seems mellower now, since the stroke," I said, referring to our father, always the number one topic of conversation when we were visiting home.

"Yeah, but it's so sad. I almost miss his crotcheti-ness."

"Not me," I said.

"You're still angry at him, after all this time?"

"Yeah. Not sure I even know why. It's not just poli-tics anymore, though he's still to the right of Reagan. I'm still scared of him. It goes back to that time in my hippier days when he said to Mother right in front of me, 'He's gone against everything I've ever stood for.'"

"That was what, twenty years ago, Barney? Can't you forgive him?"

"I can. I have, but the hostile feelings remain."

We drove past Holy Hill, an iconic Catholic basilica

and convent perched on the highest hill in the region, visible from miles away.

"If it weren't so hot, I'd suggest we climb the tower. Such an amazing view," Pookie said.

"If it weren't so hot."

A few hills farther was Heiliger Huegel, German for Holy Hill, the ski hill that our parents had been instrumental in developing, and where we'd spent many a winter weekend, riding its rope tows and shushing down its two runs, usually on insufficient snow.

"Now those were happy times, skiing with the family," I said, inspired by Pookie to dredge up happy family memories, seemingly few and far between in my memory banks.

We stopped for lunch a few miles to the east at my favorite restaurant, the Fox and Hounds, a sprawling, rustic, but gourmet eatery nestled deep in the woods in the middle of nowhere.

I ordered the mixed German sausages with sauerkraut and potatoes, with a Beck's beer. Pookie ordered the Caesar salad.

When we returned home, I found my father dictating his memoir in his study, a project he was just beginning. He complained of being stuck. Using my newly learned co-counseling, I sat with him and listened while he talked about the structure of his work—early years, medical stories, sailing stories, romantic stories, war stories. He said, "I'm not proud of everything I did."

I suggested, "You should tell the whole story and edit it later. I can get it transcribed for you, and you can read it yourself before you let anyone else read it."

"Thanks, Barney." He smiled and started up again speaking into the microphone in a voice made halting by his emphysema:

"Recollections of early childhood, particularly after the passage of many years, can be a real mixture of fact and fiction. One is inclined to tell stories about one's childhood to the point where the truth can easily be obscured by the imagination of the storyteller. My father frequently told the story that he could distinctly remember the house he was born in, even though he and his family had moved away from it permanently when he was nine months old . . ."

He paused and looked at me. "I'm OK now, Barney, thanks," he said as if he would be just as soon I left. So I left.

It had been a relatively drama-free visit so far, nothing like the previous year where Father made a drunken attempt at suicide. Working on his memoir seemed to be helping.

Father seemed to forgive my older brother Charlie for being gay, the revelation of which had inspired the prior year's drama. Charlie had retired from his high-tech job back east and was now teaching programming at the local junior college. He and his longtime companion, Mike, a poet, had moved into the old farmhouse up the hill. Father had bought the farm with his best friend

Otto many years ago, and then sold his share to Otto when Otto came into some money. He could be generous, our father. Charlie bought it from Otto's widow Bobbie, and now he and Mike had settled in to be the primary caretakers for the aging parents, thank God. Not something I wanted to do.

The whole family was there at the house on the lake, a rare occasion. Me. Charlie now in his fifties, curly hair graying. Pookie, forty-five. Mike had gotten past his HIV scare of the previous year. He was now asymptomatic and jocular as ever.

All the "kids" helped Mother, herself eighty-one, put dinner together: roast beef, fresh-picked checkerboard corn, and sliced tomato salad—there's nothing like fresh Wisconsin tomatoes in the late summer.

I called Father to come down from his study. He rode the newly installed stair lift down and walked precariously with his walker onto the porch where we had dinner as usual in the summer, muggy as it was, A soft breeze blew off the lake. Ominous clouds gathered. Father was dressed in his usual formal dinner attire of white boxer shorts, his fish-belly white stomach hanging over the elastic. He sipped his bourbon but would only have one.

Mother was starting to have short-term memory issues, but she was a trooper and still kept up with house and husband, assisted by various helpers during the day. She seemed happy to have her whole brood around for a change.

A flash of lightning lit up the sky, followed ten seconds later by a crash of thunder. We all jumped. "About two miles away," said the old man, an amateur meteorologist.

"How can you tell?" said Mike, a pudgy, befreckled boy—he seemed like a boy to me—about Pookie's age of forty-five.

Father smiled. "I'm guessing. The closer together the thunder and lighting are, the closer the storm is to us."

"Because sound and light travel at different speeds!" Mike enthused. He was baiting Father.

Charlie glared at him. "Be nice, Mike," he said quietly.

There was a moment of silence at the table, filled by the vigorous chirping of crickets. The quiet was a canvas for Mike. Ever the goad, as if our family needed one, he went on, like a seven-year-old sharing his excitement over Disneyland. "Did you know that you can tell the temperature by the frequency of cricket chirps?"

The polite family feigned interest. I jumped in. "Yeah. We learned that in Algebra I. A straight line graph. Count the number of chirps in fifteen seconds and add thirty-seven. You should get an approximate value of the Fahrenheit temperature."

"Such a brain, Barney," Mike said. "Just like your brother. All right, who's timing. Who can time fifteen seconds?"

"I can," my father, brother, and I all said at once, making us laugh.

"OK boys, synchronize your watches. Pookie, Trudy, and I will count the chirps. On the count of three . . ."

The three of us all started the stopwatches on our

wrists. Everyone counted. At the end of fifteen seconds, we compared counts. "Sixty" I said. "Forty-five," "sixty-three," "fifty," various people declared. I said, "Let's say sixty. Add thirty-seven, ninety-seven degrees. That's about right."

"Remember when a storm like this would shut the electricity off?" Pookie asked.

"I remember those times," I said. "They're, like, my fondest memory. We would dig up the kerosene stove and light candles. And you, Father, would drag out that big book of poetry and read us some Kipling or Robert Burns."

I don't know why, but he zeroed in on me. "Barney, I think your mother wishes you'd become a doctor or a lawyer or something. But teaching preschool? That's about the most important job there is." He tilted his glass as if toasting me.

"Thanks, Pop." So rare was an appreciation like that from him that I was truly moved.

THAT NIGHT IN the knotty pine room, which had been my room for forty-odd years (most of them odd), I was lying on the big double bed I had artfully angled out from the corner when I was twelve. I was smoking a fat joint of my favorite Thai Stick. The rain poured down, the wind blowing the trees outside my picture windows—four of them, two at each outside corner.

The heat had been broken by the storm, but I felt

warm and fuzzy in my bed. I stared at the ceiling and remembered how, as a child, I had been frightened of the pine knots that, in that hypnagogic state before I was fully asleep, resembled frightful monsters, snakes, dragons, and gorgons. And now, they looked like knots.

Except one. There was one directly above my head composed of two small circles with a long thin triangle protruding from them. It looked like . . . a prick.

I shook as a new memory tumbled into my brain. I was little. I was in the shower with my father.

Really?

Would he have ever taken me into the shower? He did, this time, I was sure. And he stuck his thing in my mouth. I gagged.

Really?

I could see it happening. I could feel that thing in my throat. My body spasmed with horror. I flashed on the other memory of wanting to die. Could that have happened?

I couldn't have been more than two. Who remembers things that far back? There were people in cocounseling that remembered things that happened when they were inside the womb. No wonder I've hated him so over the years. No wonder I have never felt comfortable inside my own skin. This explains everything.

Really?

The next morning, I told Pookie about the memory. "Really, Barney? No, you're making this up. He would never do anything like that."

I recalled that Pookie claimed to have no memories

earlier than age five. What might have happened to her?

I called Charlie and told him. "That son of a bitch," he said, not doubting me for a second.

This happened. This couldn't have happened. No wonder I went crazy. No wonder about everything.

That afternoon, I secured myself in the downstairs bathroom, where our odd family idiosyncratically kept the phone, and called Kate. We exchanged a five-minute session. "I think I remember what happened to me to make me want to die, Kate," I said in a trembling voice.

"Oh?"

"Right before that little death I told you about, my father took me in the shower and stuck his dick in my mouth." I trembled some more as I spoke.

"Ouch," Kate said.

"Ouch. I gagged."

"Ouch," Kate repeated.

"Could this have even happened? And if it did happen, how could I remember something so early? It's not like there were witnesses. Maybe it's a false memory that I made up to justify my hatred of him."

"Maybe. Why would you need to do that?"

"I don't know. It just explains so fucking much."

"So fucking much. You know, whether it actually happened or not isn't nearly so important as the emotional release that you can squeeze out of it."

I let that happen over the phone, the tears running down my face. "That's the theory. But somehow whether it actually happened or not, the uncertainty surrounding it is the essence of the memory. This happened.

This couldn't have happened. The phrase that comes to mind is 'ontological doubt at the dawn of consciousness.'"

"Ontological doubt. You have a way with words, Barney." I heard the beep of her timer. "Oops. That's time."

"OK." I pulled myself together.

"You like absurd comparisons as attention-outs, as I recall. Which do you prefer, Barney? The moon or ice cream?"

I laughed. "In this heat? Ice cream."

"Chocolate or green cheese?"

"Strawberry."

EIGHTEEN

THE OTHER WORLD

— 1 —

*T*he world is perfect, he thinks, as his mama fingers his belly button and coos to him, "Bu-bu-bu-bu-bu-bu-boo!" He's dry-diapered again, and now she holds his fluffy stuffed raccoon in front of his face and then disappears it behind his head. "Where's Coony, where did Coony go?" she says. He tries to turn his head to look. "You're getting it, Barney boy? You remembered him? Good boy." She shows him the raccoon again. He laughs. *It's not lost,* he thinks.

She picks him up from the changing table and holds him close to her yummy cotton candy smell. She plops down with him in an easy chair and gives him her breast to suck and suck the sweet warm milk.

He fades back into her softness and travels through her to the other world. In the other world he floats on a gentle black ocean, cradled in the petals of a shimmering white, bowl-shaped blossom, under an orange sky.

Small, laughing birds, with soft lavender plumage, spiral down from the sky and proffer to him bits of succulent fruit in their curved beaks. As they leave their gifts in his mouth, they sing to him in the clear tones of the bells that hang from the mobile over his crib. Their notes are without words, yet the meaning is crystal clear. "Barney, the world is yours."

— 2 —

The day was hot, gray, humid, stultifying. Robert had spent it in an enormously frustrating, unsuccessful attempt to re-attach the detached retina of an ancient World War I veteran. As he handled one bit of tissue, another would crumble, as if he were trying to repair a tottering brick wall. His hands shook. He needed a drink.

He stopped the old DeSoto in front of the barn-like front of his father's house, but he couldn't move. He didn't want to face her, them, the smell of baby shit. Slumped over the wheel, his stomach tightened as though squeezed in a huge surgical clamp. Sadness clenched his jaw. What would he do?

A year ago, he'd returned all the way from China for his father's funeral and stayed two months later for the birth of his son, Barnard II, named after Father, and now he was back again, had been for a week, and the war was over, but he couldn't get the taste of those metal army plates out of his mouth. He still wore his uniform, though his discharge was imminent. He was proud to have been promoted to colonel, even though his contribution to the war effort seemed to him dubious, frustrating. He'd spent the war removing cataracts from the eyes of Chinese warlords, whom the army hoped to prevent from collaborating with either the Japanese or the Communists, but who ended up doing both. Meanwhile, his colleagues in Milwaukee who had avoided the army were flourishing. He would have to start his practice over, and, at forty-three, he was no longer a young man. His hair was nearly all gray now, even his chest hairs and newly sported mustache.

Finally, his craving for bourbon overcame his inertia, and he tiptoed into the house through the back door. He didn't want to see her, yet he was pissed that she wasn't in the kitchen to greet him. He poured himself a big slug of whiskey, downed it, and then poured another. The clamp on his stomach loosened three whole clicks.

Trudy came gingerly into the kitchen and greeted him as if assessing his mood. He pecked her cheek. She busied herself with the dinner. Both of them struggled in silence to bear the weight of the atmosphere between them.

She was a small, mousy woman with short brown hair, cute but timid. *Christ*, he thought, *I can hardly look at her. After those lively Chinese concubines, sex with her would never be the same.*

He heard the baby fussing in the next room. Charlie, his thirteen-year-old son, dragged the one-year-old Barney into the kitchen.

"I think he's hungry, Mom. Oh, hi," he said to his father.

Robert patted both boys on the head. *It wasn't always like this*, he thought. *Something about the new bastard.* Even though he accused her, he supposed it was his. They did screw that one time. He was too old for another kid. He wanted to be free. That's one thing he had loved about the army—he had been free from her and the family. He could do what he wanted over there. He could even have a man if he wanted, too. Of course, he didn't want to. He wasn't *that* way, not like her brother, that fat faggot, Fred. How he hoped his kids hadn't picked up Fred's damn genes.

He was suffocating here. He couldn't stand it. He didn't know what to do with kids. His mother hadn't known, for Christ's sake. The older ones were just a pain in the ass for him, Trudy's territory. Trudy didn't seem to know what to do either. It didn't help that he'd been away so much. The goddamn war. Charlie was smart, but kind of a mama's boy. He hoped he wasn't . . . Maybe it was already too late for him. He'd do anything to prevent Barney from turning out that way. Anything. Pookie was, how old? Four. She was cute. He liked how soft her skin felt. Sometimes it felt like he could . . . God, how could he think such things? He hated himself for having such thoughts. He tried to shake them but they wouldn't go away. Times like this he scared himself. He wondered what he was capable of. What he had seen men do in the war, though not done himself. Kill for fun, rape.

Suddenly he saw the strange blue light again. The light approached from the distance like the headlight of an oncoming locomotive and completely overtook his brain in a way that obliterated his ability to act. Something about judgment. He couldn't face that kind of terror. He gritted his teeth against such feelings. He would try his best. He could make it work. He was a good man. She was a good woman. Everything would be fine. He poured himself another drink.

He sat down heavily at the breakfast nook table where they always ate, except on special occasions.

Trudy put Barney in his high chair.

The boy still hollered.

"OK!" she yelled at him, losing patience. "Stop all that fuss now. Feed him, Charlie, will you?" She handed Charlie a jar of strained peas. Barney continued to holler.

Blond, curly-headed Pookie in her yellow pinafore bounced into the room.

"Hi, Daddy," she squealed, hugging his legs and forcing him to smile. "I'll feed him," Pookie said to Charlie. She took the spoon from him and did the choo-choo thing into Barney's mouth. He stopped fussing and smiled at her.

After a dinner of roast beef, bourbon, and silence, Robert's mood shifted. He got sentimental. His eyes teared up.

"It's good to be home," he said to Trudy.

Trudy, too, seemed to relax. "We missed you," she said.

"It was hard," he said. "Once when I was flying over Burma, the plane got struck by lightning. There was a horrible crack. The plane filled with this strange blue light, and I saw you all there. I thought I was dead.

"When I got real lonesome, I remembered that song we used to sing." He started to sing, off-key:

"Show me the way to go home . . .

Trudy joined him, while Charlie laughed in embarrassment at such sentiment.

". . . I'm tired and I want to go to bed,

"Well I had a little drink about an hour ago,

"And it went right to my head . . ."

Barney II banged his spoon against the tray of his high chair.

"Time for your bath," Trudy said to him.

Robert looked at the boy, whose face was smeared with peas. He was suddenly overcome with affection. "I'll give him his bath."

"What?" Trudy said.

"I'll take a shower with him."

Trudy laughed. "That's all right, Bob."

"No, I mean it." His face turned fierce again and stopped Trudy's argument.

"If you insist," she said.

Robert grabbed the boy and began to pull him from the high chair roughly. The boy's leg got caught. He squealed.

"Why don't I bring him up to you?" Trudy said.

"OK." Robert staggered up the stairs and pulled off his clothes.

Trudy brought the baby to him naked. "Hold on to him tight," she said, as if to both of them.

The noise of the shower seemed to scare the child. He started to cry. "It's all right, Son. It'll feel good."

What happened next was not clear. Robert held the boy to his chest and was filled with an upwelling of warmth toward him. The boy stopped hollering. Robert closed his eyes. He felt his heart ache with a longing that went way, way back, before the war, before Trudy, before the dawn of the world. His brain clouded over with the red steam of desire. He felt himself getting hard.

Robert soaped the child's little body. He felt dizzy. Suddenly, he lost his grip. The boy slipped down his father's front. Robert panicked with the image of the boy's brains spattered on the tile floor. The red steam in his brain transmuted instantaneously to the strange blue light. He'd do anything to keep this boy alive and pure. He grabbed the boy's hand and just caught him, stopping the boy's fall at his thigh.

The strange blue light obliterated his mind. It was like an accident. He was still hard. The boy's other hand gripped his erection like a handle. *Now is my chance to save the boy*, he thought. *I'll inoculate him against homosexuality.* He lifted his knee and the boy's mouth just sort of caught there. The boy choked. Then he screamed.

My god, what am I doing? Robert thought. Robert's brain finally registered. *What kind of monster am I?* He quickly got out of the shower.

Trudy, who must have heard the cry, took the hysterical baby. She dried him and took him to his room. It was a long time before he stopped screaming.

Robert had trouble falling asleep, despite another drink, but in the morning, he remembered nothing of the night before. Still, when he saw the baby again, he resolved from then on to keep his distance.

— 3 —

B arney notices that when the man they call Daddy comes home, the sky goes dark. He doesn't like the dark. But now the man is cooing. He looks softer.

Now the man holds him naked in his strong arms against his naked chest. The curly hairs there tickle him pleasantly. The man is warm. The water roars like the music of doom in the background, but he is safe.

He looks at the window, covered with steam. He can see where big green petals of paint are peeling from the sill, showing the white underneath. The steam soothes him and the water music washes away his fear. He begins to glimpse the gentle black ocean as he slips into the other world. His floral boat rocks gently. The small lavender birds swoop from the orange sky.

Suddenly, the boat dumps, rock-a-bye baby, and the ocean shatters like the mirror he once dropped.

He slides down, down, down, through the orange sky, under the water, ready to shatter, ready to drown.

The whole bird leaps into his mouth. He can't breathe. He gags. He chokes. Then he screams.

Mama, Mama, Mama, holds him. Will it be all right? He can't stop crying. She holds him. She sticks her breast in his mouth. He spits it out. He squalls, he wails, he bawls, he hollers, on and on and on. Every nerve in his little body fires off full force.

She keeps sticking her breast in his mouth, but it's no use, he won't be consoled. Then he looks up at her. She has this look on her face. He's never seen her look like this before. The fierce mean look of the wolf in those stories. Her eyes as round as moons. Flames around her face. He has to stop crying to breathe but he can't stop.

Her voice screeches at him like the shattering of the mirror, like the screaming of the water.

"Stop it! Stop it now!"

She stuffs her breast in his mouth so that he can't breathe. Again he gags. In a desperate gulp for air, his mouth fills with milk and it flows down the wrong pipe. It tastes like blood. His little body convulses, and then he freezes himself silent in the crib. He catches hold of the milk. He lies there frozen, a long, long time.

The other world. Where is it? Where did it go? He looks and looks. He keeps on looking. He doesn't find it. It's lost.

NINETEEN

PARAGRAPH

An hour before she discovered her husband Robert dead in the bed across the room from her, Trudy awoke, awash in a sea of puzzlement. She blinked her eyes and sat up in her own bed, the bed she had slept in for forty-three years now, just over half her life. She thought, *Where has the time gone?* Astonished, as if time were a cherished earring that she couldn't believe she had lost, as if she had forgotten something but couldn't remember what it was, or even what kind of thing it might have been. Was there something she was supposed to be doing? The children?

All grown, she remembered, grown, married, divorced, living with lovers, she had given them her all, but that hadn't quite been enough. One son, gay. A daughter, an unsuccessful artist, constantly in need of money. And one son, a twice-divorced communist. No doctors like Robert, or lawyers, or professional much of anything, more like her own family of ne'er do wells. As if her genes had polluted the pure strain of Robert's socially prominent family of professionals and business people.

She loved them, her children, of course. A mother loves her children no matter what. But she wished for more for them. More what? Happiness? Financial security? Happiness was an elusive quality. She imagined she would feel more of it for herself if she could see more of it in her children. If she could shake the nagging feeling that she had done something wrong as a mother, that she just hadn't been good enough. And yet they were, all of them—what?—thinkers. Questioners. She supposed that was good, or that there was something good about it. She probably wouldn't have been that pleased if they had all towed the line and become boring business people like the children of most of her friends. She had experienced her own years of wildness, in Europe, before she was married, when she was in love with an artist and danced with Scott Fitzgerald. She hadn't been as pretty as her sister, who had stolen her artist away from her, but she had a pleasingly round peasant face that matched her humorous personality, her quick laugh. But she had outgrown her wild ways and settled down. Way down. Her children, it seemed, would never settle down.

As she walked to the bathroom, she caught a glimpse of the view from her window in the pre-dawn light. *It has been a good life*, she thought. *I have a lovely home.* She giggled at that thought as she looked at the frosting of fresh snow on the branches of the trees, on the vast expanse of frozen lake just below the hill outside their window. Her favorite thought: "I have a lovely home." She was fully conscious, even in her state of diminishing consciousness as her short-term memory slipped away, of the delicious irony. She was no devotee of women's magazines. What was she doing? Oh, yes, the bathroom, her bladder reminded her, thank God for bodily functions, reminding you what to do next. Breakfast? Did she cook it or did someone come and do it? People did come. Sometimes Charlie, her son. Others. Nurses. Every day? Some days? These were the details that wouldn't stick in her head anymore, and it was frightening, as if she might one day exhale and then forget to inhale again. There was a slight pain as she urinated, a reminder of her kidney problem of the previous year, the one that had almost killed her, a reminder, too, of her own fragility, of the fragility of life. As she returned to the room, she thought of Robert. Where was he? Oh, still in bed, still asleep. *Better leave him, let sleeping dogs lie,* she chuckled to herself. You never knew what kind of mood he would be in. Yes, they would be here, the nurses, because he needed help. Bathing, getting into his wheelchair, getting downstairs, even though they'd put in one of those stair lifts.

Robert. It was so hard for him, losing his faculties one by one. Losing his dignity, his independence. She looked at him. He was so still. His hair white since he was in his thirties. Sharp features, not sagging with age. Asian eyes that she hadn't noticed until he got back from China and spoke so adoringly of the Chinese, the "smartest people on Earth." He had a smirk on his face just now. An odd smirk.

How long had they been married? Close to sixty years. *That's a long time not to know someone,* she mused. It was funny. She couldn't remember what she was doing one minute or even ten seconds ago, but she remembered him taking her out to Maeder's, Milwaukee's finest German restaurant, in his shy and boyish way. She had ordered the sauerbraten. She'd loved him right away. She knew he liked her. He would work on loving her, but she knew the way a woman knows these things, that there had been someone else he loved who had turned him down. He never talked about it, but she knew.

Still, she had warmed her way into his heart, *warmed, wormed,* she giggled. Thanks to the Depression and her father's illness, they had married in a small family ceremony at her mother and father's dreary apartment in the Schroeder Hotel. They had honeymooned at Virginia Beach and got too sunburned to do what they were supposed to be doing on their honeymoon, but that was OK, because they had done that way before, on their first date even. Young people today think they invented sex.

She listened. It was so quiet here in the country, by the lake. The sun was just rising, and the birds were welcoming it back from its journey through the night. It had taken her a long time to get used to the quiet when they first moved here, but the birds had helped. And the flowers. She had come to love the flowers. Her gardens won prizes. Even now, in the dead of winter, she could imagine the daffodils, the tulips, the petunias, the geraniums, the bluebells bursting forth into the spring with the help of her loving care. Did she still garden? Or had she gotten too old? She couldn't remember. In the spring, she would try again. If she didn't forget.

She looked at Robert again. He hadn't moved. His expression hadn't changed. *Maybe he died in the night,* she thought, and a wave of terror swept over her. Maybe he had even killed himself as he'd threatened to do from time to time. A member of the Hemlock Society, he believed that people had the right to choose the circumstances of their own demise. But she would know, wouldn't she? He would tell her, say goodbye, wouldn't he? If he had told her, would she have let him go through with it? Or would she have called Charlie to come and help her talk him out of it? Even if he hadn't told her goodbye, she would still know. Her intuition would tell her. Wouldn't it? She was scaring herself. She called his name.

"Robert?" Her voice creaked from lack of use.

He didn't move. Still lying in her bed, she called, louder this time, "Robert?"

He didn't stir.

She got out of her bed and crossed over to him, hesitating, seriously frightened now. "Robert!" she called sharply at a distance of six feet. Nothing. Not so much as the flutter of an eyelash. She put her ear near his face to listen for his breath. Nothing. Panicking now, she touched his cheek. It wasn't cold, exactly, but it wasn't warm enough either. "Robert!" she screamed. She tapped his shoulder roughly. "Wake up!" Tears welled up from inside her as her legs gave out from under her.

She grabbed the phone. She knew Charlie had fixed

it so she only had to press one button to call him.
Which button? She tried the letter A at the top.

It rang. Charlie answered.

"I can't wake him up," she blurted hysterically.

"I'll be right down," Charlie said. He lived a quarter
mile away.

Why was it taking so long? Where was he? She
didn't want to touch Robert any more. She lay on the
floor, crumpled in a heap, hoping against hope that she
was dreaming, that this wasn't happening. She was
breathing heavily, perhaps for the both of them. *Please,
God, no.* She remembered that she didn't believe in God,
but what difference did that make now? *Please.* Her
chest ached with the awful sorrow of raw probability.
He was eighty-seven years old. People die. Why people
die was a mystery. So was why they live. Why suffer
through life for eighty-seven years, only to die? It made
no sense. But he probably wasn't dead, anyway. More
likely it was some trick of her own decaying mind mis-
perceiving the situation.

She heard the Jeep in the driveway.

Charlie stormed into the room with a scared look on
his face, a little boy again, running to Mommy after a
nightmare, his gray hair windblown from the cold wind
off the lake. He grabbed her hand as he rushed to
Robert's side.

"Dad?"

He shook Robert's shoulder with his other hand, still
holding hers.

"Dad?"

He put his ear on Robert's chest to listen for his heart. He shook his head. He felt for a pulse on his wrist. He shook his head again.

He helped Trudy up from the floor and held her for a long time, while they both shook. Charlie cried shamelessly. She wanted to, but couldn't quite. Charlie was a big man now, tall with a big, soft belly. She was small and withered, and she sank into his roundness, round face, round horn-rimmed glasses. She was the only one of the family who didn't wear glasses, except for reading. He half-carried her over to her own bed.

"He led a full life," Charlie muttered. "At least he died in his sleep." He pressed a button on the phone. "Can I speak with Dr. Greenthaw? This is an emergency. One of his patients has died." He said more into the phone, but Trudy didn't hear him. She was gradually and carefully trying to let in the reality that it wasn't a trick of her mind after all, that it was finally happening, that it had finally happened, that he was dead. Whatever that meant.

With the reality, too, crept in the numbness. The cold fact of her husband's death pressed upon her in the pit of her stomach, as if her bowels had turned to lead. The grief clogged her pores like a bath in cold bacon grease. She felt nothing—nothing except that nagging sensation she was forgetting something. *Robert's dead*, she kept reminding herself, a fact she wished to forget, but could not. *Feel something*, she ordered herself.

Dr. Greenthaw came. Should she tell him? *"Doctor, I can't feel anything,"* she practiced in her mind. He was addressing her with the awkward solemnity people reserve for the surviving spouse. No one knows what to do with death, not even this fine, experienced doctor who dealt with it all the time. In the end, she forgot to tell him of her own condition, and he left her some pills. Sleeping pills. Tranquilizers. He didn't understand that it was her calmness that disturbed her most of all.

Charlie was solicitous. "Are you OK, Mom? Can I get you anything?"

I can't feel anything, she wanted to shout, but she couldn't say anything. It was too embarrassing. She deflected his solicitations. She wanted to be left alone. She wanted her feelings back. Hadn't she loved him all these sixty years? The bad times flooded back to her, oblivious to the decorum of her situation. His cruelty. He could be vicious, putting her down with vicious sarcasm for not having worked in her life, a point around which she was particularly vulnerable. Oh, she'd worked all right, keeping his house, cooking his meals, raising his children, even if she'd had help, but it wasn't real work, not like *his* work, attaching detached retinas with minute movements of his unsteady hands, giving sight to the blind. Blaming her for making a "mama's boy" out of Charlie, which was a joke really, because Charlie was anything but a mama's boy, gay or not. Which was even funnier because of that other thing, that thing she couldn't remember.

"Mom," Charlie shouted from the next room, alarm in his voice. *What else*, she thought. "I think you better hear this."

She struggled to get up from the bed again, her joints

especially stiff. She glanced at Robert, horrified that that smirk was still seemingly aimed at her from his inert face. She followed Charlie's voice into what they called the "maid's room," though the maid had gone some forty years ago, and the room now served as Robert's home office. Or used to, before he died. She shivered.

Charlie was seated in Robert's chair, huddled over a cassette tape recorder. He got up so she could sit in the chair. She read the note taped to the machine, in Robert's inimitable left-handed scrawl, extra shaky since his stroke: "Play the tape." She sighed, bracing herself for what she was about to hear. It couldn't be good.

Dear Family,
I've done it, I've taken all my euthanasia pills, and I am now asleep, on the way to death. It will take some hours before I die, therefore do not call Dr. Greenthaw for at least twelve hours after you discover me. Just let me sleep in peace. Paragraph. . . .

Paragraph! She shuddered. *He's dictating his suicide note! To what ghostly secretary?*

I've had a good eighty-seven years of life, but the past year has been torture, and I do not wish to continue. I have only two regrets. One is that I did not show enough affection, which I truly felt for my wife, Trudy. . . .

His voice cracked. *Was he crying? He did care.* A lump came to her throat, too, and she held it in, no fan of emotional displays. She remembered seeing him cry only once, a couple years ago when his dog, Ferdinand, a lazy basset, like the bull, was hit by a car.

> . . . and the other is that I did not spend enough time with my children as I should have. . . .

She winced at the diction, "*As much* time . . . as I should have," she corrected, angry at herself for being petty.

> Otherwise, it has been a wonderful life. I want my funeral to be a simple family affair, with perhaps Charlie saying a few words. I want to be cremated, and I want my ashes to be buried with my family in the Blatz lot. This can be done in the spring; there's no hurry. Also, if you want a memorial service in the spring in the city, that's all right with me. I don't think that Pookie and Barney should be expected to come to my funeral, but that's up to you to decide . . .

Even as he regrets spending too little time with them, he pushes them away. Is he merely scared they won't want to come, that they are too mad at him? Yes, they may be mad at him for a multitude of sins, for not letting them in, but he has . . . had . . . no idea how much they loved him, poor man.

If you have no further use for the rowboat, or the iceboat, or the sailboard, I bequeath them to my cousin Walter to do as he wishes with them. If you wish to keep them and use them, that's fine with me. Also explore with Walter whether he is interested in the copies of *Wooden Boat,* which I have from the beginning of the publication of the magazine fifteen years ago. Adios. Your husband and father. Don't call the doctor for twelve hours.

She stared blankly at the machine as his voice went . . . dead.

Wooden Boat magazine. An odd detail. For all his international reputation as a surgeon, one who pioneered the use of lasers to re-attach retinas back in the 1960s when no one had even heard of lasers, his proudest accomplishment was building a lapstrake rowboat, steaming each plank in his workshop so it fit just so. The boat was ugly, sloppily built even, and it leaked. He had given it to Barney when he finished, but Barney never used it. She doubted Walter would want it. How odd what finally seems important in a too-long life. Perhaps the boat would get him across the River Styx. If it doesn't sink first.

So he did it. She never believed that he would, not even after he'd tried it a few years back, drunk as a skunk, when Charlie first contemplated moving back from New York and there was no longer any denying that he was gay. Oh, they'd suspected for years, but pretended it wasn't so.

Now what did she feel? She felt, for one thing, like she needed to monitor her feelings, as if they were vital signs, as if they might slip out of control at any moment, and, on the one hand she wished they would, but on the other, she needed to contain them somehow, to maintain decorum, or something. She felt . . . wooden . . . like the boat. Except where his voice cracked, when he was talking about her, he was so damn *rational* about it. *Wooden Boat.* It reminded her of when she was in a car accident, when someone came out of nowhere and slammed into her car (no, she hadn't been paying attention), the glove compartment popped open and spilled its contents onto the floor. The first thing she did was start picking up the maps, manuals, flashlight, receipts, registration, old lipstick, nail file. If he really regretted not showing his affection toward her, why not wake her up and hold her as he slipped away? She chided herself for being uncharitable. Then she remembered the smirk, which was still on that face in the next room. It was directed at her, somehow, she knew. It chilled her.

Finally, she got up the nerve to look at Charlie, who sat in the other chair, the same chair where he had sat as he had listened to his father dictate his memoir a few months ago. It was good that Charlie got him to finish. Charlie looked tense and pale. Trudy jumped to the rescue, an old habit. "It was a brave thing to do, you know," she said weakly, not quite believing her own words, but eager to defend him to the end . . . beyond the end. "He was in a lot of pain."

"Yes, he was," Charlie said, noncommittally, not about to reveal *his* feelings.

We Germans don't wear our feelings on our sleeves, she thought. She could tell that Charlie's feelings were decidedly mixed.

They'd been close in the early years, Robert and his first-born son, as close as anyone could be with Robert. He'd been an only child himself with distant parents and lived in his own world much of the time, with vast territories shared with no one, so it seemed. But he had taught Charlie how to ride a bike and catch a ball. So it must've been *her* fault that he turned out to be gay. She had fussed over him. She enjoyed dressing him up in cute little outfits. Of course, it couldn't have helped that he had gone off to the war when Charlie was in puberty. But most likely it was those genes he had gotten from her, the same ones that had made her brother Fred gay. Genes weren't really her fault, of course, but a good part of her felt she was to blame for just about everything wrong with the family. Unless it was that thing with Robert, that thing she couldn't remember, her mind an aged slab of Swiss cheese.

"I'll call Barney and Pookie," Charlie said. "I'm sure they'll want to come, no matter what he said. Are you OK? Do you want to go back to bed? Get dressed?"

"What about . . . him?" Would he just stay in bed with that smirk on his face for all eternity? What did they do with the dead, anyway? Why couldn't we just drop wherever we were like other animals and let the flies and worms and crows feast off us? Though come to think of it, that wouldn't be so pleasant to watch in her own bedroom. Could Charlie take him into the woods out back? He'd said he wanted to be cremated. How she wished to avoid the horrid funeral people.

"The undertaker's on his way," Charlie said.

"Then I better get dressed," she said. The last thing she wanted was to be seen in her flannel pajamas with the little pink roses on them.

Fortunately, Charlie handled the nurse, the under-takers, and the others who came. Trudy sat in her wicker rocking chair in the playroom looking out at the lake, a misty blank tableau of snow and ice, quiet and still. The ground was white, the trees were white, the frozen lake was white, the sky was white, blank, the way she felt inside. There was a purity to the blankness. In many ways, her life was over, too—her life as a wife, which was her life. Yet she lived. She felt light, a bit obscenely so. She was not supposed to feel this much relief.

Ignoring the noise in the background of them re-moving the body, she tried to remember the good times. Skiing. She'd never learned to ski very well, but she liked being outside in the cold, and she'd learned how never to fall. First, there was Austria. Then, Aspen, be-fore it was a major resort. They had to climb using climbing skins, sealskin strips strapped to the bottoms of their skis. Going uphill, the fur was brushed upwards, breaking the downward pull of the slope. Downhill, the fur slicked back and provided little resistance; 1937, she thought it was, when they were offered to buy half a block of Aspen for $500 they didn't have. Who knew what skiing would become? Who knew if the world would ever recover from the Depression? It seemed likely that it would not. But Robert had been happy when he was skiing, and the after-ski *gemütlichkeit* was a high point of German-American culture, such as it was. Yes, they'd get drunk, but it was a happy drunk, not like the solitary, maudlin binges of later years. Then there was Heiliger Huegel, Holy Hill, the ski club they developed with their friends near the convent in the nearby Kettle Moraine area of Wisconsin—not a mountain, but a nice hill. It had been fun to buy the land from the farmer, trying to explain what they were going to do with it. Then there was clearing the trees, putting in the rope tow, or providing logistical support—coffee, beer, and sandwiches—for the men while they did this manly work.

Having loaded the body in their hearse, the undertakers came to speak with her, two men in dark suits and oily hair, stereotypes of their profession. Trudy tried briefly to see beyond their too-personal, soft-spoken solicitations, to see them as just people doing a job, but when they got out their leather-bound catalogues showing the ten-thousand-dollar caskets, she dug in her heels. "We want the basic service," she said, over and over, with Charlie backing her up. "We want the basic service." She was not normally an assertive woman, but here she stood her ground.

"We will have a memorial when the family arrives at the end of the week," Charlie told them. "We don't need to have his body on display. People will believe us that he is dead." At this blasphemous phrase the two men looked at each other somberly and gave up.

Charlie went to make more calls, to arrange the church, the caterer. Trudy sank back into her reverie, wishing she could remember more. With a greater burst of deliberate activity than she was accustomed to, she went into the living room and found the manila envelope containing the typewritten pages of Robert's memoir. She sat on the couch, under the framed watercolors, abstractions in the manner of Paul Klee, painted by her old lover, Hans Reichel. As her short-term memory had receded, she'd gotten out of the habit of reading. It was difficult, but she could still do it, if she focused her mind.

She read the opening lines:

```
My earliest recollection is of my
grandfather taking me to Oconomowoc for a
haircut in the horse and buggy. This was,
of course, an all-day affair, which
included the haircut and lunch. I loved
riding behind the horse for two reasons.
One was the almost perfume-like smell of
horse manure, which still, to this day,
delights me; and the other is the
astonishing beauty of a horse's anus as
he ejected his horse apples, outfolding
into the picture of a beautiful, flesh-
colored rose.
```

That was so Robert, in all his perversity, she thought. She skimmed through the rest. Sometimes, she would read passages over and over, forgetting that she had read them already. She read of making ice cream in a machine with a crank with fresh strawberries and unpasteurized cream, of getting drunk on beer at a nearby farm's threshing bee at the age of five, of running in the woods, knocking down dead trees, and finding woodpecker nests, squirrel nests, raccoon habitations, some with living animals still in them. She read of sailing accidents, bicycle accidents, motorcycle accidents, of building pushcarts and ham radios, of playing with the "shanty Irish" in Milwaukee and getting caught stealing, of nearly failing calculus in college, curtailing a promising engineering career. There were numerous medical stories, war stories from his stint in the Asian theater during World War II, sailing stories from cruises in the Caribbean and Mediterranean Seas, Chesapeake Bay, Lake Michigan. Much that was interesting, little that was new to her, much that was just plain boring.

One passage jumped out at her about the war when they lived in Texas where he was stationed:

> In the spring of 1944, my father and
> mother came down to Texas to escape the
> winter weather in Wisconsin and stayed in
> the towns north of San Antonio. In April,
> they came to visit us for a short period
> before going home. Father was obviously
> quite ill after his third heart attack.
> He would get up in the morning, take a
> brisk walk to test out his heart, and
> come in panting with lips very blue. He
> was trying to make his heart work
> normally or else not at all by this type

of exercise. They went home by train, as
I remember, and Father was hospitalized
at Milwaukee Hospital and died within
three days. They strongly suspect that he
elicited the help of a medical friend to
assist him in a form of euthanasia. He
was seventy-six at the time of his death.

So that's where he got it, this voluntary euthanasia, she thought, *like father like son.* Then she came to the end, where he talked about her:

I first met Trudy, along with her sister
Hannah, at the Milwaukee Yacht Club when
she was about sixteen, when a friend of
mine, Starky, and I were exploring the
place, looking for female companionship.
Both of them were charming girls, full of
fun, and Starky and I double-dated them
for the next three or four years off and
on. It was not so much necking and sex
between us, just good companionship. We
both loved jazz; we used to go to Sam
Pick's as often we could, as often as we
could afford it, and at one time Starky's
father followed us out there and insisted
that we go home from that den of
iniquity.

Lots of drinking, she remembered, but she hadn't minded. She was used to it; her father and brothers drank a lot, too. She did like him on those double dates, though he was so shy, even shyer than she was. There could have been more necking. She remembered wanting to hold his hand but not having the nerve. The jazz was good, and he was a good dancer.

> I dated her once or twice while she was
> at Smith and I was at Williams, and later
> we had a few dates in Madison, Wisconsin,
> when I was in medical school and she was
> living in Madison with her family. She
> left for Europe in 1925, at the time when
> her sister was married and was over there
> for five years. When I came back to
> Milwaukee in 1930, I was a very lonely
> young man. I tried to look up Trudy and
> had quite a bit of difficulty finding her
> family. However, I eventually located
> them and learned that Trudy was returning
> from Europe in the fall. I can remember
> meeting her that September at the
> Boulevard Restaurant just north of West
> Park and being overjoyed to see her.

And that was a mutual joy. She thought that in the intervening years since those first dates, they were each looking for something better. Then he got his heart broken by that girl Ann he mentioned in the memoir. Trudy had her heart trampled on by that "novel" they'd lived in Europe, when she was in love with the artist Reichel, and her sister Hannah, her married sister, stole him away from her, while they all—she, Hannah, Hannah's husband, and Reichel—lived in the same Munich flat. But, she knew, it was Maeder's Restaurant, not the Boulevard, that marked her first real date with Robert, when love was born.

We dated regularly after that and finally
decided to get married. We were married
on May 23, 1931. This lady became my boon
companion and the love of my life for the
next fifty-eight years. She was always
good company and always had a terrific
sense of humor. Her willingness to
participate in any of the sports that I
was interested in was phenomenal.

Now she started choking up. It felt good, the little
tears that formed by themselves in the corner of her
eyes, but scary, too, because she feared she couldn't
control them. Oh, people were allowed to bawl their
eyes out when their husbands died, she supposed, but
she so much didn't want to make a spectacle of herself.
There was something else as well—something prevent-
ing her from feeling her loss, which she couldn't quite
put her finger on.

There were only two times in our fifty-
eight years when she buckled in to a
fear, to a real fear. Both times we were
skiing. Once was the trestle crossing in
Innsbruck, and the other was coming down
the Roche Run at Aspen in the middle
1930s. Both times she survived and was
just as jolly at dinner as ever.

Oh, God, let's not dwell here. How well she remembered the fear. How well she remembered both times
the stark terror and hating herself for being afraid, irra-
tionally, she knew, and hating him for forcing her to

confront it. Though, he did talk her down. He was good at that, with his deep, calm, reassuring voice, not the voice on the tape.

> Her ability to mix in a friendly way with
> all kinds of people was also a great
> asset. I remember going to parties when I
> would hold on to her skirt. If I jerked
> twice, this meant that I couldn't
> remember the name of the person we were
> going to meet next, but she managed to
> get around that and introduce me without
> any social error.

Yes, well, that was the easy part. She was well versed in the social graces. She was good at running interference for his shyness.

> Other affairs with women were mostly
> short-lived and relatively casual. I
> don't even remember their names.

That probably wasn't true. Certainly, there was one secretary. She had held her breath over that one. She'd taken up biting her nails while he was away at those late night "meetings." Notice he said "mostly" and "relatively." She supposed he was protecting her here, or himself. But at the time her instincts had told her to wait him out, and she had been right, she supposed.

The next passage took her aback:

> I also had a couple of brief episodes
> with transvestism. As a sixteen-year-old,
> I was terribly shy and could hardly look
> a girl in the face. Living alone one
> summer in my grandfather's house, I
> found, on exploring a closet, some
> clothes that belonged to my grandmother.
> I had a desire to dress up in them and
> did so and found that it gave me a sexual
> stimulation. In other words, dressing up
> in women's clothes gave me a stimulus to
> masturbation. I think that's the basis
> for most transvestism, at least in the
> beginning. I reverted to transvestism for
> a short time in my sixties, although this
> time it did not seem to have the same
> sexual stimulus that it previously had.
> So much for women and sex.

Her mind went blank over this one. Her face turned hot with embarrassment. Why put this in your memoir? What had Charlie and Barney and Pookie thought when they read this? She hadn't remembered reading it at all when the memoir came back from the transcriber. In fact, she hadn't, she remembered now. Charlie had mentioned that he had had to sanitize the final draft for the relatives. "It wasn't so bad, what I took out," Charlie had said to her over the phone. "Something about masturbation." Her mouth tasted of tin, the taste from over-ripe tin cans. Panic coursed through her.

She forgot where she was. "Robert?" she said out loud. *Robert's dead,* a calm voice whispered to her from inside her head. But she called again.

"Robert?"

Charlie came into the room with his scared look again. "You OK?"

"Where's Robert?" she asked. She knew the answer. She just needed to be sure.

"He's dead, Mother," Charlie said softly. "Remember?"

"Oh." She smiled, weakly, amused by her ability to forget something so momentous.

"Do you want to go into town with me?" Charlie asked. "We have to put some kind of obituary in the local paper."

"Do I have to?"

"No, but it might do you good to get out of the house."

"OK." Safely ensconced back in her fog, she put on her heavy winter coat, fur hat, boots, and gloves. She followed Charlie to the car, her car, the big, white Buick. They drove in silence through the trees. The road wound through the silent, snowy woods for more than a mile.

"You were reading the memoir?" Charlie asked.

She couldn't answer. The sobs welled up in her throat uncontrollably. She buried her face in her gloves. Finally, she spoke in an emotion-wrought voice not her own. "I caught him once. Dressed up. He looked . . . so ridiculous." She was crying fully now, for the first time. "I couldn't handle it. I made him stop."

Charlie took her hand and gave her a tender look. She bawled for a long time, her body jerking in great spasms of sobs.

"If only I had let him talk about it," she said, finally, quietly.

She understood the smirk now. She supposed that was why he did it this way, why he felt he needed to kill himself without saying goodbye. He was getting even. Her understanding reinforced every bad thought she had ever had about herself, that she was to blame for everything. It felt unutterably horrible, yet the realization made her feel lighter, too, as if she had just confessed her sins to a priest.

"We were never too good at communicating," she said. She suddenly wanted to tell Charlie that it was really OK that he was gay. But—she stopped herself. It wouldn't be seemly.

"It wasn't your fault, Mom," Charlie said.

"No, I suppose it wasn't," Trudy said. "Not really."

TWENTY

TERM LIFE

— 1 —

Why come back to Wisconsin to die? I hate Wisconsin. The weather sucks, compared to California. The flora and fauna? Prissy woods versus majestic redwood forests. Pitiful lakes versus the roar of the Pacific Ocean. Muskrats and badgers versus coyotes and bears. Memories of heartbreak don't help either. Yet here I am.

California dreaming, my eyes pop open where I lay in my old VW Eurovan camper, parked off the road by the clearing in the woods on this one-acre plot we withheld from the sale of the rest of the ancestral homestead, up the hill on the farm across the road from the big house on the lake. This spot where we spread Father's ashes thirty-five years ago. The sky glows with the impending sunrise on my last day on earth.

My prostate the size of a grapefruit, stage four cancer, I'm on my painful way out anyway. The worst is the urgency. Having to piss all the time, triggering toilet training trauma, perpetually squirming. I could have had my prostate removed, but I was unwilling to give up my sex life.

I turn seventy-five next month, and my million-dollar term life insurance policy will expire. I am still a small "c" communist after all these years, why give a fuck about money? It was a bet against myself. I took out the policy from Transamerica Life the day I got the diagnosis ten years ago, before it hit my medical record and the rates hit the roof. One of my better investments, but I have to die to collect. I made sure the suicide clause wouldn't invalidate the policy after the first two years.

I've kept the policy secret from my family, paying the premium with royalties from my novels, as well as various credit cards. I want it to be a surprise.

It isn't just about me, though I mostly live as if it is. I have a family. Mariah, I will miss the shit out of her. "The third time's a charm," my brother Charlie said when he met my miraculous third wife, a Latina from Mexico who bubbles like the Piper-Heidsieck she loves, skin as smooth as mango lassi, eyes that sparkle like Mexican fireworks.

Our son, T-Jay, in his twenties, a warrior for the planet, a quiet mestizo beauty who has left a trail of broken hearts and had his own broken too many times.

Jason and Ramona, children from my first wife, Sasha, both with Ivy League PhDs, thanks to their mother's smarts, opposite sides of the Cartesian split; he a genetic scientist, she a classical philosopher. They're both flourishing, but Jason's wife Susanna also has stage four cancer—of the liver. She's holding her own, but the prognosis is terrible.

We aren't that poor, Mariah and me. But Mariah should have something. And T-Jay wants me to put some serious money in the movement to save the f-ing planet, which was heating up fast—both the movement and the planet.

And, the most compelling reason: Jason has gotten Susanna into an experimental program that *might* save her life. But it costs half a million dollars. Susanna is forty-six, the love of Jason's life, a belly dancer, fire-eater, terrific mom to my grandson Zeke. Surely it's worth exchanging my dwindling life for hers, even for the chance of hers.

The August heat is sweltering. I drove here for a family reunion that ended a few days ago. One of my cousins has been able to keep a section of the Great-Grandfather Blatz homestead and generously hosted the other cousins to come swim in Pike Lake and reminisce about the old days. It was a warm and pleasant gathering of people with a lot of history, no matter where we stood on the partisan divide in the country. It was a blessing that we got rid of that horrid president last year.

But I wasn't really present. I was busy plotting my own death.

I inherited some money from the sale of the Pike Lake property and the farm. Mariah and I invested heavily in real estate: an apartment building in Oakland, our 1910 Craftsman dream house, also in Oakland, and a sweet little house in San Miguel de Allende in Mexico where she and I met thirty years ago.

I was staying in my camper on "my" acre during the reunion. I said my goodbyes to everyone, not forever goodbyes, just my leaving-for-California goodbyes. Except I didn't leave. I'm holed up in this thick but wimpy forest, where the fox used to hang out, or so it was rumored.

As soon as I got here, I carved out a parking area in the woods for my camper, surrounded by pines and birch, invisible from the road. They might see my light at night, so I stay in the dark. It's hot. I don't need a fire.

I brought my grandfather's World War I vintage .45 automatic. I reach for it in my little closet. It's in its leather holster, snapped to an army-issue web belt, along with a case with two clips, about sixteen bullets in all. I will only need one. It's amazing how little the technology of death has changed over a hundred years. I knew there was a reason I didn't sell the gun to my grade school friend Jeffery, now a gun dealer.

Does it bother me to be following in my own father's—and his father's—footsteps with this voluntary euthanasia business? You bet. For seventy-five years I've resisted his influence, ever since that psycho shower scene when I was two—that's another story. I am the antithesis of my father—he to the right of Ronald Reagan and me to the left of Mao Zedong—and now here we are at the synthesis.

I fold the bed in my camper back into a seat and set up the little table, my cozy little nest. I make my French roast French press coffee on the built-in stove. I fry up some bacon. Eggs over easy. And, left over from my steak dinner last night, potatoes with onions and red peppers fried in bacon grease. I'm having several last meals.

I deserve them. As Randy Newman says, "You ain't been a bad man / You ain't been a good man / But you've been pretty bad."

I will miss bacon and coffee cooked outside.

I have two phobias: one of being buried alive and one of being burned alive. I know where they come from. My first experience of death was a toddler drowning when I was five, son of my cousin's maid next door on the lake. I remember seeing the mother wailing on the dock. Since then, panic smothers me whenever I feel deprived of air. Even though I grew up on the lake, I never learned to swim well.

The burning alive fear comes from our house burning down when I was four. Pookie, aged all of seven, and I were home alone with the caretaker Clifford, more of a drunk than a child-development specialist. Pookie noticed the smoke oozing out of the shingles. We went to find Clifford, who was down the road in the tool shed. He tried to call the fire department using the new-fangled dial phone, but had to go next door to get the neighbors to help. Turns out a squirrel had shorted out the wires. Many of my toys that didn't get burned up retained that inimitable smell of the fire for years.

So I refuse to be cremated or buried whole in a claustrophobic coffin. Who knows when sensation really ceases? Just because you flatline out on the electroencephalogram doesn't mean you won't feel pain.

I want to die just like any other animal, drop dead where I am and rot on the forest floor, food for the buzzards, the flies, and the worms. And I have the means to do it, this single acre in the Wisconsin woods.

A year ago, I asked Jason to drive me out here in the trunk of a car after I died and unceremoniously dump me—or even ceremoniously if they wanted. Jason laughed at first.

"You're not serious?" he asked.

"Yes. Yes, I am."

Jason scoffed. "That's disgusting. You want to subject Susanna and Zeke to that?" he said. Zeke is now fifteen.

"I wouldn't have asked, until I saw *Little Miss Sunshine*," I said, referring to the movie where a family drives to Los Angeles with the grandfather dead in the trunk so the girl can meet the deadline to enter the beauty pageant. "But it's OK if you don't want to do it."

Silence. And then a sudden outburst. "Why do you always have to be so damn *different*? Why can't you just be normal?"

From a son who was usually so loving, such a rebuke cut like a razor, and I hung my head. It was a judgment against my entire life, and a chill came between us, which hasn't fully healed to this day.

Jason and I had another fight as well. While still in Mexico, I overheard Mariah and Jason plotting over the phone to throw me a surprise party for my seventh-fifth birthday. Nostrils flaring, I picked up the extension phone.

"Don't either of you know me well enough to know that's the last thing in the world I would want? Just the thought of all that embarrassment makes me want to throw up."

I was being unreasonable. I should be flattered they would go to all that trouble for me. But I remembered my last surprise party, when I was nine. The afternoon of my birthday, I was climbing a tree by myself in the yard, horrified that they'd forgotten my birthday. I fell out of the tree, only a few feet. I wasn't hurt, but I landed in a fresh pile of dog shit. I ran in the house to change when a bunch of my friends and classmates materialized from nowhere and yelled, "Surprise!"

I burst into tears.

Everyone got a good whiff of me before my clueless mother smelled me and realized what was wrong. She whisked me away to change, but the mortification lingered for days, months, years. I had earned a nickname among some of my peers: Dogdoo.

Without Jason's cooperation, I decided I would just do it myself when the time came, come here on my own and end my life. The time has come.

I pull out my vape with the cartridge of Premium Jack. I don't usually smoke this early, but today is different. I pop open a Negra Modelo from the fridge. I set up my laptop on the table. I open a blank page. I begin my final journal entry:

August 15, 2020

"I've done it, I've taken all my euthanasia pills...." That's how *he* started, isn't it? My father. But I don't want to copy him.

The sliding door to the van is open for the heat. Outside a birch tree flutters in the breeze, with its jagged, heart-shaped leaves and its white bark that the Indians made canoes out of, birch bark canoes. Down at the foot of the tree is a whole universe of grubs, bugs, bacteria, fungi, all communicating through the exchange of CO_2, I heard on NPR. Grubs that will soon be eating me.

What do I need to tell the world that it doesn't already know? I used to cross-dress, dress up in women's clothes. And I'm confessing it at the end just like Father did in his memoir. Is there a fucking gene for this? A lot of people know this about me, Mariah, certainly, but not my kids. What I like about cross-dressing is that it gets me in touch with those marvelous female characteristics that, thanks to sexism, are denied to men. Why shouldn't men be able to enjoy the feel of silky fabric across our private parts? Why shouldn't men get to cry our eyes out when we need to? Why shouldn't men be able to care deeply without having to work at it so fucking hard?

I'm going to burn this journal entry before I check out. Delete it.

Then I write the suicide note:

Dear Family,

The time has come to end this amazing journey that has been my life. I love you all and will miss you more

SQUIRRELS IN THE WALL

than I can imagine, but the pain has become too much.

In the drawer of the roll-top desk in Mexico is my insurance policy. I'm hopeful the money will come in time to save Susanna's life, to invest in saving the planet, and to leave you all with something.

I have three nuggets of wisdom to impart on my way out the door.

One: Life is death's dream. I know this is true, that it's my deepest thought, but I don't really know what it means.

Two: In the last nanosecond of one's life, time slows down so that it is experientially just about as long as the previous idea of one's life, in my case almost seventy-five years.

Three is speculation: Time moves forward as the universe expands, but once it reaches the limit in about a trillion years and starts collapsing, time will reverse direction. In another trillion years of human/ earth time, we will return to the present and live our lives backward, until we end up in the eternal coziness of our mothers' bellies. But since we won't be conscious, those two trillion years will go by in a flash, and, experientially, it will be like waking back up again even as we just fell sleep. So, catch you on the rebound. See you soon.

Love to all,
Barney

I do delete the journal entry and leave the suicide note up on the computer for them to find when they find me.

I pull on my jeans and T-shirt over my fuchsia panties

with the lace waistband. I look at the gun belt, consider donning it, decide I'm not ready. I step out onto the clearing, which is carpeted with dried grass. I pull my camp chair out of the back of the van and set it up by the circle of stones that serves as a campfire site. I walk to the edge of the clearing to pee against a birch tree and nearly fall in a big hole, which is overgrown with poison ivy, recognizable by its trinity of leaves. After relieving myself, I examine the hole. I fetch my camp shovel from the back of my van and clear away the poison ivy.

The hole is about five feet by two feet, but over six feet deep. I'd forgotten about it, but now I remember when Father dug it that time with the idea of building an outhouse, which, typically, he didn't follow through with. The outhouse never got built. But what a perfect grave!

I've always been a fan of synchronicity, Jung's idea that meaningful coincidence is as dynamic a force in the world as the cause-and-effect model upon which science is based. A concept Jung developed in conversations with Einstein in the early twentieth century, later validated by the idea of quantum entanglement, which I don't pretend to understand. I sit on the edge of the hole with my legs dangling inside. I lower my eyelids and clench and release my Kegels in time with my breath, counting to seven, one for each of the chakras I don't believe in. I activate my inner smile, that little curve in the back of my head along the edge of the cerebrum as it borders the cerebellum.

I breathe the air from the hole, a fecund bouquet of decaying life.

I gradually slip all the way inside. It's deep enough so that the rim is at least an inch over my head. Inside, it's dank and cool.

I lie down on the leafy bottom. It's cozy, as soft and supportive as my Tempur-Pedic mattress at home in Mexico. I can die here, just like this.

A colony of potato bugs scurries among the rocks and roots of the hole's walls, each of them a point of consciousness with its own trials, tribulations, joys.

The image of a girl hovers over me, her skin pale as ivory, long blond hair, the bluest of eyes. A wry smile. "Jennifer," I whisper her name. My stomach gurgles with fear as the memory washes over me like vomit from the sky.

I was on duty that night at the psychiatric halfway house where I worked for my alternative service as a conscientious objector during the Vietnam War. My job was to watch over a dozen or so heavily drugged residents attempting to transition back to normalcy from their time in Napa, a notorious "insane asylum."

At about nine, I made my rounds, and all seemed well. I even took an extra minute by Jennifer's room because her vulnerability touched me. She made no effort to hide the deep sadness she felt. She too seemed to be resting peacefully. At eleven, I was supposed to make another bed check, but I was sleepy myself and the house was quiet. I was sure everything was fine.

The next morning as my shift was about to end, I greeted the residents as they shuffled into the kitchen for breakfast. Each cooked his or her own meal, or settled for Lucky Charms, part of the independence regimen. By nine in the morning, everyone was accounted for, except Jennifer.

I rushed up the stairs, checked her room and the bathroom, softly calling her name so as not to alarm the others. No Jennifer.

With a sinking feeling, I returned to the kitchen, worried about how I would explain this disappearance to my boss. I asked a loud but casual question to the group. "Anyone seen Jennifer?"

A wave of anxiety swept the room as this gaggle of crazies tuned into worst-case scenarios.

I stepped out on the back porch for a gulp of air. I managed three gulps before the broken refrigerator caught my eye, stored there by someone unclear on the concept.

I opened the old-fashioned door, with no inside release. Her body rolled onto the porch floor with a sickening thud. There was shit on her flannel nightgown with little Eeyores all over it. There was blood under her fingernails. There were scratches on the inside of the door.

She had changed her mind!

If only I'd made that final bed check! Of course, I told no one that I had skipped it.

I close my eyes against the memory and let the sobs come.

Breathing into the loam, my thought-dreams follow the birches and pine trees into the sky. Something clicks inside, in spite of the enormous guilt weighing on me. I smile.

Why die? a friend of mine, now dead, once asked.

Why indeed. Certainly not something to choose, when life burbles through one so exuberantly. I remember the present. The Present. The eternal now, a cliché. That's all there is. That and the joy of my hunger. I've always chosen life over money, so how can my final choice be any different?

Jennifer changed her mind but was helpless to reclaim her life as the oxygen level in the icebox dissipated. But I am still free. I can change my mind.

A lingering flash of guilt: am I condemning Susanna to death then, without the money for the experimental program? That might or might not work? Luckily, no one knows about the money, so no one can blame me for betraying Susanna. Except me.

I begin thinking of my next steps, to cook something. In the fridge back at the van, there's a salmon steak, an artichoke, a cob of corn to grill, some miniature potatoes to roast. My mouth waters as the energy of life percolates through my veins. Why die? Why indeed.

I persuade my joints, stiff despite years of glucosamine, to lift my body to standing. A flicker of doubt as to whether I can get out of here sweeps through my mind. I stick my toes in the soft wall of the hole and reach out for something to grab onto on the surface. Poison ivy and black raspberry vines with their vicious prickles have me surrounded. My foot slips, and I crash back into the hole, laughing. I try again. I grab a long tuft of grass, but it just comes out by the roots. I tumble back in the hole. A few years ago, this would have been so easy. This time I grab the raspberry vines, piercing my hands like Jesus' stigmata. My left knee hooks the edge when the vines give way and hurtle me back into the hole. The snap of my right leg jolts me with pain. "Yeow!" I yell for no one to hear.

Still bubbling over with life, I laugh. I know right away that my leg is broken. Shit!

For how many people are these their last words? *Oh, shit.*

— 2 —

I 'm fucking stuck. Be careful what you wish for. *I changed my mind,* I silently holler at the universe.

My phone is in my van. I yell, "Hey, Siri," but then I remember it's out of juice.

I call, "Help!"

But I know the farm has been abandoned for open space, and the nearest neighbor is a mile away. Maybe if I were on top of a hill, but little sound escapes from this dank hole, my putative grave.

My enormous prostate throbs. I have to pee. The urgency is enough to justify suicide.

I unzip and pee so it doesn't all go in my pants, though some of it splashes against the wall of the hole and wets my panties anyway.

Now what? My tongue measures the dryness of my mouth. I begin to calculate how much time I might have left if I can't get out of here. In my reservoir of useless information, I find the rule of threes: three minutes without air, three days without water, three weeks without food. I regret wasting my pee. I've read how shipwrecked people drank their own urine to survive.

I grit my teeth against the pain, derrick myself to my left knee, but without my right leg, I can't stand. As I slip back into the loam, tears flood my eyes. I cry for a while; the healing tears help me think.

What is there to think? Send telepathic messages to my family? To Mariah. I ache for her in my heart with all the pain in my leg. Oh, we've had our struggles. She could be critical and judgmental. I understand how her critical patterns hook with my pattern of never feeling as if I'm good enough. But all that seems trivial now. I would give anything to be with her again, to bask in her laughter, her Latina liveliness. We fought ferociously over the years. It surprises me that we're still together.

Five years, ten years, twenty-eight years my three marriages have lasted. The great epochs of my life: Pliocene, Pleistocene, Holocene. Like the strata of rock on the sides of my hole. I regret none of them, I love all my wives—Sasha, Linda Jean, Mariah—and never stopped, something that drove Mariah crazy. If it were up to me, I would stay close to all of them, but Mariah couldn't handle that. She felt like the third wheel, she said. And yet it's she I achingly long for now. She with the Marilyn Monroe beauty mark on her cheek, she with the astonishing open-mindedness, she who shares with me a certain morbid fascination with death, with our own peculiarly wistful notions of immortality.

In *The Shining*, my favorite movie, that weird little

boy Danny was able to send a long distance shine to the Scatman Crothers character. I try it now with all my might, beaming my thoughts of love, longing, and desperate cries for help to Mariah through the sky like radio waves, bouncing off the ozone layer to Mexico, where I imagine her on the patio overlooking the beautiful colonial town with a client, wheeling and dealing. We have different attitudes toward money (she likes it), politics, music, literature, movies (she hated *The Shining*), but none of that matters now, if it ever did. We share a consuming love for our son T-Jay: a sweet, sullen boy who gave up meat at the age of ten after passing the charnel house stench of the slaughterhouses of Coalinga on the desolate highway to Southern California. He couldn't stand to think of how the animals were treated.

My hunger grows beyond hungry, something like what happens when one fasts. I haven't eaten since those bacon and eggs. What, eight hours ago? It was now about three in the afternoon.

The pain in my leg is now a dull thud, manageable. I decide to breathe. Deep, yogic breaths into my abdomen. I lower my eyes to half-mast and try to let go of my thoughts. I'm not very good at meditating, though not for lack of trying. Chants, mantras, creek sounds, sheer acts of will, nothing seems to silence the chatter of thoughts that keeps my consciousness trapped in time, rather than liberated in the eternal present. I try to focus on the energy streams, yin up my spine with the inhale, yang from my crown back down my back on the exhale.

A chill comes over me despite the heat. Fuck dying! No fucking way. Way too early. I have at least ten years, prostate or no prostate. My mouth is parched with the taste of death. Moisture. The moss and the dirt have moisture. I nibble at the moss straight off the wall. It tastes like shit—which is a hell of lot better than death. I scarf up the moss and dirt until I choke. In choking, my heart kicks into emergency mode and gallops bravely toward life.

Breathe. I'm not dead yet. Perhaps I have only a few hours. I might as well enjoy them.

How do you do that?

Well, you leave your body a little bit.

That sounds suspiciously like the seductive cry of death, now one of my selves. There are a lot of selves in this hole.

Breathe. Listen to the forest. Silence. The noisy silence of tree cracks and birdsong, myriad cells pumping. How many cells? How many living cells in the walls of this shithouse grave?

It's only pain. Relish the pain because in this moment pain is life. I push myself with the power of the proverbial mother lifting a truck off her child. Up onto my good, or at least better, left leg. Clawing at the earthen grave walls like a zombie in a horror movie. Willing with all my might my body upright, my busted right leg gingerly poking the grave floor with the ounce of energy left in it to stabilize myself, with lightning bolts of pain. Tears streaming down my cheeks, I grasp at the edge of the shithole grave. I grab at the blackberry bush with a mighty thrust from my broken leg, but the lower half of the tibia bone shoots through my skin toward the sky like a broken arrow and with it a gusher of blood, and my body slips helplessly back into the hole. My life. My life blood.

— 3 —

A s I collapse back into my grave, I pray for more endorphins to kick in to dull the pain. No such luck. Only pain, pain worse than burning alive.

Breathe.

Slowly the suffocating pain becomes part of the landscape. A hopeful note, if the pain doesn't dull soon, death will be most welcome. Your last vote for the lesser of evils.

Start leaving your body, says a voice. The voice of my dead self again.

Don't worry. You are in complete control, says the soothing voice. Witness consciousness. Remember? From Tantra 101?

Breathe. Let go a little. Rise out of the pineal gland two inches above your head. What a view! The pineal gland. What a cliché. Death, please, be as cruel as you wish but don't be a mass of clichés. Please. No lights. No tunnels. No welcoming waifs. Please be something I don't expect.

The blood still throbs from my leg with each heartbeat. The heart, in emergency mode, slows everything down to staunch the pulsating flow of blood.

I dig at the walls of the grave for dirt and bury my gaping leg in soil turning muddier with each blood spurt. The dirt turns into clay and slows the bleeding to the trickle of a mountain spring in late summer.

I eye the stalks of poison ivy that I dragged back into the hole in my last fall—literally, my last fall. My hunger overpowering my sense, I stuff the leaves in my mouth, chew and swallow them with relish even as my lips puff with the toxin in the sap.

I need the sustenance of the poison ivy plant badly enough to tolerate the itch. But I hadn't anticipated quite such an itch. My lips, my cheeks, inside and out, my tongue, my throat. What if the hives grow in my throat so big they cut off my air?

Breathe.

I need to pee. I need my pee. I rip my leg out of its premature grave. The blood resumes its previous throbbing gush. I squirm my way around the hole so that my feet are in the air, my right leg a crimson rain-forest waterfall. I got my dick about level with my face and hose a fountain stream in an arc through the air and into my mouth. I chug it down. It has an acrid taste, a salt syrup, ammonia. They say it's sterile, not that it matters any more. I slurp a good cupful before the fountain goes dry, waste a few precious drops on my jeans, but only a few. That ought to be good for another half hour of life.

The phrase puzzles me. What's a half hour? I reach a spot two inches above my pineal gland where time has stopped. Not stopped exactly. It's like you've been steaming along on the railroad of time, and you suddenly jump the tracks and take a sharp turn to the left. Time scoots by behind you, like a passing train.

I watch my body slump down in its dying heap. I scoop the earthen tourniquet over my leg, re-inter it, as it were.

Breathe.

I'm in an interesting place. Time has either stopped or slowed so completely that it's passing as imperceptibly as the turning of the earth. I'm looking at this otherworldly sky, designer orange and black, more like a negative sunset than a fire. It's slightly familiar, this place. Sometimes in the past, when I stood up too fast from my writing, the blood would rush out of my head leaving this view behind. The words that came to me then and come to me now: I've never been *here* before.

Birds come swooping down from this twi-night sky; not birds, angels. Swarms of angels. Oh fuck. I prayed for no more clichés. But I remember these angels from those acid trips years ago. Moments of consciousness, I called them. Little ribbons of memory wrapped around a dream. These are the units of the skein of being, colorful little thought-dreams recorded in neuromolecules, the technology of the body. They dance about, flaunting their dimensionality like wings, angels' wings.

Breathe.

It's getting harder, breathing. The paranoia of my throat clogging with pustules of poison ivy seems to be validated. Just because you're paranoid and all that.

Maybe my unconscious drove me to this point. This

thought does a little shooting star twirl. The Death Wish. Thanatos. Granted me with the Transamerica magic wand. It's not my unconscious. It's the Pavlovian reward of a million dollars.

The capitalist system was sacrificing me on the pyramidal altar of Transamerica Mutual Life. They put a fucking ransom on my ass. Which one of my multiple selves will stand up to the lure of riches, posthumous or otherwise?

Then come the yellow jackets. Miniature buzzards in search of carrion. Yet another poisonous hors d'oeuvre— whores' ovaries, my sister calls them. I sweep one from the air with my hand and stuff it in my mouth. It stings me on the tongue. Tongue stung. Try saying that in an hour. A what? A memory of my bee-keeping adventure with Jake, another story.

It's annoying. There's just no time here. It's like you're always missing something, looking around for something, for some leaf falling off a tree to indicate the passage of time. My teeth grind the bee to a honey-masticated crunch. Insect granola. How many seconds does that buy me? Seconds?

Newly focused, I squeeze my pineal gland and create an arc of light between it and the center of my consciousness that hovers now three inches above my head. Wait. If I'm rising then time is passing. There will come a point when the tendril connecting the rising self with the corporeal self will snap.

I focus on the radiance in the glow of the arc from my center and my pineal gland. I lower my figurative eyelids. Breathing. Watching to see if the center rises, to prove the passage of time. So maybe you do get a whole other lifetime before the last tendril snaps, pondering the gradual receding of being, the river of life as it flows out to sea.

It's like standing on a mountain searching for evidence of the rotation of the earth. Oh, it's there: the sun, for one thing, except it sure as hell seems like it's the other way around, that the sun does circle the earth; the way the stars move over the course of a night; the necklace of planets spiraling between the setting sun and the rising moon. On the edge of the universe that I now inhabit, there is a moon, about the size of a virgin pencil eraser. The same color, too—the orange we call blood.

Breathe.

I'm pretty sure I'm alone, but I don't feel alone, because the multiple selves I'm unraveling keep each other company in a morbid dance. Alone doesn't mean anything either, I note. Everything is connected to everything else. This is not a new insight. What the fuck. Maybe it is all one big Oprah show. A revelation of the obvious, as one of my ex-wives used to say.

I'm flitting about like a hyper-evolved invisible butterfly, a firefly, the firefly from the center of things. By perching on the shoulder of one of these angels, I can relive the entire experience. Shit. Why the fuck would anyone want to do that? To stave off the inevitable.

To heal the hurts from the past, says another voice, that of the "why die" guy, a man of wisdom.

I heave a long sigh. A wave of fatigue sweeps over me on the next inhale. I don't think I want to pick apart my life and feel all the unfelt feelings. I'd rather die.

Breathe. There's no hurry. I look down at my body and squint my eyes. I can't for the life of me detect any movement, no passage of time. "You have all the time in the world," the wise "why die" guy said.

So the angels are the only entertainment here. No internet, no movies, only these convoluted thought-dreams mostly linked to pain. Whoop-de-do. Can't wait to feel that pain. I'm a ways beyond feeling physical pain, but emotional pain? The skein of being spirals around me like the DNA double helix, another cliché. Why so snobbish about clichés? Maybe death is working class. Corny. Full of tired routines and exhausted one-liners. *The Way*, the Taoists call it. The zone of proximal development, someone else calls it. Everyone is saying the same thing.

I notice that in general the multidimensional skein of being is fashioned of whole cloth, so to speak, a silken sari that shimmers as waves of energy roll through it. There are only a few places where the fabric is torn, snags interrupting the undulating flow.

Only a few places that need to heal.

Breathe.

Sins. Oh, fuck, still another cliché. I can't stand it. I have to look at my damn sins that I don't for one fucking second believe in. Well, maybe a fucking second. I was, after all, raised by my loving grandma in the bowels of the Episcopal Church.

The first angel I alight on butterfly-like is the girl in the icebox. If only, if only, if only, I'd done an extra bed check; I'd had an intuition, but I had, in all laziness, ignored it. *Nothing will happen*, I thought then. *Everything's fine. Nothing to worry about.* But everything wasn't fine, and my laziness killed her—worse than killed her because she had changed her mind, like me.

How do you heal them? The smell as I opened that fridge, with the girl's body in it. Shit and death. My God, I can't breathe. This is it. Fuck. I melt into a flow of wax-candle tears, flowing from the flame.

The light doesn't die, the dead girl tells me. *It's OK. It wasn't your fault. I wanted to die. Besides, I was still in bed when you would have checked at eleven.* She smiles the kind of smile she might have smiled as a three-year-old child who fell in love with every stranger.

Breathe. Turn off your mind, relax, and float downstream. To the next snag. This one is close in time, the story of my cousin Jimmy, who at first lived next door on the lake in the summer in the red cottage. Later his parents built a new house in the woods. Jimmy was the goat. All my friends and I bullied the shit out of him, making up cruel songs, treating him as some kind of monster. Until I became the monster. I was seventeen, having a beer bash of a party on the fourth of July at my house (what were my parents thinking?), with dozens of the Milwaukee's private school denizens, the cool people, when uninvited Jimmy comes to the door. I greeted him warmly, grabbed his hand, and burned the back of it with my Marlboro cigarette. He ran home screaming.

At the reunion, I told him I was sorry for everything. He said it wasn't so bad.

The next snag is a big one: how I hurt my second wife, Linda Jean, a working class black woman who deserved only love, love that I couldn't give her, even as we struggled against the system together. I had an emotional affair with another woman, Cali, and to make matters worse, I wrote that novel about them, the two women, *Dark Night*, changing things to make my autobiographical protagonist look better and the women worse, for the sake of the story, of course. Writers can be assholes.

Was there racism involved? Sexism? White men drink this shit with our mother's milk and carry it around for life. We can fight it with all our might, but traces of it linger. In Linda Jean's case, I had to go crazy to pretend I had no choice. For a while, I believed I was possessed by a turtle.

I was a shit to you, Linda Jean, I told her. *You deserved to be treated so much better.*

She flashes her shy smile. *About time you realized this, Barney. You know it's not like me to use such language, but fuck you!*

Ouch. I have to pause in my travels to take that in. It's oddly healing that she can say this to me.

The river of consciousness where I am surfing consists of waves of vibrations, strings of every color, including those way beyond the visible spectrum. The visual is no longer such an ineluctable modality, LOL. A Wikipedia image of string theory. But there's something else. It's as if this silken roadway were a river of energy flowing through space, which isn't empty and lightweight as we usually think of it, a near vacuum. It's a nothingness beyond nothingness, a palpable nothingness made of uranium Jell-O, way denser than you can imagine.

What scares me is maybe there is a right path. Maybe the choices you make matter to how you will spend eternity. Another cliché, yes, but even clichés have a speck of truth at the center. Language is metaphor, close to reality only in the most poetic of moments. It's like everything everybody says and believes is true, if you smushed all the endless words together, you would have a moment of transcendent radiance, which might last for a while. Pure imagination, the creative force—an imagination so powerful, it has imagined itself. The palette of infinite possibilities. I am navigating this wave of waves of waves of waves as if kayaking down the Wisconsin River. And yet at any moment, I can be sucked into the uranium Jell-O that makes up the banks of this river.

The next snag is different. It's a hole in the fabric of space-time. But it's covered in what looks for all the world like dog shit. And who should pop his head out but Herzie, the caramel brown dachshund, the love of my life. I want to jump at him and wrap my arms about him, rub my cheek against his fuzzy neck, but there's some kind of membrane between us.

Be careful, Hmmm, Herzie says.

Oh, you can talk now, I say.

Always could. You just couldn't hear me.

Oh, I say.

Don't pierce the membrane. You'll be all the way dead. Now you're just half dead.

Where did you learn English?

Human, we're not speaking English. We are sending direct messages to each other's souls.

Cool!

I got elected to lead you to the other side because of how much we loved each other.

I fall silent.

You should probably know you are making this shit up as you go along. I am a figment of your imagination. But there's no shame in that. Everything is a figment of your imagination. Imagination is the stuff that the universe is made of.

You're telling me that life is death's dream.

Something like that, the dog messages.

With a cock of his head, he bids me to follow him along a path through the woods—so many paths in the woods—with the translucent membrane on one side and the mountain of uranium Jell-O on the other. I can see people who have died. They are just there in the fog. I can engage them. I go to my mother first, of course. We smile at each other across the chasm left over from when we were both alive.

I remember when she got it. I was in my forties, and she was saying something vaguely critical of my career choices. I said to her, "Mom, you don't have to judge me anymore."

She stopped and smiled. "Oh," she said. "OK."

Then she sticks her fingers into the membrane and plays piano on my body, just like she did when I was a toddler. What sweet music!

There are other shadows in the mist, my grandmother, my brother Charlie. But suddenly sucking up all the attention as he did in life is my father, my antithesis.

I was about to kill myself like you did, I say to him. But I changed my mind.

And yet here you are, he says.

Shit happens.

It does.

We stare at each other for a long time, willing ourselves over the Mariana Trench between us. I want him, but I need to get this out of the way:

I think you molested me when I was a baby.

He looks away, sadly, guiltily. *Did I? I don't remember. I could have. I was a little nuts when I came home from the war.*

It was in the shower.

Barney, if something like that happened, I am truly sorry.

I can't cry anymore because I've left my body behind. But I can vibrate at a mournful frequency.

The next moment we are doing an air hug so as not to tear the membrane, and I see he is wearing a white nylon slip over bulging breasts. I start to laugh when I see that I am wearing a pink teddy and fishnet stockings.

Some kind of spherical music buzzes around us as we dance to the tune of healing affection, some solid recognition that, in the words of seven-year-old T-Jay, *we are all one.*

Maybe these last nanoseconds won't last seventy-five years. The speck that is left of me is receding away from my body, and everything is growing fainter.

A disturbance in the skein. A Roman candle goes off and spreads its sparks all over whatever universe I am in at this point. I'm drawn toward the fire, as if paged at the airport. I'm up against the membrane again, face to face with Susanna.

Are you dead? is the first indelicate phrase to leave my parched lips.

I don't know, Susanna says matter-of-factly.

It's hard to tell, I say. *It's good to see you, I think.*

She has flaming blue hair and a body covered with belly-dancing jangles. *What about you? Are you dying? Are you fucking killing yourself?*

I lower my eyes. *You know I wanted to kill myself to help save you, but I changed my mind.*

What?

My term life policy was supposed to pay for the experimental procedure that could save your life. I won't apologize for that. Changing my mind? Well, there was about a 5 percent chance of the procedure working.

Why did you change your mind?

Honestly? I was afraid to die.

Oh. That's good, actually, because I need you to take care of my boys. She's referring to Jason and their son, Zeke.

Yes! I could do that. Except I'm fucking stuck in this shithouse grave.

You'll get out.

You think so?

I know so.

We stare at each other lovingly.

With a burst of pliered-fingernail pain, I slip back the other way, toward my body. I can move both ways. That might extend my stay here on this planet. Still as the pain washes back over me, so does the great fatigue.

I can flutter like a butterfly in the twi-night universe, darker than before, as the earthbound sun slips behind the trees. In this observation there is a hint of the amount of real time that has passed since I fell into this grave. It's somewhere between one and five in the morning, I suppose with a weary pedestrian awareness.

The more I move back toward my body, the more pain I feel, and the intolerable thirst intensifies. Yes, I can prolong the agony, but why? It's time to let go. Oh yeah, I need to think of Jason and Zeke. I'm now about five inches above my crown. Another wave of tears rolls over me with the resignation. Tears of grief for the loss of my life, for Susanna, for the people I love and will see no more, for the people I've hurt, for the thought of a world without me in it, yes, but there is something else here.

The sky is lightening. That old crystal orb, another old friend from my acid trips, the clear blue light, everything I know I learned on LSD. "Starkling beauty," I think Nina Simone called it. The electron dance. It isn't so bad, this dying, really. I still can't tell whether a part of me will somehow retain consciousness, selfness, but it seems to matter less and less. I am still a point, the still point of the turning world. I still have a point of view, and a rather remarkable one at that, full of other-worldly vistas, most of which are indescribable in words, and without apparent meaning, but who cares? Meaning is overrated. Bursts of color way beyond the visible spectrum, energy spikes cavorting in a sea of pure imagination, I—am I still *I?*—can get used to this.

Looking down now from high in the pine branches, I can barely make out my corporeal self. I shed my selves along the way, seemingly left now with just one self that has escaped the skein of being as if it were a chrysalis. I can choose my viewpoint. I can be the tree. I can be a passing bird. I can alight on anything and fleetingly become that thing so that I become all points of view at once, how interesting. This is sweet.

Then I freeze. From what now seems like miles below me on the forest floor, I hear a voice. "Barney?"

Barney. Who is Barney? Whose is that voice?

"Barney?"

My consciousness snaps like a rubber band back into my old brain, and with it excruciating pain.

"Barney. I'll get you out of here." Jimmy. My cousin, my childhood nemesis.

— 4 —

*T*he next thing I know I'm waking up in fiberglass bondage, my leg tied to a pulley, catheter in my dick, a drip, presumably morphine, in my arm.

Vague images of paramedics and an ambulance. Another segment has been surgically excised from the tissue of time. Once I am back in my body, what happened when I was outside of it is a dream, much of it forgotten.

For some days, and I can measure days now, I float on a narcotic fog, not giving a shit about much. I feel . . . dead. I completed the process of dying, but my body didn't die. It's a spent feeling, like on those rare nights when you had sex and came three times.

People in my family come and go, but I can't really see them, or feel them, or remember them. This is a sad feeling, like reaching for your lover's hand as you fall off a cliff and missing by just an inch. At least it isn't cold. There's something warm in the beep of my heartbeat on the monitor, scientific evidence that I am indeed, still alive.

It's Jason who first comes into focus. He stands by the bed and smiles.

"Hey," is all I can say.

"Hey, Dad. We thought we'd lost you."

"I was about gone. But I'm back. And I'm glad. What about *her*?"

He gulps back tears. "She died a week ago."

Jason hugs me awkwardly, given the casts, and we sob together.

Jason lifts his head. "You always said you were going to do this, die like an animal, drop where you are, food for the buzzards."

"Yeah, but I changed my mind. What's the hurry? We all get there soon enough as it is." I feel the need to defend myself. "My idea was to do it for her, so you guys would have the money for that procedure."

"Really? It would've been too late."

"Yeah." I let that sink in. "Where am I?"

"You're at the hospital in Oconomowoc. They want to keep you at least a couple of weeks to get your strength back."

I try to move, but realize I am in traction. A wave of claustrophobic panic rolls over me.

"Easy, Dad. They actually saved your leg, but you're going to have to stay still for a while."

"Not my strong suit."

Time ceases to exist again, but this time it disappears in an opiate fog. And yet, I still have that inner smile I rediscovered when I was in my shithole grave and decided not to die, that smile that lives at the back of my skull.

At first, I find the parade of well-wishing relatives irritating, an unwelcome interruption of my opium dreams. It's partly how they treat me. There's a solicitousness usually reserved for Alzheimer patients or the mentally ill, the kind of nursing-home sing-song, *And how are we feeling today?*

Jason, and even Ramona, talk down to me as if I am pitiful. At the same time some resentment lurks in their saccharine sentimentality.

It's my fifteen-year-old grandson Zeke who gives it away. He comes with his father, but when Jason is in the bathroom, Zeke says to me, "Papa, you really tried to do yourself in?"

"Is that what they told you?"

"Not exactly. They didn't tell me anything. But that's what it sounded like."

I've always had a good relationship with my grandson, a sunny, enthusiastic child, the first natural athlete in the family for a long time. Blond, flowing locks, more straight like his mom's than curly like his dad's, blue eyes full of joy, even at this time of unfathomable sorrow, losing his mom.

"Well, no, I didn't try to do myself in. I was thinking about it, decided against it, and then fell in the damn hole and broke my leg."

So that's why all the mushiness. Damn, Jason. But it does look suspicious. Why would Jason necessarily believe that I had changed my mind? I smile at Zeke. "Thanks for the intelligence, Zeke. Now I understand why everyone is treating me so weird."

Yes, I've decided to live, but that means I have to *live*. I tell the doctor to ease me off the morphine so I can think. I think about how to connect with them. Those angels I've healed are guiding me.

"Jason, I know you think I was trying to kill myself down there, but I wasn't. I had thought about it, only a little more than one does every day, but I decided that life was too precious."

"It's OK, Dad." Jason squirms, trying to avoid the heart-to-heart embarrassment.

"No, it isn't. I learned some things when I was close to dying." Tears come to my voice. "I can't be sure, but I don't think you actually die. Something of you, even it's just an atom, something remains and merges with the universal consciousness, yet stays ever so slightly distinct. Susanna is still with us."

Jason sighs impatiently, his scientific mind no friend of spiritual gobbledygook.

"I know this is uncomfortable, Jason, but I have to say it. I'm sorry I wasn't there for you when you were young."

"It's OK, Dad."

"Yes, it is OK. It's OK because you took the right lessons from it. You have been there for Zeke in ways that I wasn't there for you, and maybe that's the way it works, we learn from our parents' mistakes. I think you're a terrific father."

"Yeah, OK, I learned from your mistakes, but from your strengths, too. I remember when I was about fifteen and you tried to give me The Talk. You said, 'Your mother thinks I should talk to you about sex. Well, that seems pretty embarrassing. I'm sure you know all about it. Here.' And you handed me a three-pack of condoms. I loved you for that. You told me everything I needed to hear: that you trusted me."

"OK."

"OK."

We hug. We cry. One down, I think.

Next comes Ramona, with her mother's dark eyebrows, deep, brown eyes, pools of wisdom. "I know it's late, Mony, but I was a jerk about money back when you were in college."

"Yeah, Dad, you were, but I forgave you a long time ago. You were an OK dad, really."

"Really? It doesn't feel like it so much. All those divorces must have been hard on you."

"Yeah, but you know, I never felt in the slightest that it was my fault, like a lot of kids of divorce do. There was a way I knew that it had nothing to do with me. And I almost always felt that you did a decent job thinking about us, that you were careful to give us enough freedom so we learned self-reliance, but not so much that we ever felt unsafe, you know?"

"I'm incredibly proud of you, Mony."

We, too, melt into healing hugs and tears. It is a little Hallmark, but near-death has reconciled me to the cornball.

T-Jay flies in from San Diego.

"My youngest son."

"Barney." Annoyingly, he'd taken to calling me by my first name at age eleven.

"Will you grant me a dying wish?"

"I would, but you're not dying."

"Still the literalist. Really, one small thing."

"Maybe."

"Tell me for real how you are doing."

"OK."

"OK as in you're doing OK, or OK as in you will tell me?"

"OK."

I sigh and glare at my son.

"I'm sick of going to school," he said then. "I'm going to take some time off before I go to graduate school, if I go to graduate school. I want to be a photographer, like Stieglitz or Man Ray. And I met this girl. OK?"

"OK." I grab T-Jay's hand and hold it. For the first time in twelve years, T-Jay doesn't pull away. OK.

Finally, Mariah bursts into the room in a swirl of joyous laughter—face like the moon, hair still short and girlishly butch at sixty-one, body still small and trim, deliciously soft now. Knowing me as she does, she crawls right into bed with me. I kiss her Marilyn Monroe beauty mark, remembering that birthday sex video we made years ago, when she sang, "Happy Birthday, Mr. President."

"You look good in bondage," she whispers, recalling our erotic connection, placing her hand on my balls and squeezing.

"Ouch. Be careful of the catheter."

She kisses me hard and tongues my mouth.

"Don't you dare die on me, Barney Blatz," she says after a while.

"It did occur to me that you could use the money."

"What? I can't believe you think I cared about the money."

"It wasn't that. It's just that I had a chance to leave you with something,"

She suddenly pulls away from me. "I don't know what kind of monster you take me for, Barney Blatz. Do you think I married you for your money? That's disgusting. If I wanted to marry someone for money, it certainly wouldn't have been you. You hardly had any money then, and you have no money now. It's like after all these years, you don't know me. I fell in love with you because you always made me laugh and because I knew you would be a good father to our children, which you have been, you know."

"It's true I felt distant from you for a while, and I wanted to feel like I'd led a successful life by leaving you money. But when I was dying, it was thinking of you that kept me alive. I'm sorry I got confused about the money. I was doing it for Susanna, too. So she could have that procedure."

"I know. That is so sad." She warms back up to me.

"Will you marry me?" I ask. This was a running joke with us. Two weeks after we met in San Miguel twenty-seven years ago, I asked her to marry me, and we said our abbreviated vows to each other before the altar of the famous Parroquia church. We repeated this ritual frequently in the first few years, even after we were actually married, decreasingly as time went on.

"Yes, I will, yes, I will, yes," she says in a sultry whisper.

A wave of contentment washes over me such as I've never felt before. After 74.9 years of visceral discontent, this state of bliss seems to have been worth waiting for.

"So, no surprise party," Mariah says. "You'll still be in here on your birthday anyway."

"OK."

That evening, they all gather in my small room. The love in the room is palpable. My eyes tear up. This is my party and I can cry if I want to. "This isn't about me," I say. "I'm good. I'm happy to be alive, to be with all of you. This is about Susanna, who left us way too soon. I saw her wherever I was when I was dying. She has a message for us: it's not about how long you live. It's about how well you live."

Jason says, "Yeah. She got her money's worth."

Ramona says, "She crammed about eighty years of life into her forty-six years."

Mariah says to Jason and Zeke, "She loved you guys so much."

— 5 —

Slowly my decrepit body heals. They take me out of traction. I can hobble about the hospital on crutches. The family retreats back to their lives, mostly to California where they are planning a big memorial for Susanna. My state of bliss degenerates into boredom.

A week before my birthday, I can't take it anymore. Life is too short to languish here. They wanted a surprise party, by God, I'll give them one. I'll show up at Susanna's memorial myself.

I convince the doctor I'm ready to get out. The doctor is skeptical, but most likely mindful of the expense of keeping me longer, so he agrees to release me as long as a family member would meet me.

"Of course," I lie.

Instead I call AAA. I crutch my way to the front, awaiting the tow truck. For a hundred dollars extra, the truck drives me to the clearing on the farm by Pike Lake where my VW camper van is still waiting for me with a dead battery. With a jump from AAA, the van starts right up.

Just before starting off, I throw the .45 automatic in the shithole grave.

One-legged driving is a bit of challenge, but my body is percolating with the joy of freedom. I can do anything. I head down the road toward California, my encased right leg leaning on the drive shaft hump. I use my left leg for both the accelerator and the brake. Luckily the transmission is automatic. This arrangement works fine as I hop on the freeway and head toward Madison and points west.

Thirty-one hours to Oakland, Google says. It's now three in the afternoon. I set the camper on cruise control and relax into the long haul, with its excruciatingly boring scenery. There's a reason we coastal snobs call this flyover country. Luckily, I've got plenty of Vicodin.

I fill up on coffee at various truck stops along the way, those markets with CB radio equipment, fancy belts, knives, every kind of auto gadget. At the first stop, I buy a box of Depends, which, apparently, a lot of truckers use to minimize pit stops. I've known for a while that wearing them would help my problem, but until now, I've stubbornly resisted. I make a decision to have my prostate cut out when I get to Oakland.

I keep going into the night, three hours to Dubuque, stop for a Southwest Skillet at Denny's—fried potatoes, peppers, mushrooms, onions, cheese, and chorizo topped with two poached eggs—and more coffee. Another hour and a half to Iowa City to hook up with Interstate 80 that will take me all the way to San Francisco. Two hours to Des Moines. By midnight, I'm outside of Omaha, and sleep is catching up with me.

I find a rest stop and curl up in the back of my van.

The hot summer sun peaks over the endless cornfields around six in the morning, and I'm off. By noon, approaching Cheyenne, I'm getting sleepy again, and the road narrows to one lane in each direction in a long construction zone. There's no place to stop.

Still on cruise control, I see a string of red lights ahead where the traffic has stopped. I slam on the brakes, but my cast-swollen foot hits the accelerator, and I have to swerve into the east bound lane to avoid rear-ending the car in front of me.

Where a huge semi is barreling toward me.

I hear the blast of its horn.

On impact, my camper van bursts into flame.

I leap out of my body to avoid the pain of burning alive. The tendril snaps. With a final guffaw, I merge with the silken skein of being.

My last thought: *Cremated, after all. Oh, fuck.*

About the Author

HENRY HITZ grew up in a habitat similar to Pike Lake. He taught pre-school for thirty years and organized public school parents for another fifteen years. He has published stories in *Cube Magazine*, *Magnolia Review*, *Scarlet Leaf Review*, and *Moonfish*. His first novel, *Tales of Monkeyman*, won the Walter Van Tilburg Clark Prize. His novel *White Knight* was published in January 2016 by Wordrunner Press. He blogs at henryhitz.com. He lives in Oakland, California, with his wife, son, two older sisters, two dogs, and a cat.

ALSO by
HENRY HITZ

A midquel to *Squirrels in the Wall*

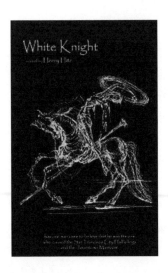

White Knight, or how one man came to believe that he was the one who caused the San Francisco City Hall Killings and the Jonestown Massacre

———

Available on Amazon

In 1977, a fireman named Dan White saved a woman and her babies from a fire in the Geneva Towers apartments in San Francisco. It is this scene which opens *White Knight,* the story of one witness to that fire, Barney Blatz, and his entanglement with the political and personal catastrophe that followed. With the November, 1978 Jonestown Massacre of 912 people and, nine days later, White's murder of Mayor George Moscone and Supervisor Harvey Milk, the city and Barney unraveled. "There's a bumper sticker that reads, 'Time is nature's way of keeping everything from happening at once,' but this November, it isn't working."

"A powerful tale set in San Francisco during the turbulent late '70s. Hitz makes you feel that you were there, and shows how we came to grasp that 'the personal is political' and, alas, vice versa. An elegant debut novel."

—CLIFFORD IRVING, author of *Final Argument* and
The Autobiography of Howard Hughes

"Interweaving San Francisco's twin civic traumas—the massacre at Jonestown and the murders of Mayor George Moscone and Supervisor Harvey Milk—with the tumultuous inner life of protagonist Barney Blatz, *White Knight* captures the frenetic scene of late 70s San Francisco. This fast-paced novel melds the revolutionary zeal of political activism with personal turmoil that both feeds it and results from it. A great read!"

—RUHAMA VELTFORT, author of *The Promised Land*
and *Strange Attractors*

"Barney has only the best intentions. A community organizer and pre-school teacher, he just wants to save the world, starting with the children (and women) in a dilapidated housing project on the outskirts of San Francisco. But in this engaging tale of internal and external implosion, the best intentions of many decent people are destined to go awry. Beyond well researched, this is the story of someone who was there and has the scars to prove it."

—MARK LAPIN, author of *Pledge of Allegiance*

SELECTED TITLES FROM SPARKPRESS

SparkPress is an independent boutique publisher delivering high-quality, entertaining, and engaging content that enhances readers' lives, with a special focus on female-driven work.
www.gosparkpress.com

Seventh Flag: A Novel, Sid Balman, Jr. $16.95, 978-1-68463-014-1. A sweeping work of historical fiction, *Seventh Flag* is a Micheneresque parable that traces the arc of radicalization in modern Western Civilization—reaffirming what it means to be an American in a dangerously divided nation.

The Sea of Japan: A Novel, Keita Nagano. $16.95, 978-1-684630-12-7. When thirty-year-old Lindsey, an English teacher from Boston who's been assigned to a tiny Japanese fishing town, is saved from drowning by a local young fisherman, she's drawn into a battle with a neighboring town that has high stakes for everyone—especially her.

Pursuits Unknown: An Amy and Lars Novel, Ellen Clary. $16.95, 978-1-943006-86-1. Search-and-rescue agent Amy and her telepathic dog, Lars, locate a missing scientist who is reported to have an Alzheimer's-like disease—only to discover that someone wants to steal his research for potentially ominous purposes.

Bedside Manners: A Novel, Heather Frimmer. $16.95, 978-1-943006-68-7. When Joyce Novak is diagnosed with breast cancer, she and her daughter, Marnie—a medical student who is on the cusp of both beginning a surgical internship and getting married—are forced to face Joyce's mortality together, a journey that changes both their lives in surprising and profound ways.

Love Reconsidered: A Novel, Phyllis J. Piano. $16.95, 978-1-943006-20-5. A page-turning contemporary tale of how three memorable characters seek to rebuild their lives after betrayal and tragedy with the help of new relationships, loyal corgi dogs, home-cooked meals, and the ritual of football Sundays.